THE KEEPERS

ALSO BY JEFFREY B. BURTON

The Finders
The Eulogist
The Lynchpin
The Chessman

THE KEEPERS

A MACE REID K-9 MYSTERY

‡

JEFFREY B. BURTON

MINOTAUR BOOKS
NEW YORK

First published in the United States by Minotaur Books, an imprint of St. Martin's Publishing Group

THE KEEPERS. Copyright © 2021 by Jeffrey B. Burton. All rights reserved. Printed in the United States of America. For information, address St. Martin's Publishing Group, 120 Broadway, New York, NY 10271.

www.minotaurbooks.com

Library of Congress Cataloging-in-Publication Data

Names: Burton, Jeffrey B., author.
Title: The keepers : a Mace Reid K-9 mystery / Jeffrey B. Burton.
Description: First Edition. | New York : Minotaur Books, 2021. | Series:
Identifiers: LCCN 2020056381 | ISBN 9781250244567 (hardcover) | ISBN 9781250795861 (ebook)
Classification: LCC PS3602.U76977 K44 2021 | DDC 813/.6—dc23
LC record available at https://lccn.loc.gov/2020056381

Our books may be purchased in bulk for promotional, educational, or business use. Please contact your local bookseller or the Macmillan Corporate and Premium Sales Department at 1-800-221-7945, extension 5442, or by email at MacmillanSpecialMarkets@macmillan.com.

First Edition: 2021

10 9 8 7 6 5 4 3 2 1

To Amber—
How she knocked down and snarfed up those twenty-three large gingersnap cookies in the two minutes it took me to bring in the rest of the groceries was truly amazing. It was the Australian shepherd version of *Cool Hand Luke* and his fifty eggs.

There is honor in being a dog.

—Aristotle

THE KEEPERS

PROLOGUE

I spent the bulk of the call with my eyes shut, thinking I was still asleep and in some kind of lucid dream. I may have even called the night sergeant out of the Chicago Police Department's 12th District "Mom" before he barked at me to *wake the hell up* and *get* my *ass* to the address he was texting me. He said as soon as I got west of the river, to follow the noise and the glow—the sound and the fury—and that I'd *be a damned idiot* if I missed it.

I sat up in bed, wiped eye snot off my lashes with both forefingers, and then opened them. Elvira, my golden retriever puppy, stood on the opposite corner of the bed, tail wagging and staring back at me as if she'd been a participant on the call.

"No way I'm starting you with a blazing warehouse fire at," I peeked down at my cell phone, "three o'clock in the morning, Vira." I'd been training her as a cadaver dog and, considering her age, she'd been showing remarkable ability. And endless enthusiasm. "You're getting there, girl, you really are, but let's have you and Maggie hold down the fort."

My name is Mason Reid—I go by Mace—and I specialize in human remains detection—that is, I train dogs to hunt for the dead. My HRD pups and I help the authorities—the Chicago Police Department and various sheriffs' departments—in their searches for the missing and presumed dead. In fact, I've knighted Vira and my pack of cadaver dogs *The Finders* and would have that imprinted on business cards had my kids opposable thumbs in which to hand them out or pockets in which to place them.

It was a quarter to four when I parked my F-150 a couple city blocks shy of the address the sergeant had provided. The streets were littered with fire engines for pumping water and chemical flame-retardants as well as fire trucks for hauling ladders and rescue gear, a line of squad cars, and an ambulance or three idling, empty. There were more flashing lights than on bingo night at Caesars Palace. My wake-up call had informed me that CFD—Chicago Fire Department—had spent a chunk of the night fighting a warehouse blaze in the Fulton River District, which is situated on the border of Chicago's downtown and considered part of the Near West Side. The area had once been known for transportation and industrial warehousing but had, in recent decades—like many other quarters in the Windy City—turned residential.

Sue, my alpha male of a German shepherd, and Delta Dawn, my farm collie, and I threaded our way around local news vans, cameramen, and huddling reporters as we came upon a white-haired man standing next to a fireman. Both stared fixedly as the crew of firefighters finished hosing down the burned-out warehouse through a haze of smoke and steam, ash and soot.

"How long has it been vacant?" The fireman, whom I took to be a lieutenant or captain, asked.

"Two years," White-hair, whom I took to be the warehouse owner, replied. "A company that shipped aluminum rented the spot for twenty years before going under."

"You got a homeless problem?"

"Once a space that size goes empty," he nodded toward the smoldering facility, "you'd have to live here around the clock to chase out any transients." White-hair shrugged. "I call the cops now and again."

Our trio continued onward with Sue, as always, in the lead and ID'd ourselves through a series of officers acting as sentries. The scent of smoke hung heavy in the air. I found myself blinking the grime from my eyes every couple of seconds, wishing I'd brought along a quart or two of Visine. As we approached I could tell from what remained of the structure—ruins to be more accurate—that the inferno had been devastating. The place resembled old newsreel footage of Berlin in 1945, and I wondered if some kind of electrical or lighting or heating equipment had triggered a flame that soon met with combustible materials.

I spray a protective film on all of my dogs' feet in order to protect and toughen their pads and paws. I hope the darned stuff works. I wasn't worried about the hot concrete, as the facility had been doused in an ocean of water. I was more concerned with any smoldering or sharp debris my pups might step on.

Once we'd advanced to the front line, we were instructed to hold our horses as another forty minutes passed until the fire commissioner himself gave the all clear for us to enter and search for human remains in the wreckage of the burned-out facility.

By daybreak, Sue, Delta, and I had worked our way through the scorched remnants of the Fulton River District warehouse. The kids, as though working in unison, had led me to the northeast corner, opposite from where we'd been allowed to enter. It had taken my dogs all of five minutes to weave and wind about the soaked and steaming wreckage, leading me around twisted metal, busted rubble, and blocks. Delta tapped at the wet concrete in front of her with a single paw while Sue just stared back at me—pawing at the ground was beneath him.

I flagged a handful of firemen over and, as they pushed

aside the blackened debris, they uncovered charred human remains.

I followed the story in the *Chicago Tribune*. Originally, it was thought to be the work of idiot kids playing with matches or maybe that homeless fellow we'd found tried cooking himself a chicken dinner and, poof, everything went to hell in a handbag. However, a couple days later, the fire commissioner confirmed that accelerants were involved—both on the victim as well as on the floor and walls of the warehouse. It had been intentionally set . . . arson. And though he'd not been accused or arrested, White-hair—whose real name turned out to be Howard Costa—protested his innocence, "Why would I torch my own building?" he said to the press. "It wouldn't make sense to burn it down in some kind of insurance scam when I've had a ton of offers—developers wanting to spit up even more and more of them goddamned condominiums."

Without intact fingerprints, it took investigators a couple more days to match dental records and DNA to a man by the name of John Averbeck. Turns out Mr. Averbeck was anything but homeless as had initially been surmised. Averbeck was an employment lawyer who'd gone to pick up Chinese carry-out for dinner earlier in the week, never to return home or be seen alive again. He'd been reported missing by his wife. As it turned out, the fire hadn't killed Averbeck. There was no smoke in his lungs. Mr. Averbeck had been stabbed to death and his body dumped in the warehouse prior to it being set ablaze.

In other words, he'd been burned postmortem.

Another week or two passed and, eventually, the *Tribune* had nothing more to say on the matter of the deceased employment lawyer John Averbeck.

Just another murder in a city of unsolved murders.

PART ONE

THE SPECIAL PROSECUTOR

If you pick up a starving dog and make him prosperous, he will not bite you. This is the principal difference between a dog and a man.

—Mark Twain

CHAPTER 1

David Siskin wondered why he bothered checking into the Courtyard Marriott on his bimonthly trips to Chicago as he always worked late into the evening at the office suite off North Dearborn. A cot in the copy room would save the business money as well as save Siskin mucho time since booking a room at the Marriott for the equivalent of a lengthy nap didn't help the bottom line.

And, as a real estate investor, David Siskin was all about the bottom line.

His wife, Cherie, had knighted Siskin a *workaholic* decades ago, before the two had even tied the knot, but she didn't mean it in a bad way. Cherie had her book clubs, her quilting classes, her floristry, her fundraising for the Alzheimer's Association—the disease that first stole her mother's mind and then her life—as well as a half dozen other public-service hobbies that never registered on Siskin's radar but kept her busy now that the kids were grown. By contrast, outside of work, Siskin had no hobbies. Sure, he suffered through endless rounds of golf as that was part of the game you played to rub elbows with investors and property financiers, but the actual pastime never took hold of him. However, when Siskin hit middle age and began fretting over the expansion of his midsection, he took up biking. Siskin even dumped a couple grand into a Cannondale CAAD. Siskin's hobby lasted all of a week. He was biking around Lake Nokomis one beautiful summer evening, enjoying both the exercise as well as life in general—until the debacle. Some hothead in a yellow Corvette laid on the horn and didn't let up. It startled Siskin, sending him into the curb and from thence ass over teakettle onto the sidewalk. Bruised and bleeding, Siskin glanced up in time to witness the Corvette speed past with a middle finger salute held high out of the driver's side window.

The road bike had been gathering dust in the garage ever since.

Siskin lived in Minneapolis, had all of his life, and—like loads of other business commuters in the Twin Cities—he took the United Airlines puddle jumper to O'Hare and, two or three days later, took it home again. Siskin's Chicago partners, venture capitalists one and all, didn't burn the midnight oil like he did. Siskin's Chicago partners were more clock-watchers—golf-playing nine-to-fivers.

That didn't bother Siskin. There were no hard feelings.

Siskin's Chicago partners did their jobs.

They made money. They invested money.

Rinse. Repeat.

Siskin heard sounds from the outer office and wondered who in hell that could be. Margie, the spinster admin who drenched herself in so much perfume that her fragrance lingered long after she'd exited your office, had waved goodbye hours ago. And the night janitor, Juan or Raul or whatever, had already passed through the office suite with his trash cart and vacuum cleaner and dust wand. Siskin glanced at his Rolex Explorer—a gift from Cherie given about the time of his biking debacle—and figured it was time to head over to the Marriott for his nightly siesta.

It was then a throat cleared and Siskin's head snapped up.

An impossibly large man filled the doorway of Siskin's office. The unannounced visitor was not basketball-player tall but appeared to be seven feet in height, possibly aided by the pointed-toed cowboy boots on his feet as well as the black fedora on the top of his head. The unannounced visitor was dressed in a classic black suit, cut well for his size and height. The unannounced visitor also sported an unbuttoned brown raincoat that hung down to his ankles and appeared to contain enough fabric to sail a small skiff to China. The man was a living chiaroscuro, a Goliath of light and shadow, and looked as though he'd just muscled his way out of an old black-and-white Humphrey Bogart movie.

"Is this a bad time?" the unannounced visitor said.

Siskin hadn't been this startled since the unfortunate biking incident at Lake Nokomis. "The office has been closed for hours."

The unannounced visitor glanced about Siskin's twenty-fifth-floor office. "You don't say."

Siskin saved and exited the Excel sheet he'd been working on and leaned back in his chair. "What can I help you with?"

"Do you mind if I sit?"

Siskin motioned to the guest chair in front of his desk, hoping it was sturdy enough to support the man's bulk. *Mike McCarron* flickered through Siskin's mind. Michael J. McCarron was one of his Chicago business partners and the president of the investment company in which he currently convened with the unannounced visitor. Michael J. McCarron and that Irish sense of humor of his, always ready with an off-color joke, always filling dinner conversation with the high jinks he'd pulled on his wife and children, friends and neighbors, and even some of the raunchier practical jokes he'd pulled during his years at Columbia University. Siskin thought he heard light rustling coming from the outer office and imagined McCarron and one of the other partners hiding behind the door, keeping their chuckles to a minimum after imbibing a single malt or four at a nearby tavern where, evidently, they'd met this guy who looked like a film-noir version of Paul Bunyan and convinced him to participate in some kind of office prank.

"So . . ." The unannounced visitor spoke again after cramming his heft into the cushioned armchair. "You're the Jew from Minneapolis?"

"Yes," Siskin replied, now convinced this stunt was more of McCarron's tomfoolery, "I'm the Jew from Minneapolis."

"My name is Cordov Woods, as in a *cord of wood*." The big man smiled. "I shit you not. My father laughed his ass off every time he introduced me. But everybody calls me Cord."

Siskin definitely heard rustling in the outer office. "What can I do for you, Mr. Woods?"

"Do you like idioms? You know, a turn of phrase that contains a *special meaning*?"

Siskin shrugged. "I haven't given them much thought, one way or the other."

"I find idioms fascinating—what they mean, how they came into being. And you've no doubt heard the one that goes 'don't upset the apple cart'?"

Siskin nodded.

"It's basically the same expression as 'let sleeping dogs lie.' Both idioms generally mean—and pardon my French—don't *fuck* with the status quo. Because, if I'm selling apples, I've stacked my cart in a tidy structure—an orderly manner—which keeps the merchandise from rolling off the cart and all over the street. Do you see what I mean?"

Siskin nodded again. He felt goose bumps forming, the hair on the back of his neck began to prickle, and he was no longer so certain this encounter was a Michael McCarron–hatched gag at all. He began to suspect that *other* thing . . . the one he'd been assured—not assured but promised—would be kept in the strictest of confidence.

"So, if I'm out selling my apples, trying to make a decent living for myself and my family, and then some shit-hog comes along and pulls an apple out from where he shouldn't. And before you can say fuckity-doo-dah, my employer has me chasing runaway apples all over the goddamned street." The unannounced visitor stared at Siskin a long moment. "Now why did you have to go and yank that apple off my cart, Mr. Jew from Minneapolis?"

It took Siskin a second to speak, but when he did, he spoke fast—a nervous habit that kicked in whenever he came under pressure. "This is insane. You had to have checked in with the lobby guards at the main desk. They've got cameras all over the building . . . they even track your card in the elevator at this time of night."

"Tell me about it." The big man shrugged. "Makes me pine for the olden days. A simpler time. I've got several friends, colleagues to be more exact, I'll never see again unless I visit them at the Stateville Correctional Center. And I ain't visiting Stateville. Now, all these old colleagues of mine had to do was stay current; just enter the twenty-first century for crying out loud, and they'd have never seen a second inside of SCC." The unannounced visitor who called himself Cord Woods tried leaning back in his chair. However, considering his bulk, there wasn't much room to maneuver. "But to your point, I didn't come in through the lobby and I didn't sign in at the guard station. As for cameras and elevator cards and all that jazz—another idiom by the way—I've got a world-class IT guy that has my back."

"You'll never get away with this," Siskin spoke again, not so fast this time, now feeling as though he were about to vomit.

"You don't know Jethro. The guy's an awful conversationalist—don't even get me started on the lost art of conversation or I'll wax on all night—but Jethro's a true magician, he really is, although he may be somewhat autistic or, what's that other thing that's not as bad? Asperger's syndrome? Jethro's probably more Asperger's than autistic, but, bear in mind, I'm no expert, and I doubt Jethro's ever been tested. You see, as long as Jethro kept fetching daddy's ice beer from the fridge, his parents didn't give two shits about any *irregular* behavior on his part. A sorry state of affairs that was, quite frankly, but they're both now out of the picture—figuratively and literally—since back when Jethro proved his worth. Dear old dad's ice-beer days are gone forever." The big man added, "I saw to that myself."

"What do you want from me?" Siskin knew he'd never be able to retrieve his iPhone from the breast pocket of his suit jacket, so he inched some fingers toward the desk phone.

"First off, I'm not going to hurt you." The unannounced visitor flicked his head toward the outer office. "Jethro's going to town on your network server. And he'll need your laptop, of course, when he's done with that. If I were you, I'd just sit back and relax."

Siskin closed his eyes and thought of Cherie. He thought of that crooked smile of hers, and he thought of the kids—the kids who were now adults but would forever be his kids—and he knew that *sitting back and relaxing* was out of the question. Siskin seized the phone off the cradle, pressed the number nine with a forefinger, but that was as far as he got before the unannounced visitor towered above him, guest chair flying backward into the wall.

"I told you I wasn't going to hurt you." The giant who called himself Cordov Woods kicked at Siskin's desk with a boot, sending desk, phone, laptop, yellow notepad, and a couple of Mont Blanc pens soaring across the room.

There was now nothing between the two men.

"But I am going to kill you."

CHAPTER 2

That was the year that was, that was
And I am the was of time

Vira and I made our way toward the northwest side of Chicago.
Vira sat in the passenger seat of my F-150, her face outside
the window, soaking in the sun of another beautiful April
morning. We listened to my smartphone as it slid about the
dashboard and cranked "The Was of Time"—a Grammy win-
ner from decades back. I caught myself singing along with the
chorus I somehow knew by heart.

File me a memory
And put me in your past
File me a memory
Never meant to last

The song continued playing for another minute. I grew mel-
ancholy and blinked back moist eyes.

That was the year that was, that was
And I am the was of time
That was the year that was, that was
You left me far behind

Throughout the separation and eventual divorce from my
wife, Mickie, and in the immediate aftermath—or aftershocks
as it felt like at the time—no matter what station I had the radio tuned to, a one-hit wonder song would come on and knock
me on my ass. I'd be minding my own damned business,

maybe even having a mediocre day, and then I'd take a right hook to the chin by "Seasons in the Sun." Then, a day or two later, I'd take a shiv to the guts from "Brandy." Then, I'd be driving home with a bag of tacos for dinner and "In a Big Country" would come on and dropkick me in the seeds.

However, the one that tore out my guts and tossed them back in my face was "The Was of Time" by Jonny Whiting and The U-Turns. Whiting's theme, as far as I could decipher, was how time wasn't necessarily linear but more reliably measured in intensity of feeling and, as such, even if I lived to be a hundred, Mickie's leaving—her kicking of me to the curb—would always be first and foremost in my mind . . . my reality . . . my cross to bear.

Freaking music.

Of course, per Officer Kippy Gimm's hushed phone call, that very same Jonny Whiting of Jonny Whiting and The U-Turns now lay dead on the tile floor in the kitchen of his Avondale condominium, evidently battered to death with his own electric guitar.

I grabbed my iPhone, tapped a few times at my Maps app so it could zero in on the address Kippy had provided, and tossed it back on the dashboard so the voice could wave us in like an air traffic controller. Kippy worked out of the 17th District—Albany Park—on North Pulaski. Her and her partner, Officer Dave Wabiszewski—or *Wabs* if you'd managed to advance to his inner circle—had been dispatched to Whiting's address after a hysterical 911 call from the singer's condominium manager and immediately discovered that the condo's manager had every right to dial 911 and had every right to be hysterical.

Jonny Whiting was quite dead.

The singer-songwriter grew up a north-sider—local boy makes good—and moved back to his old stomping grounds after a couple decades of making music in New York City. He'd bought a top-floor condo off Addison Street, overlooking the north branch of the Chicago River. Whiting had been back five years and set up his nest in Avondale as part of Chicago's process of renovating deteriorated neighborhoods per the influx of more *well-to-do* residents—*gentrification* I heard a newscaster once term it.

I parked my pickup in front of a fire hydrant, the only open spot I could find on Addison Street, half a block away from the mounting bustle of police activity. Kippy and her partner were nowhere to be found, so I Googled Jonny Whiting, came back with a million hits, and began tapping open articles of interest.

I was the Daily Double under One-Hit Wonders—fuck you Alex Trebek. Ain't nothin' the matter with being a one-hit wonder. You write "Tainted Love" or "Take On Me," and Soft Cell and A-ha should get their asses kissed forever. The Proclaimers and their 500 miles, Nena and her red balloons, The Knack, even Looking Glass, their songs—their one-hit wonders—are fucking great. But I'd quibble with Trebek as "Bar Maid" was on the Billboard chart for a week or two and "Chainsaw" did okay as well.

I looked up from the interview Whiting had given *Rolling Stone* magazine back in the day. For the life of me I couldn't place any songs called "Bar Maid" or "Chainsaw," but I sure as hell could—and without the aid of a karaoke display—belt out maybe two-thirds of the lyrics to "The Was of Time" correctly. I figured Whiting was deluded and that the *Jeopardy!* answer had been spot on.

Jonny Whiting should have embraced his status as part of a late-eighties one-hit wonder band.

I stared at Vira, who shot a questioning look my way, and then hung the CPD notice from the rearview mirror. The notice would keep my pickup from being towed away as the closest spot I could pull into for the brief time Vira and I would be here was, in no uncertain terms, a no-parking zone.

Officer Gimm, Vira, and I had found ourselves in a bit of a pinch last fall—had come face-to-face with a man of most unpleasant means—but we'd fought back and, with no small assist from Vira, had somehow managed to stay alive. Kippy and I had since become friends and even chummed about for a few months—catching a dinner here, a movie there, even explored some off-leash dog parks about the city. But—as *just friends*—it'd become more and more difficult for me to be around her . . . and I'd pulled back since the first of the year.

So, with recent personal dynamics in mind, imagine my surprise when Officer Kippy Gimm called my cell phone first thing this morning and requested our presence at the scene of Chicago's latest homicide . . . at the scene where rock-and-roller Jonny Whiting had, in fact, become the *was* of time.

Kippy stepped out onto the building's stoop, stood next to the officer who'd been stationed there, and glanced toward my pickup truck.

That was our cue.

CHAPTER 3

Special Prosecutor Peter Feist finished his cup of dark roast and wondered if he could make the trash bin near the entryway to the conference room from his perch at the head of the cherry wood table. But that would be rude. And, after all, he was the genius who set in place the biweekly meetings in which each attorney, or team of attorneys, would present a status update on their ongoing investigations.

Feist headed the Special Prosecutions Bureau inside the Cook County State's Attorney's Office and the staff seated around the table—with their mugs, legal briefs, and notepads at the ready, with their smartphones set to not disturb—as well as those seated in chairs lining the walls was his crew.

Yup, what a genius he'd been—gather together a group of lawyers and give them each a shot at out razzle-dazzling their colleagues with their legal brilliance and wit. What could possibly go wrong? Even as an attorney himself, Feist would glance at his watch and contemplate Shakespeare's old adage "Let's kill all the lawyers." The first few rounds of biweeklies had dragged on an eternity—Feist spotted eyes glazing over, his included—so Feist switched gears and informed his staff that in the interest of getting everyone back to their desks before lunch, these palavers would become more huddle-like in nature than meetings, more sprint than marathon. And unless there was a major accomplishment, a cause for celebration, or a request for all hands on deck—everyone's status update would be limited to five minutes.

Feist almost brought in an egg timer.

Plates on his team were perpetually overflowing as investigations inside the Special Prosecutions Bureau jumped from white-collar crime to street gangs, from consumer fraud to organized theft and fencing, from human trafficking to public corruption, from identity theft to a wide assortment of other inquiries tossed in-between. Steve Cowart, Raj Patel, and Jennifer Sporre had sailed through their case updates with time to spare, as expected. Anahita Esfahani was currently in the process of rattling off bullet points from her yellow legal pad. She paused briefly between topics to glance about the room, make eye contact, and see if anyone had any questions or comments. Anahita led the Consumer Fraud Unit and Feist had no fear that she'd come in under the wire. In fact, Anahita was currently rounding third with some of the more interesting cases her unit had screened off their consumer and home repair fraud tip line—the submitted complaints they actually planned to pursue, but on deck was Arthur Behr.

Good old Arthur—a nicer bore you'd never meet. He worked in Andrea Hayes's group—but Andrea was out this morning, a private matter at home—and she'd appointed Behr as her stand-in for today's meeting. Art had a brilliant legal mind—but good god the man could wax on, and he'd be presenting on the impact of legislative reforms as they relate to mortgage fraud.

Christ wept.

Windbag or not, Arthur Behr could think on his feet. As could Andrea Hayes and Anahita Esfahani and Steve Cowart and Raj Patel and Jennifer Sporre and all the other attorneys Feist had handpicked for the Special Prosecutions Bureau. He'd seen them all in action—whether conducting a direct or cross-examination in a courtroom or grilling a witness during deposition. Thinking on your feet was a gift, not something they can teach in law school. Sure, locating previous judicial decisions, the case law, and legal precedents is vital. If you can't do that—if you lack technical dexterity in utilizing Lexis-Nexis or Westlaw—well, enjoy your student loans. Additionally, one must be well versed in the law, also vital, but—and Feist took this as gospel—it's essential for an attorney to be able to think on his or her feet in order to spot each potential issue, however minute, that could make a case or break it wide open. And then dig in, relentlessly probing and prodding the newly discovered issue as though you were a master surgeon with a mental scalpel.

And speaking of thinking on your feet, Feist might have to take a quick stroll down West Washington Street just to clear his palate after listening to Arthur's soliloquy on mortgage fraud. Feist's own plate was full—beyond full considering the situation to which he was personally attending. He needed the week to focus on that case alone. Feist glanced around the room and wondered again where in hell Marty Kolles was? Marty had the ability to nudge the Art Behrs of the world along with a wink in his eye, a smile on his face, and a song in his heart . . . so the Art Behrs of the world would exit meetings not knowing they'd been given the bum's rush or that their toes had been thoroughly stepped upon.

A second later Feist's internal query was answered as Kolles opened the conference room door quietly, caught Feist's eye, and jerked his head toward the hallway.

Feist stood as Anahita took her chair. He grabbed his empty coffee container and briefcase. "Please excuse me." He glanced at Behr. "The floor's all yours, Art."

"What do you mean Siskin is dead?"

Kolles had refused to tell Feist what the hell was going on until the two of them were alone in Feist's corner office with the door shut. "I caught a blurb on the news about a death last night at the office of the Michael J. McCarron Investment Group and called a guy I know at the Bureau of Detectives."

"What the hell happened?"

"Jesus, Peter," Kolles said, face ashen. "The man was murdered."

CHAPTER 4

I leashed my golden retriever and killed the Jonny Whiting music video I'd been watching on YouTube—Vira refuses to exit the F-150 if tunes are in play. She gave me a *Dude, I was jamming* look, so I said, "Kippy's here."

That got her tail wagging.

We slipped out on the driver's side, peeked for traffic, crossed Addison and did another forty yards on the sidewalk, got ushered by Kippy into the building's foyer, and from there into a side stairwell. We took the steps up to the eighth floor—the top floor—which, per Kippy, was the only floor in the complex that housed two units. Whiting's executive condominium took up one side of the floor; an affluent gay couple, currently vacationing in Italy, resided in the other side.

Taking the steps gave more time for Kippy to fill me in. She stooped between Vira and the fire door leading to the eighth floor, shook an offered paw, and looked up at me. "Ames thinks it's drug-related or maybe a John Lennon thing."

"A John Lennon thing?"

"You know, Lennon was killed by a crazed fan."

"Wasn't Lennon shot outside his apartment building when he came home? This building is secured, so even if a *crazed fan* got inside, why would Whiting let him into his home?"

"He knew whoever it was well enough to let the guy in, even fix him up with a cup of coffee—there are two cups and cream on the island—before things got ugly." Kippy shrugged. "It could be a drug thing. He was in the music business—you know how that goes. From what I've heard, Whiting spent much of the nineties snorting cocaine."

"How much would you have to owe a drug dealer to get beaten to death?"

"This is Chicago, Mace—it could be five bucks." Kippy added, "I got you in here on the illicit drug angle. Walk the periphery, stay out of the way, but make sure Vira gets a glimpse in the kitchen." Kippy stood up. "So she can do her thing."

I nodded.

"And Mace," she said, "it's not a pretty sight."

Vira and I traipsed behind Kippy, heading toward the open doorway of Whiting's condominium, when a figure stepped into the hallway.

"So nice of you to rejoin us, Officer Gimm," a detective by the name of Trevor Ames said. "And how sweet of you to bring your boyfriend."

"He's not my boyfriend."

I shook my head in agreement.

Detective Ames looked as though he'd stepped out from a grooming infomercial on late-night TV. Barring the occasional mustache, most police officers are clean shaven. Cops rarely sport beards as beards could get grabbed at in a skirmish. Plainclothes officers, such as Ames, are granted additional leeway when it comes to facial hair as long as their beards remain neatly trimmed. And neatly trimmed Detective Ames's beard and mustache were, as well as conditioned, combed, waxed, and, most definitely, dyed since Ames was in his mid-forties and there wasn't a hint of gray in the mix.

The guy took better care of his beard than first-time mothers their newborns.

After a brisk greeting, Ames whispered, "If Fido finds a stash, come get me. Otherwise, I don't want to hear it bark or smell a fart. And stay the hell out of the kitchen—men at work." The senior detective turned his attention back to Kippy and jerked a thumb toward the outer hallway. "We need to talk."

After my dismissal, I kept Vira on a tight leash as we strolled down the condo's foyer and took the first right into what had to be Whiting's home studio or music room. I stood inside the doorway and stared at the awards in a glass display case in the corner of the room, but the busybody in me tried to hear what Detective Ames was saying to Kippy as they stood outside the apartment's entryway. All I could make out was a string of intense and one-sided murmurs. Evidently, Ames was imparting pearls of wisdom, and his condescending pearls sounded exasperated in nature . . . and possibly having to do with yours truly.

I took in the singer's music room. Album covers were mounted in frames on all four walls, a Moog synthesizer sat on a table with a stool in front, and a sound system with four speakers took up most of the far side of the room. Two Grammys—Song of the Year and Best New Artist—sat in the display case, along with an array of less-recognizable plaques and awards. An acoustic guitar sat upright in an armchair while a twelve-string slept on a leather couch. An empty guitar stand stood between the furniture with a gold nameplate reading *Tabitha* fastened along the bottom.

A *Billboard* article I'd scanned while waiting in the pickup spoke of Jonny Whiting's first Gibson Les Paul Custom—mahogany with a maple neck in wine red—which the rocker had nicknamed Tabitha.

I listened as the detective finished whatever harangue he felt the need to impart on young Officer Gimm. Kippy'd made a big splash in the headlines last fall—and she was gunning for detective—so he probably got off giving her a tongue lashing for items real and imagined. He obviously didn't know Kippy, and I hoped Ames wouldn't keep pushing it lest Whiting's Avondale executive condominium became the scene of a double homicide.

Human remains detection dogs like Vira are trained to

identify the distinct odor of decomposing human flesh. Decomposition starts when microbiome and enzymes begin the breaking down of an individual's body postmortem, and the unique aroma of a human corpse—its death scent—differs from all other animals. A dead body kicks off some five hundred different chemicals, including such charming compounds as putrescine and cadaverine—the binary compounds chiefly accountable for the vile smell of putrefying flesh. Putrefaction is the fifth stage of death—trailing pallor mortis, algor mortis, rigor mortis, as well as livor mortis—and can be described as the ensuing breakdown of the cohesiveness between tissues . . . and the liquefaction of nearly all organs.

Yeah, I know—whenever I tell folks what I do for a living, they think I slept through Career Day in high school.

Alas, Vira and I had a different job to perform today, and it had nothing to do with locating human remains. Kippy had gotten us into the rocker's condo—the murder scene—under the guise of Vira sniffing out hidden drugs—illicit drugs—but our real purpose was for my golden retriever to take a gander at what lay motionless on the kitchen floor as we probed about the outer edges of the investigation.

We passed a guest bathroom as the entrance hall came to an end. A family room sat on the right, the now-notorious kitchen and another corridor leading to bedrooms lay on the left. Whiting's family room had a high ceiling, multiple fans, and hardwood floors with complementing floor-to-ceiling windows letting in an avalanche of natural light. A flat-screen TV the size of a drive-in theater lined the far wall.

I then did something I'd not done at crime scenes before. I'd been concerned about my dog's *occurrences* since the get-go, and increasingly so as we began to figure out what exactly they might signify. At one and a half years of age, my golden retriever was still relatively new to being an HRD dog . . . and then there's this whole *other thing* tossed into the mix. When Vira leads me to a dead body, she has these brief episodes or spells or double takes—a moment of shakes and shudders—like a terrified puppy at the sound of thunder. So I lifted my golden retriever into my arms, all sixty pounds of her, and edged left, my back sliding against the wall. I held Vira close to my chest as I side-stepped past a kitchen island the size of a catamaran—sure enough, there were two coffee cups and a creamer carton on the side containing a row of stools—until the murder scene came into view, until I felt the trembling kick in, until I felt my dog convulse.

A first-year law student would rip me apart if I ever attempted to explain Vira's *other thing* to a jury, but let me give it a shot.

Dogs inhale scent particles into their nasal cavities. The massive number of scent receptors in a canine's nasal cavity allows them to identify thousands of different smells. Then, like running a software program, those odors are processed by their sensory cells, by their hundreds of millions of olfactory receptors as well as by that mystical sense of smell receptor known as the Jacobson's organ, which is an olfactory chamber that allows dogs to both smell and taste at the same time. Some canine breeds have three hundred million scent receptors, whereas human beings, weighing in with only five million, got shafted.

Ultimately, this is what makes for great sniffer dogs, whether it be finding survivors after a natural disaster, locating illicit drugs, discovering explosive materials . . . or leading the authorities to human remains.

And Vira is an excellent sniffer dog, but—and here's the part where I'd get all twitchy on the witness stand—I've observed her on several occasions take it up a notch with this *other thing*.

Murder's an intimate act, right, and killers leave behind a mountain of physical evidence and DNA for the CSI teams and medical examiners to sift through—fingerprints, footprints, skin under nails, hair, saliva, blood, semen, and so on. So why wouldn't there be scent DNA—some kind of scent aura, I'd tell the courtroom before getting ripped to shreds on cross-examination—left at crime scenes as well? Vira—and perhaps all cadaver dogs—receive this tsunami of stimulus, this landslide of scent data, and Vira then takes the art of human remains detection to the next level . . . the Sherlock Holmes level. Vira discovers a body, or visits a crime scene, and then attempts to process this data, to perform some kind of forensic analysis on the various smells and odors—the scent DNA—and decipher their meaning.

Let's say there's a road rage incident and, as a result, I follow some poor sap home and beat him to death with my tire iron. Perhaps I leave behind some blood or hair or finger-prints or even fibers from my clothes for the crime scene investigators to ferret through. Hell, knowing me I'd screw up a homicide six ways from Sunday—probably wind up dropping my driver's license in the puddling blood for CSI agents to find. Anyway, all of this forensic evidence would point in my direction. Similarly, if Vira came across the body of my victim, she'd try to piece together whatever forensic scent exists at the scene . . . up to and including any trace of the murderer.

In other words, Vira'd sniff out my driver's license in the pool of blood.

Any additional explanation to the courtroom would find me humming the theme from *The Twilight Zone* as the judge called a mistrial and sent the bailiff in search of orderlies and a straitjacket. How-effen-ever, the scent receptors in a dog's nose are beyond the wildest episodes of *The Twilight Zone*, Your Honor. If Horton can hear a Who, my dogs can smell them. And if the jury wants to delve into the supernatural—those canine scent receptors are supernatural and they enable dogs to identify thousands and thousands of different smells and, in Vira's case, she interprets these odors.

Vira makes links, relationships . . . connections . . . she connects the dots.

So, ladies and gentlemen of the jury, is Vira a ghost dog? Hell no.

Vira's just Vira—a canine savant and the Tom Brady of cadaver dogs, that's all.

I rest my case.

Vira's convulsing ended as suddenly as it had begun.

And then multiple sets of eyes turned my way, all questioning what the hell I was doing there on the edge of the kitchen, gaping at the dead rocker, and carrying a golden retriever.

CHAPTER 5

Frank Cappelli Sr. finished his second cup of macchiato—a strong shot of espresso with a dash of steamed milk—at the same time he finished scanning the *Chicago Tribune*. Nothing in the morning's paper butted up against any of his business interests . . . his commerce . . . his concerns.

And he liked it that way.

Cappelli Sr. took off his new pair of bifocals—they were straining his eyes, driving him batshit—set them on the side table, leaned back in his armchair, placed his feet on the ottoman, closed his eyes, and thought for the thousandth time about the harshness of fathers.

He'd made himself a promise—no, he'd made himself an oath—decades back, before he'd ever met his wife, that he would never raise his offspring in the manner in which he'd been brought up. A first memory—flying across the hardwood floor when he was five. Jumping up, his face a mask of tears and snot and blood, begging forgiveness from his father for having *needed* to be slapped. Another memory—his mother had been ailing and his father heated a can of chicken noodle soup for dinner. He'd made the mistake of asking dear old dad if they'd be having soda crackers as well. The empty soup can hit him right below his left eye. If Cappelli Sr. looked closely in the mirror, he still saw the mark where the can's tin edge split open the skin.

And so it went—more and more memories, year after year—right on up until that glorious day when the malicious bastard went down for the count after suffering an SCA—a sudden cardiac arrest—a week after Cappelli had turned twenty-one. As the priest prattled on at his old man's funeral, Cappelli bit his lip to keep from leading cheers as though he were at a pep rally, cupped his hands together, and swore he'd never be like the heartless *cazzo*.

It had been one of the few oaths that Cappelli Sr. ever kept.

He'd heard tell that certain genes skip a generation. Things like cancer, alcoholism, even Alzheimer's can be passed on down the family tree. But all these decades later and Cappelli Sr. now knew there were other things, nonmedical things . . . colder, *harsher* things that also got passed on down the tree.

He'd seen it in his son's blue eyes—when things weren't spinning the kid's way, when his boy was angry, when he was pursing his lips, and on the verge of lashing out. Cappelli Sr. knew that look all right. He knew that portrait of rage and anger. It'd been burned into his soul as a child.

And though they'd never met, Cappelli's son—Frank Cappelli Jr.—took after his grandfather.

Of course, Frank Cappelli Sr. had been harsh in his business affairs. He couldn't deny it. In his line of work, you had to be harsh. After his father's premature demise, Cappelli Sr. had been schooled by the very best—Uncle Niccolò or, more affectionately, Uncle Nic, God rest his hard and wise soul.

But when it came to family, when it came to his only son—Cappelli Sr. had lived up to his long-standing oath—he'd been soft. And whether it was part of the bloodline or just part of some cosmic joke, Cappelli's son had grown into a somewhat taller version of Cappelli's father; different looks, same demeanor. Cappelli Sr. hadn't turned a blind eye toward the stories about his boy. Word had gotten back to him, all right—how could it not?—as well as several firsthand accounts from his men at the various scenes.

When his son was in his early teens, they'd had him treated for ICD—impulse-control disorder. That was soon followed with treatment for ADHD—attention-deficit/ hyperactivity disorder. And before long came the treatment for anger management.

But therapists and drugs like Prozac and Zoloft bounced off Cappelli Jr. like balls off a backboard.

Like he did in all his business affairs, Cappelli Sr. collected information, and he'd once read in a medical journal that the male brain doesn't fully develop or mature until age twenty-five. That had bought Cappelli Sr. a glimmer of hope as the years passed by; alas, his boy would be twenty-six in December. *Hope springs eternal in the human breast,* that English poet said, but, so far, there'd been no perceptible change in Cappelli Sr.'s kid.

Not one iota.

Nevertheless, Cappelli Sr. loved his son—unconditionally, as the saying goes—and though his boy was not the aptest of pupils, Cappelli Sr. did his best to mentor him in the family's profession, to tutor him in the ways of their *unique* world. He tried to be to his son what Uncle Nic had been to him. It had been an exhausting uphill battle. If only Niccolò were still alive, the man had been a genius, and Cappelli Sr. could assuredly benefit from his counsel.

One of four cell phones vibrated on the side table next to his bifocals. Cappelli Sr. had the phones arranged in such a manner that he knew immediately whom this particular phone represented. He slid the cell on, brought it up to his ear and said, "I've been waiting."

"It's done."

"Any issues?" It was an essential question, one which Cappelli Sr. always made sure to ask.

"None at all. Minneapolis is off the table."

"And phase two?"

"Phase two will require a little more finesse," the voice replied, "but it's on track."

"Let me know when it's done."

Cappelli Sr. tapped the cell phone off, set it back on the side table, leaned back in his armchair, and continued pondering the harshness of fathers . . . and sons.

CHAPTER 6

Two CSI agents from the Crime Scene Investigations Unit had been busy creating a photographic record of Jonny Whiting's last stand—one with a camera while the other worked a video recorder. A third agent knelt over Whiting's bruised and broken body, notebook and pencil in hand. Additional agents in blue booties, white coveralls, disposable gloves, and hairnets orbited the body while a couple of detectives edged ever closer.

"Drug sniffer," I announced to the room.

"Not in here," the agent on the floor said and went back to scribbling in his notebook.

I set Vira down and we moved quickly toward the back bedrooms.

Kippy had been right.

It was not a pretty sight.

Jonny Whiting's skull seemed at one with the kitchen tile. Dented, busted, in a thick puddle of dried blood—a flash of bone, a missing eye, clumps of brain matter. Beside Whiting's body lay the smashed remains of what I assumed to be the electric guitar missing from the dead rocker's home studio—*Tabitha*—Whiting's Gibson Les Paul Custom. Its body shattered from what had to have been repeated strikes to Whiting's head; its neck in pieces from what must have come from the final blows; its six strings now a knot of wire, strands of hair, and blood.

No amount of restoration would ever make Tabitha sing again.

The stench was equally bad. Decomposing tissue releases gas, both methane and hydrogen sulfide, and lungs expel fluid through the nose and mouth. Kippy mentioned that one of the detectives had cranked up the air-conditioning although it might have made more sense to toss open the windows. Of course, it could have been worse; Whiting could have had the heat set at ninety degrees. The CSI agents also wore medical face masks, and I'd be surprised if they'd not smeared a dab or two of peppermint oil on the inside of their masks in order to hamper any pungent odors.

I'd once quizzed a medical examiner on how he and his colleagues were able to handle working on a bad decomp. *You just have to deal with it* was all he told me. In my line of work, I've gotten used to it—to a certain degree—but am elated that once a body has been discovered, me and the kids get to step back and, in cases like these . . . step far back.

Current articles I'd scanned referenced how Jonny Whiting had been spending his days composing music for film and theater, something he'd been doing in recent years. In the *Rolling Stone* interview, Whiting mentioned he liked to keep busy, twenty-four/seven, lest his old habits—his old demons— return. He'd missed studio work on Monday. Calls to Whiting's iPhone and landline had not been returned; neither had text messages or emails. He was a no-show again on Tuesday and Whiting's agent gave the rocker another night to come down off what he thought might be a bender before he contacted the company that manages the Avondale condominium building. After ten minutes of rapping on Whiting's entryway this morning, the condominium manager unlocked the door for both her and Whiting's agent to enter.

Fifteen seconds later, the manager made haste tapping 911 into her cell phone while Whiting's agent sat outside the condo, on the hallway floor, with his head in his hands.

Kippy and Wabiszewski had arrived at the scene first,

followed by Detective Ames and his partner, and soon after by a team from the CSI Unit, which itself is part of the Forensic Services Division inside the Bureau of Detectives.

The rotting of a human corpse kicks in mere minutes after death through a process known as autolysis, or self-digestion, as enzymes begin digesting cell membranes. It starts in the liver and the brain, and ultimately works through all other tissue and organs. Body temperature drops, acclimating to the cadaver's environment, which, in this case, was Whiting's executive condominium.

As for TOD—time of death—Jonny Whiting had been in-communicado for the past two days, evidently AWOL at work, and he'd last been in touch with the studio four mornings earlier via a flurry of email and text messages he'd sent Satur-day. So if TOD weighs in at ninety-something hours, the rigor mortis would have subsided; of course that was impossible to distinguish from what I'd seen lying on the kitchen tiles as the blunt-force trauma to Whiting's face and skull had run off with the entire show.

I stood inside the master bedroom with Vira and tried to shake off the images from the kitchen. Our job here was es-sentially over, but it occurred to me—what if the CSI agents trip over a stash of narcotics in some hidey-hole? Vira was many things—cadaver dog extraordinaire, some kind of ge-nius, a sweetheart—but she'd never been trained to sniff out cocaine or heroin or other illicit drugs. What if Jonny Whiting's death truly had been a drug crime and Vira and I miss the kilogram of naughty stuff hidden in the back of a closet? Then I wondered if I should rifle through some of Whiting's stuff? Search desk drawers? Check under beds and between mattresses?

A thorough search would take hours, not to mention how something like that would leave my fingerprints all over the area.

Then it struck me that Detective Ames had handed us a way out. I show up with Vira to see if there were any drugs hidden at the scene and Ames is unreceptive—hostile, in fact. Ames even takes Kippy aside to read her some kind of riot act. As a result of Ames's antagonism, and not wanting to get Officer Gimm into trouble, Vira and I performed a half-assed walk-through in case any drugs were lying about in obvious places, and then made a hasty retreat—that is, we got the hell out of Whiting's condo as soon as possible—in order to decrease the lead detective's ire at our very presence.

A minute later—and without a further glance at what lay on the floor of the condominium's kitchen—Vira and I got the hell out.

The street now buzzed with activity. It was bound to happen as soon as the story leaked—the media had arrived in full force. I counted news vans from three different stations. Reinforcement police officers had arrived and kept the gathering throng of reporters cordoned off the sidewalk and backed into the street. Considering who Jonny Whiting had been—and considering his song heard around the world—this would not remain *only* a Chicago story.

I glanced at my watch and muttered a profanity. I had to cruise back to my two acres in Lansing, a village seven miles south of Chicago's city limits, grab my brood of pups, and then bat-out-of-hell-it to an obedience class I was scheduled to lead in Schaumburg.

And it was going to be a nightmare navigating my F-150 through this beehive.

CHAPTER 7

"I guarantee I'm pronouncing it wrong, but it's Bucatini all'Amatriciana or something like that."

Paul Lewis stormed into my trailer—spreading dog treats in his wake—dropped the foil pan on top of my stove, and began punching preheat buttons he knew by heart from dozens of pizzas while we'd watched dozens of ball games.

"What the hell's in it?"

"Bacon, tomatoes, onions, and chili peppers," Paul replied. "And bucatini is basically fatter spaghetti."

In addition to being the executive director of CACC—Chicago Animal Care and Control—Paul Lewis is my best friend. Historically, Paul's been meticulous in his attire—the only man whose job centers around animals I've ever seen in three-piece suits. However, Paul's sense of fashion had of late begun to lapse as he eased into his fourth decade. The vests had all but disappeared, suit jackets remained hidden in his office closet or shrouded about the back of his desk chair, and—most surprising of all—his dress shirts were no longer tucked in.

This was certainly not the Paul Lewis I'd met a decade back when I'd first wandered into CACC with a laundry list of questions.

And I blame Paul's wife.

Sharla's a helluva chef. It'd take death to turn down a meal at the Lewis household. Sometimes I'll phone Paul in the mid-afternoon and let the conversation ramble onward until he inevitably invites me over for dinner just to get me the hell off the line. Last time I was there, I went Winnie-the-Pooh over a four-layer berry and custard trifle with that sponge stuff soaked in sherry that Sharla had simply *tossed together* at the last second.

If I were married to Sharla, camouflaging an expanding waistline via untucked dress shirts would not suffice—I'd need stretch pants and maternity clothes.

I took out my phone. "Let me thank Sharla."

"No." Paul grabbed my iPhone and set it on the kitchen table. "She made it for my lunch all week, but if I eat this plus what she makes every night for dinner, they'll bury me in a piano case."

"Well, what are you eating at lunch then?"

Paul looked as though he were about to weep. "Leafy greens and vinaigrette."

"So you're unloading these bins every Monday?"

"I'll heat and toss them in the break room at lunchtime and let everyone know. They'll be empty in ten minutes."

"The hell with that," I said. "I'll pop in and grab the bins Monday morning."

"Don't be greedy, Mace." Paul opened his Coors Light—as part of his diet he'd made me promise not to pick up any more of his favored Guinness—and sat down at the kitchen table. "So, what's the latest?"

Paul knew all about Vira and her *unique* ability—he'd been there at the very beginning—and I suspect his true motivation for stopping by on his way home from CACC was to get the lowdown on Jonny Whiting because—as expected—it had led the news in the days since his body had been discovered.

"Kippy's having me parade Vira around at Whiting's funeral tomorrow, but—I don't know—several days have passed."

Paul stared at my golden retriever, who sat next to Sue on the family room sofa monitoring the nightly news. "I suppose, plus the poor guy had been percolating in that apartment a few days." He took a sip of beer and switched topics. "So I got ya a roller, huh? What's Billie Boy been into?"

"What's he not been into?" I replied. "Yesterday Bill was out of my sight for two seconds and he comes back a wapatui of squirrel poop and old barf. Fortunately, whenever he rolls in something and tries coming in the pet door, Sue chases him back outside." I added, "I keep shampoo by the garden hose— Bill's got his own private car wash."

Sue—my male German shepherd and our family's patriarch—had taken early retirement and been slowly convalescing from stab wounds incurred while saving my sorry ass last year. I'd put the word on the street that I was looking for some new blood. Basically, my putting *the word on the street* meant I'd called Paul and promised him a case of beer if any breed showed up at his office that'd make for a good human remains detection dog.

Bloodhounds make excellent cadaver dogs and Paul called back with a tip on young master Bill in order to forsake his beloved dark stout and lay claim to a case of light beer. After a quick meet-and-greet with the troupe at CACC, we brought the little goofball back to my glorified trailer home. I named the puppy Billie Joe after Bobbie Lee Gentry's "Ode to Billie Joe," but shortened it to Bill to make it easier to issue commands. Unlike his namesake, I can't imagine Billie Joe chucking himself off the Tallahatchie Bridge, or any other bridge or overpass for that matter; however, if there were anything dead or rotting nearby, Bill would definitely carpe diem and roll in it.

It's instinctual for dogs to roll about stink piles. It harkens back to their ancestors disguising their own scent in order to sneak up on prey. I'm sure glad us humans don't have comparable instincts. Sadly, a nearby neighbor's husband of fifty years passed away in his sleep last month and, instead of rolling about on top of him, she dialed 911 for help.

My brood or tribe or den of canines now consists of Vira; Maggie May and Delta Dawn—my short-haired farm collies; Sue; and now Bill, my three-month-old bloodhound. I tend to name my kids after country or country rock songs. Vira had been shortened from Elvira, a song made famous by the Oak Ridge Boys. Maggie May stemmed from the Rod Stewart gem; Delta Dawn from the huge 1970s hit for both Tanya Tucker and Helen Reddy. Sue, of course, from Johnny Cash, and now Billie Joe.

Sue is Old Testament and spends his retirement sitting on the couch, looking all lofty and down his nose at us lesser specimens. All my German shepherd needed was a black robe to be the Supreme Court justice he always knew he was meant to be. Good old Sue would never make for much of a therapy dog—showering hospital patients with love and affection—quite the opposite, actually. He'd have a much better go of it growling at prison inmates. In fact, if home invaders had broken in prior to Sue's injuries, I'd have sent him out to make short order of them.

However, if the home invaders wanted to be licked to death or rolled upon, I'd send out Bill the newbie. If a newborn puppy broke in, I'd send out Maggie May and Delta Dawn to be, respectively, doting mother and know-it-all aunt just as they'd been to Vira. However, if anyone broke into my trailer home armed with an IQ test, I'd send out my golden retriever.

While Vira and I sidekick about town, I count on Maggie to mother-slash-mentor little Bill—show him the ropes as well as the doggy door. And I count on Sue to keep the teething little goofball toeing the line.

Paul and I shot the bull as the dinner baked before he switched topics again, this time to both his and Sharla's pet project . . . me.

"Anything new with your cop friend?"

"Nothing's changed—as far as I can tell, she still wants to be *just friends*."

"Kind of like what we used to say in junior high."

"Good point," I replied. "Are you still friends with any girl that said they just wanted to be friends?"

"Not a one."

"Of course not."

"Just say the word, Mace, and I'll unleash Sharla." He added, "There's a bunch of single women from church who'd be up for going out."

"I don't do blind dates, Paul." We'd been over this before, but it never seemed to stick. "You know that."

I grabbed another beer from the fridge, but Paul waved off a second one as he had the drive home ahead of him. After he left, I cracked open a third and noticed the kids—Vira and Maggie and Delta, even Sue—were looking my way.

"What?" I said and took a slurp. "Why would I go on blind dates? You guys are the loves of my life."

Billie Joe swaggered over to me and I wiped some slobber off his jowls with a cheap napkin.

"Even you, Bill," I said. "Even you."

I'd been blindsided by Mickie—never saw the breakup coming—and spent the bulk of our separation scratching at my head. Old Mick is soon to get remarried and I fear I may have called her the night I heard the news of her engagement, but I'm consciously blocking that *truncated* conversation. Her fiancé runs a Mazda dealership in Oak Lawn. I wouldn't exactly call it stalking but I did happen across his picture on the staff page of the dealership's website. Mickie's fiancé looks like a Ken doll, generic good-looks with every strand of hair perfectly in place. And perhaps it might be borderline stalking, but a few months back I had trouble sleeping so I spent an hour surfing the photographs on Mickie's Facebook page.

The two of them appeared quite happy together.

When Kippy and I were hacking about in *just-friends* mode, we had a bit of fun, actually, but I dare not invade any personal proximity or reach for a hand or loop an arm around her shoulders, not only out of fear of crossing a line but, well . . . she is a cop. And I found myself living vicariously through the eyes of random strangers at movie theaters or restaurants or passersby who might glance our way and assume we were a couple.

After a few months, I couldn't do friendship mode any longer.

I think Kippy understands.

At least she doesn't harp on it like Paul and Sharla and the endless stream of blind dates they try to pawn me off on.

As dusk swept over the horizon, I ushered the tribe outside for their final sniff and pee of the evening. I sat at the picnic table, drank a last beer, and kept an eye on Billie Joe, making sure he didn't disappear into the tree line and return smelling like a porta potty at the county fair. Every time my puppy began heading out of view, I called his name and Bill came scampering back to me, tail spinning like a ceiling fan. The last thing I wanted to do before bed tonight was wash the rascal for the third time this week.

Bill the bloodhound was not yet ready for training as a cadaver dog. That would begin a bit further down the road. He and I were still busy ironing out the basics.

My clan of canines is trained to find and follow the scent of decomposing human flesh that either rises up from the soil or out from a breeze and then track it back to its point of origin . . . its source. Cadaver dogs can find human remains in the ruins of an earthquake or a fire or a building collapse as well as inside a shallow grave, even inside graves not so shallow. They can sniff out a complex and elusive scent, such as dry bone, to, well, let's just say more juicy substances. Scientist are still trying to figure out which of these various compounds really matter to HRD dogs, but whatever the chemical signature, it's present in recently deceased corpses on up to years-old skeletons.

Eventually, I'll be training Billie Joe to smell death, with my curriculum beginning as a game that he and I will play. I refer to my training regimen as *cadaver games,* and whenever the kids hear me mumble those two magic words, tails wiggle as they race out to jump into the pickup truck, ditching me to gather all the gear. I'll teach Bill to associate the scent of death—decaying human flesh and blood and bone—with one of his favorite toys. Bill loves his tennis balls. I use artificial scent tubes in a variety of odors: from the recently departed, to the decomposed, as well as the drowned. I score hair from the Lansing beauty salon that Mickie used to frequent and teeth from my local dentist. Even the tooth fairy that visits my older sister's kids—my niece and nephew—chips in now and again by tossing a few baby fangs my way. And don't get weirded out—'cause a nurse at the local clinic siphons off the occasional vial—but I also use my own blood to make the hunt as genuine as possible. At this point Bill and I will play intricate games of hide-and-seek with his tennis balls, which I'll hide in different terrains—in sunlight or under a driving rain, in snow or under leaves, in the light of day or the dark of night.

And I'll also teach Bill to pat the earth gently with his paw or sit down whenever he's discovered the scent's origin as digging or jumping up and down—or, in Bill's case, rolling about on top of it—can destroy evidence . . . plus, no one likes a show-off.

Folks often ask me how I chose this vocation. It's a fair enough question, and I'm never quite sure how to answer, but I remember when I was a child—a few days after the terrorist attacks of 9/11—I sat sandwiched between my parents in front of the television and watched in fascination as both rescue and cadaver dogs and their handlers worked tirelessly, around the clock, in the crushed wreckage and smoldering debris and dust and smoke and death in order to locate any survivors or to recover human remains in an attempt to help families find some sense of closure.

We'd always been a dog family, and I remember my father squeezing my hand that evening and saying, "Those dogs are heroes, Mace. Those dogs are heroes."

CHAPTER 8

Kippy handed me a lanyard. "Put this on and no one will dick with you."

The ID had my name with *CPD K-9 Handler* in bold type. It was printed on cheap card stock—the kind they hand out at class reunions along with a free drink ticket. I felt like a fraud . . . likely because I was.

"What if Detective Ames shows up and bites my ass?"

"Ames and company are still chasing the drug angle and want you to note anyone who may be carrying narcotics—any attendees that trip Vira's trigger."

I shook my head.

"Don't worry," Kippy said. "He's inside. We're the flunkies doing crowd control."

Although Jonny Whiting had never been much in the churchgoer department, his eighty-year-old mother was a member of Concordia Lutheran Church on the corner of West Byron Street and North Seeley Avenue, south of Irving Park Road in Chicago's North Center neighborhood. I had circled the church, found no hint of a parking lot, and settled for a residential spot three blocks out and hiked in with Vira leashed in a dog harness. Sometimes Vira can get *overzealous* in her detecting, especially if she locks in on any scent that may have a *special* meaning, scent DNA that may connect a perpetrator to a murder site. After learning that the hard way on Vira's maiden hunt, I'd initially kept her contained via a choke collar, but it rubbed against every fiber of my being and I discovered that—in situations like these—keeping alert while having Vira tethered in a harness worked just as well and without the risk of tracheal damage.

I, on the other hand, wore my only pair of dress shoes, black pants, and a new white dress shirt that made me itchy. The attire was a far cry from my usual pair of hiking boots, jeans, and a T-shirt. I even tamed my thatch of brown with a comb instead of fingers and set it in place with a few squirts from an antiquated can of hairspray that Mickie had abandoned in her haste to start anew.

I wanted to look appropriate for the day's event—Jonny Whiting's funeral—as Vira and I stood sentry outside Concordia Lutheran's main door through which the crowd of mourners would be ushered inside. We'd watch as friends and family and fans—and perhaps a particular attendee not quite so altruistic—came to pay their last respects to the north-side rock-and-roller.

Even though we'd arrived early, the news media had beaten us here.

Vira and I strolled past four separate groups huddling about the sidewalk, encroaching on the church's front entrance—video cameras at the ready, performing mic checks—and jockeying for the best angle from which to cover today's memorial. I recognized a few local anchors—plastic faces whose names I'd never learned—and two more reporters from a couple of the national alphabets whose names I'd never known.

Shit.

The last thing I wanted was to be caught on tape standing outside Concordia Lutheran, pitting out a dress shirt, face beet red, and with something unflattering dangling from my nose. Though the sky was overcast with a minor chance of rain, I slipped on a pair of sunglasses, wiped a sleeve across my snout, and headed to my post.

Concordia Lutheran was a mid-sized red-and-brown-brick church that, per their sign near the front entrance, had been *serving Chicago's North Center community for over 100 years.* And with Jonny Whiting's memorial, Concordia was likely hosting their largest gathering ever in their centennial of service. Not only was the church packed, but the sidewalk out front as well. I figured this was not only due to Whiting's celebrity status and his north-side roots, but because his death had led the news since the discovery of his body six days earlier.

Kippy alternately wandered the crowd forming about the church's periphery—those who had come to pay their respect to their fellow north-sider but would not be entering the church—and then back to her perch on the top step of Concordia's main entrance, the pinch point where funeralgoers were allowed to enter. At one point Kippy beelined it to a young guy in purple spandex and had him throttle back the volume at which he blared "The Was of Time" from his Bluetooth Street Blaster—quite possibly the twentieth time I'd heard Whiting's hit single in the past week.

Like Kippy, two other uniforms strolled among the crowd—chatting with attendees and keeping eyes wide open. Essentially, they were providing a high profile in order to deter any rebellious thoughts or wayward deeds emanating from any potentially less-upright souls hidden within the assembly.

There would be order.

Vira and I stood a step back on the grass in front of the sidewalk leading up to the church steps, as instructed—thankfully away from where most of the news cameras were centered—and watched as the progression of family, friends, and fans lined up to enter the church. I worried about the time delay—six days since we'd been in Whiting's condo, six days since Vira and I bore witness to what had become of the famed rocker. All of her previous *experiences* had fallen within rapid succession, where we'd been at a crime scene and, a few minutes later—in real time—my golden retriever had pointed us toward the perpetrator as though she were on a duck hunt retrieving some waterfowl. I worried that whatever chemical signature Vira may have gleaned at the crime scene—whatever scent might point us in the right direction—had dissipated in the flotsam and jetsam of the past week.

I also wondered if Vira had gotten any kind of a read to begin with or if Whiting lying on the kitchen floor—and decomposing for four days—would have messed up her perception or, quite frankly, if any scent DNA linked to the perpetrator would have lingered on for several days or long since dispersed.

I recognized Whiting's mother from the clip of her weeping her way through an abbreviated interview the TV news seemed to air every time an update to the story was broadcast—an aged matron trying to make sense out of the death of her only child. Mother Whiting was one of the first to arrive, surrounded by her brother and his family. Next up was Whiting's longtime agent and the man who sounded the alarm after the singer had missed two days in the studio. Vira watched silently as the mourners passed by and headed up the steps and into the church.

I'd watched enough videos of Jonny Whiting and The U-Turns this past week to keep an eye out for Chris Bjerke on lead guitar, Mike Herriges on bass, and Greg Lukkason on the drums. Kippy had mentioned the three living U-Turns would be in attendance, sitting in the front row with Whiting's mother and uncle. I scanned the sidewalk and spotted a man who had to be Bjerke. He was heavier set but had managed to keep his hair and broad smile in the intervening thirty years. The other two, Herriges and Lukkason, hadn't fared as well in their battle against gravity. Herriges looked as though he'd swallowed a beach ball and Lukkason had lost his once-lengthy mullet along with the rest of his hair.

I knelt next to Vira as The U-Turns stepped past us, making sure her heart was still in the game.

No reaction.

As the aging rockers hit the bottom steps a younger woman stepped out from the line of gatherers, crossed the walkway, and tapped Bjerke on the shoulder. The guitarist turned, his jaw down to his kneecaps, and an instant later he had her in a bear hug. Greetings and additional embraces followed suit by Herriges and Lukkason.

"Nope, you're coming in with us," I heard Bjerke insist as he grabbed her hand and pulled her along with The U-Turns, refusing to take no for an answer.

Ten minutes before the memorial service was scheduled to begin, a flustered usher came out to inform the still-incoming horde there was standing room only. Five minutes later, the same flush-faced lad returned to let the flock know the church was now filled to capacity. Kippy centered herself in front of the entrance in order to punch home the point and suggest that that was that and there'd be no run on the bank.

During the service, Vira and I threaded our way through the multitude milling about outside Concordia Lutheran, about the sidewalk and grass, about the street. We worked our way toward Officer Wabiszewski, who'd drawn the short straw and, like a master conductor, directed traffic at the corner of Byron Street and Seeley Avenue. I caught his eye and gave a quick wave. He nodded back. Wabiszewski was a different person than when we'd first met, back when he'd not believed a goddamned word out of my goddamned mouth.

Another Vira convert.

Perhaps I'd take a shot and call him *Wabs*, but I didn't want to push my luck.

We circled the church, and passed through the throng . . . again and again, but Vira kept her quiet.

It was like the Sherlock Holmes case of the dog that didn't bark.

CHAPTER 9

Cordov Woods sat behind the wheel of the double-parked Lincoln Continental intently working his way through the *Chicago Tribune*'s daily crossword. The clue for thirteen down was a single word—*Forecast*. Woods counted the white squares. Fifteen spaces and he already had a *g*, two *o*s, and a final *n* filled in. He smiled and scribbled the remaining letters for the word *prognostication* in the open spaces. Although Woods was in no way, shape, or form a cruciverbalist—that is, an expert in solving or creating these types of brainteasers—Woods loved him his crossword puzzles.

Woods had an appreciation—a deep fondness—for words and language. He figured words and language were the only things that differentiated us two-legged shit-makers from the rest of the shit-makers.

Woods glanced again at his watch. The man he worked for, or more accurately the man he *contracted with,* was running twenty minutes late. Of course, the man he contracted with didn't give two hoots if he kept Woods or anyone else waiting. *Give two hoots,* thought Woods—an idiom meaning to be concerned about someone or something; however, it was characteristically used in the negative to convey the opposite. And as for the man Woods contracted with, he'd up the idiom ante—he couldn't give two shits or a rat's ass if he kept anyone waiting.

Woods was entering *Minotaur* in the eight empty spaces for six across—clue being *Greek mythology, monster with body of a man and head of a bull*—when he spotted his employer exiting the building, striding out the revolving door, and heading his way across the sidewalk. Woods tossed his nearly completed *Tribune* puzzle on the passenger seat and then did what he despised most, what rubbed against the grain of every fiber in his extra-large body. He stepped out from the sedan, marched around to the rear door, opened it for the man he contracted with, waited until the man was seated, and shut the car door. Woods then got back behind the wheel, hit the left turn signal, and pulled into the midday traffic. Woods stayed in the right lane; in fact, he took the first right turn, and then took another as he circled the block.

Woods glanced in the rearview mirror and caught the man he contracted with staring back at him. They locked eyes for a long second before Woods took a final right, drove another half block, and then parked the sedan in the exact same spot from where they'd begun their journey.

"We're moving ahead," the man Woods contracted with said before exiting the vehicle, shutting the Continental's back door, and quickly striding back inside the building.

CHAPTER 10

Jonny Whiting had been cremated per his expressed wishes to both family and friends over the years whenever the topic of *shuffling off mortal coils* got broached. Of course, the extent of the injuries to his face excluded any type of open-casket funeral. Whiting's cremains—his funeral urn—would rest in a niche columbarium. It would be stored in a hand-carved nook in Graceland Cemetery's historic chapel.

Graceland Cemetery and Arboretum lies between North Clark Street and Irving Park Road in Uptown, just a short jaunt northeast of Concordia Lutheran Church. A recent restoration had returned Graceland's chapel of quarried red granite back to its original scale and beauty—at least according to what the brochure I'd nicked had mentioned.

The reason I'd spent time reading cemetery brochures was in order to kill the monotony. The Concordia Lutheran Church memorial had been open to the public, but the interment service in Graceland's chapel was private—invite only—just for family and close friends and the surviving U-Turns, basically the mourners that took up the front rows at Concordia Lutheran. Vira and I had performed sentry duty, much like we'd done at the church, as the handful of attendees filed slowly into the chapel. Then my golden retriever and I retired to the shade as the clouds had opened up—no April showers after all—and I sucked down water out of a bottle while Vira lapped her cut out of a paper cup.

Again, it'd been a bust . . . the case of the dog that didn't bark.

The media presence in the cemetery's parking lot had dwindled down to one news van, likely because the private service had not been advertised and the other alphabets had gotten enough footage at Concordia Lutheran.

The police presence had also dwindled down to Kippy and her partner. Kippy had disappeared inside the chapel's atrium—where I'd misappropriated the cemetery brochure—while Officer Wabiszewski sat in their squad car and scrolled Facebook. Although Kippy had told us we could vamoose, Vira and I hung out in the off chance any suspicious onlookers, hovering among trees or tombstones and gazing at Graceland's chapel, showed up and tripped Vira's radar.

None had.

We were getting ready to decamp when a red Toyota Camry snaked its way into the lot and parked in a far corner, under a thin patch of shade kicked off by an elm that'd just begun to sprout. A woman stepped out from the driver's seat, stared at the chapel, glanced about the memorial park, then nodded at me, shut the door, and headed in our direction.

I recognized her immediately as she'd been the mourner that had stepped out from the horde at Concordia Lutheran and been reluctantly drawn into the church by the surviving band members. I figured she'd arrived intentionally tardy so there'd be no chance of a recurrence at Graceland's chapel. At thirty yards out she looked to be in her late twenties, but as she settled in front of me I'd upped it to mid-forties. She had a Stevie Nicks vibe going—all lace and billowed sleeves, bohemian, her brown hair long and wavy. She could have been a model.

Scratch that—she could be a model.

"You've got a beautiful dog," the woman said, holding a hand in front of Vira for her to sniff.

And suddenly it dawned on me.

"Are you Tabitha?"

She looked at me and smiled. "Call me Tabby."

"I've not seen him in a quarter century, but Jonny was a force of nature. Some days sunshine, other days—storm clouds and thunder. The cocaine and vodka and whatever else he'd wormed his way into kept him locked in that latter class." She added, "In days gone by, they'd be arresting me for his murder."

I'd fetched Tabby a bottled water from the cooler that lived in the cargo bed of my F-150. We stood in the shade, sipped at our drinks, and chatted about her time with The U-Turns.

"Sounds like you'd been placed in an impossible position."

She shrugged. "Jonny got five years of my life. I was his agent, his publicist . . . his personal ATM. I set up gigs—bars and clubs, private parties—just to get the band a following. And I made sure Jonny showed up at these gigs, which, quite frankly, wasn't one of his stronger suits."

I knew the story from my recent dive into Whiting's biography. Without Tabitha in his corner throughout those early years, Whiting would have been nothing. But instead of paying Tabitha back in kind, Jonny Whiting took the prick route.

Not necessarily a unique story.

"Must have been difficult, living with his addictions," I said, thinking how Tabby had been little more than a kid herself and then having all of Whiting's baggage dumped on top of her.

"He was too broke for much of that in the early days. I kept us afloat, barely, and pinched pennies for that Gibson Les Paul of his." Tabby knelt by Vira and ran fingertips behind her ears. "Unfortunately, when fame and fortune came calling, Jonny'd managed to unearth this *great passion* for cocaine and speed." She stared up at me. "And groupies."

"Is that when you left?"

"I'd left him a dozen times by then. And somewhere along our civil war, 'The Was of Time' was written." Tabby stood. "I left for keeps before the Grammys. Jonny was out of control and I hated what I'd become—a cliché—the jilted girlfriend trying to find him out in each and every tryst."

I thought of Kippy. Her ex-boyfriend had, among other things, cheated on her, thus instigating Kippy's current cold war against the male gender, thus keeping her and I from progressing beyond our *just-friends* status.

The rotten bastard.

Tabby and I stood staring at our feet another minute before I said, "All these years, yet you came to his funeral."

"Looking for closure, I guess." Tabby shrugged again. "Plus, every time that song comes on, it's as though it's only been a couple of weeks . . . and not a lifetime ago."

Kippy peeked her head out from the chapel, spotted us, and hiked over. I made a quick introduction.

Tabby asked, "Any suspects yet?"

"I just know what's in the paper," Kippy said. "They found a little marijuana in a Glad bag in his freezer so they're thinking it could be a drug-related homicide, maybe a falling out with his dealer—if he even had a dealer—but killing someone over such a meager amount of cannabis doesn't make sense unless the perp grabbed a bigger stash of something else. And if Whiting owed someone a chunk of change, he had plenty in the bank, so he'd have been able to pay them off." Kippy added, "The intensity of . . . his death seems more *personal* in nature."

I noticed Kippy omitted the fact that Whiting's head had been bashed in, smashed to a pulp, with the Gibson Les Paul Custom Tabby had bought for him once upon a time—the guitar he'd named after her. I figured it was police protocol not to release details of an active investigation, especially the nasty stuff that hadn't made the papers, but I also knew Kippy wouldn't want to lay that regrettable piece of news at Tabitha's feet.

"Did The U-Turns ever get into it back in the day?" Kippy asked. "You know, arguments?"

"God yes. Once they became famous, if you ever pushed Jonny—if you even so much as bumped into Jonny—he'd go off and let you know you were only along for the ride."

"Would any of them have reason to hold a grudge?"

"Chris tried keeping Jonny on track in the studio, tried keeping him clean and sober while they recorded. I was there when Jonny ripped into him once—ripped into all of them, actually—about how he was the *hit wonder* and how Chris and the rest of them could all screw off, but Jonny used a different word for 'screw.' I imagine they fought and made amends and fought and more amends until they finally broke up," she said. "But they made good money together, which likely smoothed over any spats they'd had along the way."

"All the band members and everyone were at the funeral, right?" I asked, back to pondering Sherlock Holmes and the case of the dog that didn't bark.

Tabby nodded. "Chris and the gang had me sit up front with them, by the family." Tabby then looked from me to Kippy and added, "Of course I didn't see Eddie, but who would expect him to show up."

"Who's Eddie?" Kippy asked.

"Eddie Clare," Tabby replied. "The band's original drummer."

CHAPTER 11

"There's a phone call for you, Mr. Feist."

"There is?" Peter Feist had been lost in thought, shaking ground nutmeg—just a pinch—into his large Arco Etrusco dark roast at Caffe Umbria—his morning ritual—when Abbi, who as far as Feist could tell was Umbria's head barista, tapped his forearm. This was certainly a first. The past two weeks had been hell on wheels, and he wondered what now had so blown up at the office that Marty or Andrea or Anahita felt the need to hunt him down as opposed to waiting an additional five minutes for his arrival.

Abbi smiled at Feist, one of her regular customers. "You can take it in the back if you'd like."

Feist followed the coffeehouse barista, juggled his steaming cup of joe and his iPhone long enough to realize he'd received no calls or texts since the previous evening. Why wouldn't his colleagues, or his wife, try him on his cell phone first rather than calling for him on Umbria's landline?

Warning lights began to flash in his head. What the hell was going on here?

Abbi handed Feist the receiver for the shop's landline in an office the size of a TV tray and returned to her station behind the counter to assist her crew in serving their morning rush of caffeine addicts.

Feist stood in the open office doorway, stared at a rack of

house-brand beans for sale, and spoke into the phone, "This is Peter Feist."

"I have news about David Siskin."

"Why didn't you call my office?" Feist said sternly into the receiver, realizing how angry he'd become. If this call wasn't from work or a family member, that meant a stranger had been following him. He scanned the coffee shop's patrons, those standing in line and those sipping their brews at wooden tables. Feist hoped to spot a man with a cell phone glued to his ear and peering in his direction.

No such luck.

"Because it was a leak from your *office* that got David killed."

The accusation hung in the air for several seconds before Feist said, "Who is this?"

"It's a friend," the voice replied. "Probably the best friend you've got right now."

"I sincerely doubt that."

"You can cop an attitude, *Mr. Special Prosecutor,* or you can jot down the number to a prepaid I just picked up and call me back—from a public phone—in thirty minutes sharp."

"And why should I do that?"

"I told you—I have news about David Siskin."

"Why the cloak-and-dagger?" Feist replied. "Why not just come in and talk?"

"David got himself kicked to death because the two of you pranced about as though you were going to prom. How fucking dumb was that?" the voice said. "I'm not going to be seen with you, and I'm not going to have your calls traced back to me. I've got a family to think about, for Christ's sake. This is not shits and giggles, Feist. You need to know where I'm coming from. Capiche?"

Though he'd not touched his coffee, Feist's heart had begun to beat faster. "Understood," he said.

"If you want to waste my time," the voice continued, "I'll shred the damned documents and toss David's audiotape into Lake Michigan. And I'll tell you something else, Feist—ditching everything would be a hell of a lot safer on my end."

"I said I understood."

The voice gave him a cell number.

"You're Michael McCarron, right?" Feist said. "David's Chicago partner?"

"Oh, Christ—you're using names. How fucking dumb is that?"

"I'm calling the number you gave me from a pay phone in the lobby of the Art Institute," Feist said. "Hell, the museum's not even open yet and there's nobody here."

"Don't you read the papers?" The voice was half frantic, half pissed. "All that eavesdropping shit they can do with phones now."

"Okay," Feist agreed. "No names."

"Good. And, yes, I was in the office that morning before the police arrived and I saw what had been done to *our Minneapolis friend*. I saw the compound fractures—as though the killer snapped kindling for a bonfire."

"The ME said our friend was already dead before most of those fractures occurred."

"That supposed to make me feel better?"

Feist had memorized the police report. "They took his Rolex, his wallet, wedding ring, laptop, and a couple other trinkets to fabricate a robbery, but they left his body that way in order to send a message."

"Ya think?" the voice said. "Well, I for one got the message loud and clear."

"Yet here you are," Feist replied, "contacting me."

"You know that quote by Edmund Burke? The one about evil triumphing?"

"'The only thing necessary for the triumph of evil is for good men to do nothing.'"

"That's the one."

"What have you got for me, Mr. McCar—" Feist stopped himself. "What have you got for me?"

"I've got a nine-by-twelve envelope stuffed with some interesting documentation. Some from our Minneapolis friend and more from me. I've also got an audio recording—digital, on a thumb drive—that'll knock your socks off."

"Do tell."

"With what you've been pursuing, it'll be self-explanatory," the voice replied. "You're a bright guy—you'll know what to do with it."

"Look—let me get you into a safe house," Feist said. "I know you're scared, but we can handle this in an appropriate manner."

"I don't think so," the voice said. "My family and I—our safe house will be in, oh . . . maybe Europe or Australia . . . maybe Japan or Peru."

"But I'll need you here for the case to stick. It doesn't matter what you've done *for them* because you were coerced. I get that. We can cut a deal. Okay?"

"Like you did with David?" the voice said. "No, I think I'll follow the news online and see how it plays out before I decide if I'm ever coming back to Chicago. This envelope I'm going to hand you . . . it's explosive. It'll work like a self-cleaning oven—you won't need me. And perhaps I can call you from Moscow or Thailand and talk about immunity and whatnot."

Feist thought for a moment. "How do you want to get this to me? Mail?"

"The mail? Christ no." The voice snickered and added, "It could make it to your office, but not to your desk. It has to be hand-delivered—in person—like serving a subpoena."

"How do you propose doing that?"

"You know Washington Park?"

"Of course."

"We connect there for the two seconds it takes for me to hand you the nine-by-twelve."

"I can be there in an hour."

"Then you'll have a hell of a long wait," the voice said. "I'll see you at midnight."

"You've got to be kidding."

"I'm not meeting you in broad daylight."

"Washington Park isn't that safe during the day, much less at midnight."

"You've got all that SPB juice, Feist. Have some squads sweep it at eleven, scare away the druggies. But don't tell anyone why. I'm partial to having my fibulas remain intact."

CHAPTER 12

"He's an asshole at a cellular level," Kippy shouted across the table.

Kippy didn't swear much for a cop, but when she did, I found it impressive. And the angrier Kip became, the more colorful. I'd have to turn my head or pretend to look about for my keys or iPhone so Kippy wouldn't take any chuckling the wrong way once she'd built up a full head of steam.

"He's half Peter Principle and half Dunning-Kruger."

I'd heard of the Peter Principle, where employees get promoted to their maximum level of incompetency. "What's Dunning-Kruger?"

"It's when a Peter Principle thinks they're smarter than reality would suggest."

I learn a lot listening to Kippy, from Dunning-Kruger to cellular assholes to what she planned on having me implement tonight.

I should get college credit.

We sat at a high-top table in a forgotten corner of Clover's on North Water Street in downtown Milwaukee listening to a fair rendition of Culture Club's "Karma Chameleon." The bar featured over fifty beers, lounge seating on two levels, free pool, multiple HD TVs, Chex Mix, and live music, but—though I'd been eating Chex Mix by the fistful—that's not what made us leap into Kippy's Chevy Malibu at rush hour on a Friday evening and spend two-plus hours hightailing it to this joint in Miltown. What made us hightail it to the city that beer built was to catch Eddie Clare play the drums for Time Machine—an eighties revival band that had been touring clubs in the Midwest since late March.

Although the drummer had moved to Texas soon after his forced exodus from The U-Turns, it turned out he'd been bouncing about the Midwest for much of the past month.

I was nursing my second Pabst and enjoying the music. It was the first time I'd spent any significant amount of time with Kippy since I'd throttled back on movies and pizza and the entire *just-friends* thingamabob, and it made me realize just how much I'd missed her these past few months—those deep brown eyes, the curve of her cheek, that slender neck, the hint of citrus, and her brutally honest passion.

Currently, her brutally honest passion—perhaps ire might be a more proper word—was aimed squarely at CPD detective Trevor Ames, the man she deemed an asshole at a cellular level. Evidently, Kippy'd had more run-ins with Ames than the one I'd witnessed in the outer hallway at Jonny Whiting's executive condominium. Kippy had scored top of her class at the police academy, had killed both CPD's written and physical exam, all this in addition to showing up at the table with a bachelor's degree in criminal justice. Though Ames's position within CPD fell under the Bureau of Detectives, he'd been assigned as a detective inside the Area North Detective Division . . . and their paths had crossed on multiple occasions. It was clear she was gunning for detective; Ames knew this and, evidently, couldn't let it be.

"Did you tell Ames about Eddie Clare?" I asked.

"Yeah—he gave me that condescending smirk and told me Clare was married and living in Texas, and had been out of the picture before there was ever a picture."

"You tell him we found out he's been playing gigs in Wisconsin?"

"I shot him an email saying we were catching Clare's act

tonight," she replied. "Of course that didn't rate a response or acknowledgment or anything."

Kippy sipped at her sparkling water, not only because she was the designated driver but because she had to keep her wits about her for when Time Machine took their next break. The eighties tribute band was scheduled to perform four hours tonight with twenty-minute breaks between sets. Wabiszewski had sat with Kippy during Time Machine's first set, but got a bellyful of Duran Duran, OD'd on Van Halen and John Cougar Mellencamp, and came out to spell me with Vira so I could catch their second set.

After their first set, Eddie Clare couldn't drop his drumsticks fast enough to hustle himself outside and flare up a Marlboro. In fact, Clare stayed out on Water Street, sucking tobacco until a Clover's bartender came to fetch him for the band's second set. And then Clare did another five minutes in the men's room, much to the visual chagrin of Time Machine's lead singer and the group's other two members. Clare didn't appear to give a damn about his band partners' annoyance and ignored their dagger eyes as he situated himself behind his drum set so the show could go on.

As it turned out, Eddie Clare was a pretty damned good drummer; he *had the chops* as they say—both speed and groove—even a touch of flair when it came to the solos. The man could bang away—hitting the beat dead center—as droplets of sweat flew off his face.

He was no Neil Peart or Ginger Baker, nonetheless . . . Eddie Clare gave good percussion.

Clare was a tall man, wiry, and he sported a black T-shirt with a Frisbee-sized patch of dampness on his chest. All the Time Machine members wore mullet wigs—cheap, like the kind you'd pick up at a party store in time for Halloween—but Clare seemed the only performer continually having to wipe the monsoon of perspiration that poured off his forehead with a forearm or fistful of bar napkins. Even with that water loss,

Clare kept himself hydrated by taking hits off a twenty-four-ounce bottle of Coca-Cola between songs.

Time Machine was a good-enough bar band—Clover's dance floor was packed and you could hear patrons, both young and middle-aged, scream along with their favorite hits—certainly worth the five-dollar cover and overpriced drinks. It had been a fifty-minute set, my Pabst was down to a teaspoon of backwash, and the lead singer was doing a passable version of "With or Without You." Most of the group looked in need of a break except for, surprisingly, Eddie Clare. Clare had a certain *fuck you* intensity, a vibe avowing that as long as he had a wad of napkins to mop back the sweat off his brow, he could jam all night.

At the end of the U2 hit, Time Machine's lead fumbled about with his wireless mic.

That was our cue.

Kippy set down her water and said, "Get Vira."

CHAPTER 13

"You'd better enjoy this while you can." Peter Feist chewed at a small slice of pizza and added, "If you take after Mom and me, you'll both be getting braces in junior high and then its soup and applesauce for two years."

"No way," said daughter number one.

"Karla has braces and she eats pizza all the time," said daughter number two. Karla was their most frequently utilized babysitter.

"That's right," Feist replied, "it's candy you don't get to eat. Halloween will be canceled for two years."

Daughter number one, Annika, rolled her eyes—she wasn't buying his BS, but daughter number two, Kiley, appeared hesitant.

Laura added, "Don't you girls know by now never to listen to him?"

"Eggs," Feist said in mock surprise, "that's a horrible thing to say about the father of your children."

Whenever someone would query Feist on how he'd come up with the nickname *Eggs* out of Laura, he'd tell the truth—that scrambled eggs was the first meal she'd ever made for him. Of course, Feist kept silent on the part about how Laura had scrambled them up for him after their first night spent together back in law school at Loyola.

Feist had picked up a half cheese, half mushroom and sausage—a large—at Luigi's Pizza on the way home as a half-apology, half-excuse for him having to sneak off—back to the office for this *thing at work*—at a time when most people would be settling between the sheets for a long night's sleep. Eggs had been delighted about Luigi's, but as for his having to head out later . . . not so much.

Luigi's served up some of the best pizza in town, but to-night it went down like doughy paste. Had he gotten David Siskin killed as the voice on the phone—Siskin's business partner Michael McCarron—had intimated? If so, Feist didn't know if he could ever forgive himself. Thus it was all he could do to choke down a single slice of Luigi's and feign merriment around the dinner table.

The kids were happy but Eggs wasn't buying his act.

His wife knew something was up.

Feist worked sixty-hour weeks at a minimum. Eggs picked up the slack—breakfasts and dinners for the kids, PTA meet-ings at the school, monitoring homework, dance recitals, soccer games, trips to the doctor for any bruises or bumps incurred along the way, etcetera. And it hadn't been that long ago he'd put her through the living hell of his running for Cook County State's Attorney. He hated the politics inherent in the position and his four-year stint couldn't come to an end soon enough. So what in hell had he been thinking, allowing the powers that be talk him into heading the Special Prose-cutions Bureau?

It certainly wasn't fair on Eggs as she practiced patent law at a firm in the city, working lengthy hours her own self. She'd taken to joking lately about her life as a single parent.

But Eggs understood his work and knew that this was who he was—the man she loved, the man she married—and she supported him wholeheartedly. Eggs also felt Feist had a chance to make a difference—to actually do some good—in a city that'd just as soon chew you up and spit out the bones than ever change course.

And, hopefully, tonight would be a turning point.

Hopefully, with the packet McCarron would be handing off to him, Feist would be able to blow this *thing at work* wide open and pick up where he and David Siskin had left off. Although McCarron appeared adamantly single-minded, Feist would do his best to talk him out of fleeing the country. The prosecution would work best if he could stash Michael McCarron and his family—immediate or extended or whatever—in a safe house . . . a true safe house.

Feist would assuage McCarron's concerns—Michael Mc-Carron's *existential* concerns—by bringing the United States Marshals Service into the mix. If the USMS could run the United States Federal Witness Protection Program, they could damn well keep the McCarrons safe and sound during the course of a trial. And once that was complete, perhaps the Marshals Service could relocate them to maybe Oklahoma or Nebraska.

Feist winced.

Goddamnit.

It killed him to even contemplate that his office—the Special Prosecutions Bureau—had been compromised. He found it impossible to believe the leak that led to David Siskin's demise had originated from inside the SPB, that there was a mole hidden within the bureau. Nevertheless, Feist had spent all afternoon listing the handful of staff attorneys who were even cognizant of Siskin's existence in the first place, and then subdividing those names into a list of prosecutors he could trust versus those he wasn't so certain of.

If tonight spun his way—events would unfold in rapid succession—the end would be in sight. Then he and Eggs could take a vacation—a proper vacation—dump the kiddos with the grandparents and maybe spend a week dragging her to every snorkeling hole in Maui. Just what the doctor ordered.

"Is there anything you're *able* to tell me about work?" Laura asked after the girls had been dismissed from the dinner table.

Feist picked up dirty plates, headed to the sink, and deflected, "Andrea's filing for divorce."

"About damn time," Laura said.

Andrea Hayes, who spearheaded legislative reforms for Feist, had believed herself to be in the picture perfect marriage until she'd finally gotten around to using the wireless indoor security camera her husband, Rob, had set up to monitor the kids or pets or repairmen, or in the off chance of a burglary. And though Andrea found no evidence of Rob cheating on her or abusing drugs, what she did find was equally disturbing. While skipping through video on her iPhone, Andrea watched herself from earlier that morning as she opened the refrigerator and peered inside. Seconds later, Rob walked behind her—heading for the coffee maker with hardly a care in the world—and, as he passed by, he paused long enough to lift his right hand and give the middle finger to the back of her head. Andrea's initial reaction had been to chuckle, but as she used the motion detector functionality to skip through various indoor activities; she came to realize what had occurred that morning was far from a one-off.

Whenever Andrea got up from the couch to use the bathroom, there was Rob flipping her off. Whenever Andrea was sipping tea at the island, sure enough, there was Rob in the background giving her the bird. Whenever Andrea was vacuuming, there Rob was—behind her—middle finger on full display. It soon became clear that Rob held some kind of deep-seated resentment, some kind of inherent contempt, toward Andrea that, evidently, bubbled to the surface every time her back was turned.

"There are some odd ducks on this planet." Feist crumpled up the pizza box to fit in the garbage.

Laura added, "That there are."

Feist hugged his wife after the girls had been put to bed and read to sleep, he kissed her on the mouth, and said, "Don't wait up, Eggs."

"You know I will," she replied.

CHAPTER 14

Vira and I returned along North Water Street, slipping in and about the mass of bar hoppers, many my age—the ass end of their twenties, spitting distance from thirty—many younger, mostly just happy to be out on a mild night in late April after a long and unfriendly winter. As I approached Clover's, Eddie Clare stepped out the front entrance—he must have received feedback and used the men's restroom first this go-round—palmed a cigarette as he passed the line of windows, leaned up against the nightclub's brick exterior, popped the smoke in his mouth, and lit up. Kippy trailed the drummer at five yards back, her badge now on a belt clip, her ID in hand, ready for a quick flash. She caught my eye, nodded, and approached Clare.

This was the tricky part. Kippy and Wabiszewski were Chicago PD and we were in Milwaukee, not just a different city but state—more than a minor jurisdictional issue. Kippy was also off duty. In addition, this was not Kippy's case because, hell's bells, she's not a detective. Ergo, we had no authority to do anything beyond engaging the musician in casual conversation. And that was really all we wanted to do. It's a free country and cops can catch a concert just like anybody else. On the ride over I'd lobbied for us to act fan-like, suck up and tell Clare how great we thought he was while Vira performed her *other* thing—her sussing out any scent DNA from Jonny

Whiting's murder scene, her connecting of dots. And if it continued to be the case of the dog that didn't bark, we'd pat Eddie Clare on the back, hop in Kippy's Malibu, and book it back to Chicago.

However, I lost the debate.

The three of us worried about the time delay as it had now been over a week since we'd visited Whiting's condo. We feared that whatever scent trail Vira might have latched on to had long since scattered, dispersed into the ether . . . and been forgotten. So Kippy, with Wabiszewski's tie-breaking vote, wanted to give good, old-fashioned police work a try. She wanted to flash her badge, introduce herself as Chicago PD, and, because she was in street clothes, let Eddie Clare assume her plainclothes meant she was a detective.

Kippy wanted to rattle Clare's cage and see how he reacted. If Clare was the killer, perhaps he'd do that weird thing where his head turns one way whenever he's lying, perhaps his facial expression and nonverbal cues would go all haywire, perhaps instead of saying *that was horrible to hear about Jonny,* he'd start demanding an attorney.

I wore a dark gray polo shirt over dark jeans—my standard attire for a night on the town. Kippy had been pleased to see my shirt came with a breast pocket. I took it as her complimenting my sense of flair, but soon discovered she had an ulterior motive.

At Kippy's nod, I tapped the Record button on the Voice Memos app and dropped my iPhone into my shirt's pocket. This was what she'd wanted me to implement tonight and we'd kicked this ploy about on the drive to Milwaukee. Kippy and Wabiszewski thought it best if the *non-cop* of our trio was the one recording the conversation with Eddie Clare, lest there be any legal entanglements down the road in case Clare somehow decided to confess his guilt to a couple of complete strangers outside an Irish pub on Water Street. Kippy explained how both federal and Wisconsin law permitted something called "one-party consent," which basically meant everything is okie dokie on the tape-recording front as long as I'm a party to the conversation which—well, duh—I would be.

". . . and this is Mason Reid, one of our K-nine trainers," Kippy said as we approached.

"I'm loving the show," I said, holding tight to Vira's leash with a left hand and leaning in with my right to shake.

Clare's stench washed over me, a stormfront of whiskey, sweat, ashtrays, and armpits. I now realized what was truly in that Coke bottle he'd been sucking down between songs. Suddenly I wasn't so worried about Vira having forgotten any scent data she may have gleaned from Whiting's Avondale condominium as much as how Clare's desperate need for a shower might mask whatever Vira had picked up from the crime scene, how Clare's lack of personal hygiene might throw off her read. And I figured Clare's stretching out the breaks between sets wasn't the only thing that riled his fellow band members.

"Thank you."

I was grateful to retreat a step after the handshake, away from Clare's immediate reek. I held up my leash hand and said, "This young lass is my date, Vira."

"Well hello there, Vira," Clare said, took a long pull on his Marlboro, exhaled, and turned his attention back toward Kippy. "I bet you're here with questions about my old mate?"

Up close, you could see Clare was well into his fifties. He had a few inches on me, maybe six-foot-three, but thin, in need of a shave, and the mullet wig just looked silly. I was positioned where I could watch Clare but also keep an eye on Vira. She had her head up—was air scenting—looking at Eddie Clare and then at me.

Kippy dove in. "You and Jonny grew up together, right?"

"Since first grade."

"You were friends?"

"Best friends back in the day, not so much later on—obviously—but I had a drum set, he had a guitar, and we drove my parents apeshit with a ton of clatter from the basement."

Clare's eyes were dull, glazed over, and he struck me as someone who navigated most of his waking hours in some degree of intoxication, someone whose alcohol intake would put me in an early grave but was just another Friday night to him. The man had been working bar gigs for the better part of four decades—perhaps cocktails were on the house.

Kippy had once mentioned—over drinks, ironically—that if a person is shitfaced, it makes it damn near impossible for a cop to get a solid read when it came to any kind of serious questioning. That got me thinking—could Eddie Clare be living in some kind of alcoholic haze in order to gum up any such read?

Kippy continued, "And you and Whiting started The U-Turns?"

Another puff, another exhale. "We'd begun with a couple of sillier names, but wound up with that, yeah."

Clare seemed like a mellow enough fella, and I played mental gymnastics as to what time I'd be getting back home when Vira's head began to scan about the ground and back up at Clare, slowly, as though she were trying to remember where she'd set the car keys, then suddenly her muzzle went herky-jerky. I looped my left hand farther down the leash as Vira started in with a low growl that evolved into a snarl, her eyes focused exclusively on Eddie Clare.

Vira stood as I knelt next to her.

"What's up with your dog?" the drummer asked.

"It's okay, Vira," I said, my right hand on the back of her neck. She stood at full height, her body taut as piano string. "It's okay, girl." I looked at Clare. "She gets nervous in the city."

Vira barked once and strained against the leash.

"We know, honey," I said, slipping an arm around her shoulders, getting her to settle down, getting her out of attack mode. "We know."

I glanced at Kippy but she'd returned to her list of questions, papering over an irate golden retriever.

"They bumped you from the band you helped create?"

Clare stared at Vira. I noticed he'd pressed himself as close to the brick exterior behind him as possible. He took another long hit off his cigarette before saying, "It was complicated. Jonny was the frontman—he wrote the songs—and rock beats scissors and that was that. I got voted off the island."

"That had to hurt," Kippy said, prodding.

"You can let that kind of stuff eat away at you—at your soul—but, ultimately, you've got to let it go." Clare drew on his cigarette and slowly exhaled. "That was many moons ago, a lot of water under the bridge."

I stood, placed a leg in front of Vira's chest, and asked, "Were you with the band when Whiting wrote 'The Was of Time'?"

Clare nodded.

I thought back on my original plan—of acting fan-like and sucking up—and figured why the hell not. So then I became Eddie Clare's best friend in the whole wide world.

"That's bullshit," I said. "You were a founding member—with the band from the get-go—and they do that to you?"

"Yup."

"All you'd been through with Jonny—with all of them—and they give you the boot," I said and shook my head. "That's such bullshit."

"I showed up at the studio and there's Chris—you know, Bjerke—and a couple of security guards . . . and Chris tells me I'm out."

"Wait a minute," I said. "They sicced security guards on you?"

Clare nodded.

"And Whiting made Bjerke do the dirty work?"

Clare nodded again. "I'm stuttering *what the hell* a few dozen times and Chris is hemming and hawing but he finally lets me know it all came down to Jonny."

"So you weren't in on 'The Was of Time' recording?"

Clare dropped his cigarette and stepped on it with a Converse High Top. "No."

"They screwed you out of the hit song."

"They probably recorded it later that day," Clare replied. "In fact, I'm certain of it, but they grabbed that Greg Lukkason asshole at the last minute—fucked me over . . . and the rest is rock-and-roll."

"Jesus," I said. "That sucks out loud."

"Goddamn right it sucks out loud." Clare's eyes now seemed moist. "Fucking Lukkason got champagne and blowjobs— they all got champagne and blowjobs—but not me," he said. "I got to roll around in my own shit."

I shook my head again. "That's just not right."

"That was anything but right," Clare replied.

"You and Whiting may have had a falling out, gotten pissed off at each other, but buddies don't screw over buddies," I said. "That's an unwritten law."

"One would think." Clare had picked up a head of steam, confiding in his new pal—his new BFF. "And you want to know something else?"

"What?"

"I'm glad."

"Glad what?"

"That Jonny got his."

"Kind of like karma, huh?"

"Goddamn right it was karma," Clare said. "I'm glad some-one bashed fuckwad to death with his own guitar."

"With Tabitha?"

"Yeah—smashed that fucker's head in as though it were a goddamned pumpkin."

We stood in silence a long moment, and then Kippy asked, "How did you know that?"

"Know what?"

"That the murder weapon was Whiting's Les Paul?"

Holy shit . . . if not for Kippy, I'd have missed the Perry Mason moment.

Chicago PD had intentionally kept that gruesome part about the murder weapon out of the media, had kept that trump card up their sleeve to cull out any crazies who felt the need to confess to a high-profile crime they'd had absolutely nothing to do with—a holdback on behalf of CPD, known to them but not released to the public. It was the piece of the puzzle Kippy had withheld from Tabitha in order to spare her feelings.

So either drummer Eddie Clare implausibly had someone inside CPD leaking him specifics on Jonny Whiting's murder . . . or . . . or Eddie Clare was the killer.

I saw the realization dawn on Clare a second after it had dawned on me.

"That's what they said on TV."

"No, they didn't," Kippy said and took a step backward. I knew she had her off-duty subcompact—a Baby Glock—in her ankle holster.

We stood there in awkward silence until Vira began to growl.

And Eddie Clare began to run.

He made it almost twenty feet when Wabiszewski, who'd been leaning against the building with an ear in our direction, lifted a right arm—a perfect clothesline—and Clare dropped like a bag of rocks.

"I love it when they run," Kippy's partner said as he lifted Clare and slammed him against the wall of bricks. "It means they're guilty."

"Eddie," we heard a voice behind us call and turned to look. It was one of Clover's bartenders, a question mark sprawled across his features at the sight of the drummer for Time Machine being handcuffed; nevertheless, he completed his thought, "They're ready for you."

Somehow I didn't think Eddie Clare would be making the next set.

CHAPTER 15

Peter Feist pulled his Lexus ES into the last lot on the south side of Cornell stream, only a stone's toss from where it emptied into the reservoir, and took the parking spot next to where the jogging trail enters the tree line. Thankfully, his was the only car in the lot. As instructed by McCarron, Feist'd had squad cars from the 2nd Police District comb through Washington Park a half hour earlier, both interrupting and herding out whatever passes for commerce in the hours after the sun goes down.

It was a clear evening; a half-moon stood sentry in the night sky. A couple of streetlamps made the tableau not as gloomy as Feist had anticipated. He'd brought along a flashlight, which he'd stuffed in the left-side pocket of his windbreaker—recent police presence or not, Feist didn't plan on traipsing about Washington Park at midnight in his Brooks Brothers and Gucci Leather Oxfords. The flashlight was tactical, the kind that blinds assailants with over 130 lumens of brightness. In the windbreaker's other pocket, a Kahr CM9—his subcompact 9mm carry pistol with six rounds in the magazine. Feist figured if he couldn't hit a point-blank target with six shots, well . . . then he truly was screwed.

Although there was a mild chill to the air—with temperatures in the mid-fifties—Feist felt a sheen of perspiration form along his hairline, but he didn't wipe it off. Instead, he kept his hands inside the pockets of his windbreaker, gripping his flashlight and Kahr CM9.

Feist hit the running path hard. At five yards, the trail merged into the tree line; after another fifteen yards, the trail began to curve along with the pond and, forty yards farther on—per their brief burner-phone discussion of Washington Park logistics—sat the venture capitalist, Michael J. McCarron, on a park bench under a busted streetlamp, a lonely figure in the shadows. McCarron sported some kind of old-time derby and raincoat, likely his attempt at disguise. The investor spotted Feist, nodded, and held a large envelope above his head. Feist returned the nod, jogged the remaining distance, slid his hands out of his windbreaker in order to grab McCarron's packet of corroboration.

But the man on the park bench wasn't Michael J. McCarron.

Of this Feist was certain, after having spent several minutes during the afternoon studying McCarron's facial appearance from both his bio page on the investment firm's website as well as the image from McCarron's most recent Illinois state driver's license. The towering hulk that stood up to face him had a professional football player's thickness melded with a professional basketball player's height.

"I'm afraid Mr. McCarron won't be joining us for tonight's rendezvous," the man said in a somewhat familiar voice.

Feist pointed at the envelope now lying on the park bench. "You dropping that off for him?"

"Feel free to have at that packet of newspaper clippings," the big man replied. "Don't you remember what I said on the phone? How David got himself kicked to death because the two of you pranced about as though you were going to prom?"

Feist's heart dropped. "You made the call?"

The big man smiled.

"I've seen you around," Feist said, wishing his hands were still inside his windbreaker pockets.

"And I've seen *you* around."

The two men stared at each other.

"Might we take a moment to appreciate the irony here?" the big man said.

Feist said nothing, his right hand an inch closer to the pocket containing the CM9.

"You came out here all hell-bent and Eliot Ness–like, thinking you were being handed the Holy Grail on a fucking platter; but, in fact, you got yourself lured here for something altogether different. I hear you love fishing, Counselor, and damned if I didn't reel you in like a one-pound northern pike."

"Before you finish patting yourself on the back," Feist replied, "there's something you ought to know."

"What's that?"

"For starters," Feist said, surprised at how calm he felt, his right hand now at his side, "you're insane if you think you'll get away with this."

"Oh, I may well be insane," the big man replied, "but I've usually found the ballsiest moves to work the best."

"You do know I've got backups of my backups."

"Of course you do, and I've got this idiot savant who's in your system right now as we speak . . . taking care of the *backups of your backups*. Hell, Jethro's been wiggling about your network for much of the past week."

"Jethro?"

"Wasn't me—the kid picked it himself. He does love that name."

Feist then asked, "Do you believe in God?" It was an old lawyer trick, throw a curveball and catch the witness off guard.

"Oh, I reckon there might be something out there," the big man said after a beat. "Yourself?"

"I'm a Pascal's Wager Christian."

"Fuck is that?"

"An old French philosopher named Blaise Pascal figured we human beings bet with our lives that God either exists or He does not."

"What's the bet?"

"Well, the old French guy figured a rational man should live life as though God does exist because that way he'll only suffer a few minor losses in the here and now, but will have infinite gains in the afterlife."

"What if you lose the bet?"

Feist shrugged. "I've always tried to be a rational man."

And with that Peter Feist went for his gun—a modern-day Wyatt Earp slapping nylon windbreaker instead of leather.

But Special Prosecutor Feist never had a chance. For his size, the big man struck like a cobra, a pile driver straight to Feist's solar plexus. A second later and Feist's Kahr CMP was in the big man's hand. A second after that and Feist's tactical flashlight had also been confiscated.

"That had to smart," the big man said as he held Feist upright by his collar. "I knocked you into next week. That's an idiom, by the way. It means I hit you so hard that you'll be unconscious until sometime next week." The big man redoubled his grip on the collar of Feist's windbreaker and dragged him off the path and into the woods that shrouded the pond. "Don't worry, though, that slime water will snap you up fast because you and I are going to have a little heart-to-heart. Sure, I liked that Pascal bullshit about God and all, but now we're gonna talk apple carts."

CHAPTER 16

Kippy and Wabiszewski dropped me off at one-forty in the morning. Kip told me to do what I had to do with the dogs, then turn around and haul ass downtown to CPD's headquarters to see if us worker bees could con our way into watching Eddie Clare's interrogation. Since that wasn't something one gets to witness every day—and since my orientation class in Buffalo Grove didn't begin until midafternoon—I offered to bring popcorn and Milk Duds.

Vira and I had nodded in and out of consciousness on the trek home from Milwaukee as Wabiszewski worked the wheel and disobeyed the speed limit while Kippy used her cell phone to scale her way up CPD's totem pole—first speaking with an on-watch sergeant, and then a lieutenant, before finally settling in with a captain.

Dick Weech—a retired railroad engineer, widower, and dog lover who lived up the boulevard—had once again watched the kids during my Friday-night outing. He'd hung with the brood until ten, watching baseball with Sue and eating the bucket of fried chicken I'd left for him in the fridge. Dick, in turn, had left me a note on the kitchen table.

Had to wash Bill twice, it read. *You owe me a fistful of scratch-offs.*

Evidently, my bloodhound's fetish—Bill's unquenchable

yearning to roll about in any pile he could find, the juicier the better—persisted in my truancy.

I indeed owed Dick a fistful of scratch-offs.

I microwaved old coffee that'd been left in the pot since yesterday morning and filled a bunch of water dishes. All but Sue were willing to go outside for a middle-of-the-night sniff and pee. I swear Sue rolled his eyes as I called for him, either way he wasn't budging from his spot on the couch, not this late at night. I wasn't sure how long I'd be away and toyed with leaving the pet door open as all but Bill were trained not to wander away in my absence. I sometimes clip Bill to a thirty-foot leash attached to the picnic table that allows my bloodhound to do his business as well as sit under the table or perch on my miniscule back deck or even squat inside the pet door. If Bill makes a ruckus, Maggie May or Delta Dawn will come and sit with him until he settles down. If Bill refuses to settle down, Sue will jump from his sofa, strut outside, and have a come-to-Jesus meeting with the unruly puppy.

And, quite frankly, it would be best for all involved if Sue wasn't forced to vacate his throne.

I decided against the pet door—it'd be dark for too many more hours—and Vira, a really bad cup of coffee, and I were out the door by ten to two and at police headquarters by half past. Officer Wabiszewski was on the lookout for us in the station's main entrance off South Michigan. A night sergeant with part of his right eyebrow missing—had to be a story in there somewhere—hustled the three of us into the belly of the beast where the morning's drama had already begun to unfold.

"I belted out 'The Was of Time's chorus as I beat Jonny's brains in," Eddie Clare announced to the interrogation room. "Never felt better—should have paid fuckwad a visit decades ago."

Evidently, there'd been a minor Gordian knot getting the

rock-and-roll drummer back to Chicago, but CPD attorneys sliced through the red tape and Milwaukee PD wound up escorting Clare to CPD's headquarters building. Considering Clare's lack of hygiene, that was A-OK by me as I imagine Officers Gimm and Wabiszewski would have tucked him in the back of Kippy's Malibu with me.

Trevor Ames looked all constipated upon our arrival, but the detective's fiber supplement kicked in once he was given the go-ahead nod as lead interrogator. The rest of his colleagues were so busy slapping backs, they let us accompany them behind the observation mirror—the one-way mirror—in the room adjoining the interrogation room as long as we kept quiet or whispered any responses to questions they might have about our peculiar evening in Milwaukee.

The room was wired for sound, the tape recorder turned on. We sat silently, Vira at Kippy's feet, and watched through the mirror as Detective Ames began working his magic.

Turned out not much of Trevor Ames's magic was required. The discomfort of CPD's interrogation room—no windows, one door, bare walls, a table containing my iPhone in case Clare needed to be reminded of his inadvertent confession, and a cushionless seat on par with a 1940s-era folding chair for him to park in—didn't faze the rock-and-roll drummer one iota.

Even after he'd been notified of his rights, Eddie Clare was an open book.

Gone were the blurry eyes as Clare'd had hours to sober up on his final farewell tour to Chicago. Some paramedic along the way had cleaned the abrasions and scrapes about the drummer's mug from where Kippy's partner had introduced him to the sidewalk off North Water Street. The paramedic must have had a sense of humor as Clare now sported SpongeBob Band-Aids on both of his cheeks and forehead.

"You know I loved Tabitha," Clare began his tale.

We all leaned forward like a Busby Berkeley production as Ames replied, "This all went down because you had the hots for Whiting's girlfriend a million years ago?"

"Don't get me wrong, Detective—a lot of emotions were at play. I gave Jonny half a dozen whacks for how he treated Tabby and another half dozen on account of, you know, the fuck-over. The U-Turns—the band I cofounded—got fame and fortune . . . and I got to spend my life shoveling asbestos."

"Shoveling asbestos?" Ames asked. As if by magic, the detective had a beard comb in his hand. No kidding—he began raking it down one side of his face.

"It's a metaphor," Clare replied. "Figure it out."

"But you've got a wife back home in Lubbock." Ames took a blowup of Mrs. Clare's driver's license out of a folder and set it on the table in front of the drummer. "Was she aware of your plans for Jonny Whiting?"

"No." Clare stared at the picture of his wife. "Old RBF is in for a surprise."

"RBF?" Ames asked as he began raking the other side of his face.

"Resting bitch face." Clare's eyes widened, "Hey, can I listen in when you let her know?"

Ames stared at Clare, astounded at the man's insensitivity. "That's not how this works."

"It'll be comic gold."

The detective shook his head and began combing his mustache, oblivious to the fact that he was publically grooming. I wondered when the floss would come out.

Clare leaned back in his chair. "You want to know the real reason I got kicked out of The U-Turns?"

"Of course."

"I told Jonny I'd kick his ass if he kept treating Tabby like crap. I met her first—loved her guts out—and was dumb enough to bring her around to meet the band. I introduced her to Jonny . . . and that was that. They became an item and I had to stand by and witness his shit, day in and day out. Then, a week after I confronted him, I get tossed out of the studio. Now you've got to understand something here. Jonny and I went way back—I mean way, way back—grade-fucking-school back, and all of a sudden I'm out on my ass." Clare pounded the table with his fist. "Boom! Gone!" he said. "No girl. No band . . . nothing."

After Clare's burst of drama dissipated, we sat behind the mirror and watched as Ames wrapped up loose ends. The detective prodded—a question here, a beard comb there—and Clare's answers tumbled out unrestrained.

It turned out to be a John Lennon thing after all, only not a crazed fan as Ames had previously surmised. It was the scalding hatred of a drummer dismissed from a band on the verge of stardom, a *Pete Best kind of thing* as Pete Best had been an original member and the first drummer with the Beatles before they replaced him with Richard Starkey . . . aka Ringo Starr.

Eddie Clare didn't have to be at some bar in Madison to perform until eight o'clock in the evening so he thought—*what the hell?*—plenty of time to drive to Chicago, do the deed he'd been contemplating for eons, beat *fuckwad* to death, and be back in Madison in time for the first set with an hour or two to spare. Clare said he got into Whiting's building when an elderly couple was coming out, said he wore a baseball cap and sunglasses, and kept his head down in case of any cameras.

Clare said Whiting recognized him right off the bat, seemed authentically pleased to see his old mate—as though Eddie Clare had long been expected—and invited him inside. They talked about old times in Whiting's home studio—nothing heated or serious—and then Jonny went to make a dark roast from Costa Rica for them to sip. Clare said he had second thoughts, *reservations*—and considered backing out of his plan—that is, until he almost tripped over the Gibson Les Paul Custom sitting in a guitar stand along the side of the music room . . . *Tabitha* . . . Jonny Whiting's shrine to the girl they both loved.

That was just too much for Clare to take—the final straw—so he placed *The Was of Time* CD into Jonny Whiting's player, skipped forward to the title track, cranked the Nakamichi

Shockwafe soundbar to cover any forthcoming reverbera-
tions from the neighboring condos, and The U-Turns original
drummer picked up the Les Paul Custom . . . and headed into
the kitchen.

"I've not felt this great in decades. Finally free of all that
vile jammed down my throat. The U-Turns got champagne
and blowjobs . . . Jonny got Tabitha, at least for a while . . .
and I got to roll in my own shit."

It had been gnawing at Eddie Clare for decades—a sliver
that never worked its way to the surface, the wound that
never healed—and for over half of his life he'd kept it hidden
beneath the surface, but the grief was born anew, and ampli-
fied, every time he heard that tune.

Finally, Clare had taken action . . . and found himself at
peace.

Knowing his arrest would be splashed across the headlines, the fame that had so long eluded Eddie Clare had come
to an end.

"If you see Tabitha," Clare said as Ames gathered his papers, "could you tell her—"

I didn't get to hear Clare's final reflection as the door to our
room swung inward and slammed against the wall. All eyes
turned in that direction and there stood the sergeant with
the half-eyebrow, the one who'd hustled Wabiszewski and I to
CPD's hallway of interrogation rooms. He had a hard look on
his face and he stared my way.

"You're the dog man, right." It was more declaration than
question.

"Yes," I said, startled, thinking I was moments away from
being handcuffed.

"You're needed at Washington Park ASAP," he said in a tone
that wouldn't accept no for an answer. "Grab your dog."

CHAPTER 17

The head of the Special Prosecutions Bureau inside the Cook County State's Attorney's Office, Peter Feist, never made it home last night. When the head of Special Prosecutions vanishes into thin air, there is no waiting period: Chicago PD doesn't waste any time hoping the absent official will miraculously reappear looking sheepish from some bender in Peoria. Peter Feist's position in the State's Attorney's Office came with multiple enemies, and Feist's take-no-prisoners reputation had doubled that number.

He'd last been seen leaving the executive offices for the night and had even been captured on the parking garage video at 11:25 p.m. as he slipped into his Lexus ES. Feist told his wife—who'd grown accustomed to her husband's lengthy workdays—that he'd be home late. But when she'd not heard anything from him by 1:30 a.m.—which was quite unlike him, as he'd not called her or returned her phone calls or replied to her voicemails or text messages—she began making phone calls. Forty-five minutes later they received a break when CPD's 2nd District night sergeant caught the alert notification and informed his superiors that, in fact, Special Prosecutor Peter Feist had requested a sweep of Washington Park at 11:30 p.m. the previous evening, and that no reason for the park sweep had been provided. A pair of squad cars dispatched from the 2nd District soon found Feist's lonely black

Lexus in one of the park's south-side lots. The driver-side window had been smashed in and the glove compartment and trunk left open, but the officers were unable to tell if anything had been stolen out of the vehicle as the head of the Special Prosecutions Bureau was nowhere to be found.

CPD knew nothing good came out of Washington Park at half past two in the morning.

With a police escort, in addition to nonexistent traffic, Vira and I were at the park by 3:35. By 3:50 a.m., Vira had found the leader of the Special Prosecutions Bureau facedown in a dank fishpond, which was an oddity itself as the poor man was lying on his back. His neck had not only been broken but cranked violently backward. Vira led me to the body and, as though struck by lightning, she fell into another one of her occurrences. One paw hovered above the water by Feist's shoulder. And though I'm not sure what chemical signature she caught in the night's breeze, or if she caught anything at all, her eyes scanned back and forth like a searchlight over Feist's body, and then across the pond.

Vira's a sweetheart; she's highly sensitive, and I began to wonder if these occurrences stemmed more from finding human remains—discovering death and the brutality of murder—than any subsequent attempt at making sense of it all, of performing some kind of scent forensics. And I recalled the pounding heart and dry heaves and tears from my first year on the job.

I took a knee beside Vira and gently stroked at her still-quivering shoulder. "It's okay, Vira," I said. "It's okay, girl."

A Lincoln Continental pulled into the parkway, turned into the pond-side lot now bristling with police activity, and parked a row behind Feist's Lexus ES. The ES was being serviced by a team of forensic specialists and looked as though it were going through some kind of high-tech car wash. Somehow the press had yet to stumble upon what would become their lead story of the day. I sat at a nearby picnic bench while Vira loafed on the grass at my feet. We were waiting to see if the investigators—all currently ruining their dress shoes in the muck down by the pond—would need my statement or for me to assist them in any additional search, which, at the moment, did not appear likely.

Not often, but now and again I'm required to testify in local or state court, so I always jot down the sequence of events—from when I'm first contacted through the discovery of any remains—as well as any details or observations or items of interest that occurred along the way. And if there were ever a case that might require my testimony, this was likely the one. I'd finished scribbling my thoughts in a mini notebook and was jamming it into my back pocket when the doors to the Continental swung open and like flicking a switch Vira went livid, growling and springing forward—her leash taut in my grip—barking like a maniac, demanding I set her free. I didn't recognize the mountain-sized chauffeur in the long coat and hat who stepped out first, but I sure as hell recognized the man who exited from the back seat of the dark sedan.

My blood froze.

And as much as I despise choke collars, I wished to God I'd had one looped around Vira's neck.

"Stop it, Vira," I whispered down at her, not wanting to draw more attention to ourselves than we already had. Vira ceased her barking and lunging but stared daggers at the duo standing next to the Lincoln. Her growling continued unabated.

The man who'd stepped out from the back of the sedan glanced over—at Vira's furor—and began heading in our direction as his driver leaned back against the Continental, folded his arms, and stared at the two of us. I rolled the leash around my hand to keep it tight, to keep Vira from doing anything we'd both regret.

"Get that fucking dog out of here," the man commanded as

he stopped ten feet from our picnic table, making certain he was outside of Vira's reach, "or I'll have it shot."

"Yes, sir," I said, gripping my free hand around the scruff of Vira's neck, my other hand still tight on the leash, backing away and pulling my golden retriever with me. "Quiet, girl! Quiet!"

In seconds, Vira and I were at my F-150. I opened the passenger door, and Vira leaped in but coiled about, keeping her eyes focused on Washington Park's newest arrivals, the man and his mountainous driver; her growl continued but at a softer pitch.

"I get it, Vira," I said, sitting next to her and scratching at the sweet spot behind her ears. "I get it."

We both watched as Police Superintendent Gerald Callum strolled back to the chauffeur of his Lincoln Continental. The two men spoke quietly for a minute before Superintendent Callum turned to head down the jogging path through the strand of trees on his way toward the pond, toward the city's latest homicide scene. Callum's driver—big enough to make the Continental look like a subcompact—focused on Vira and me for several more seconds before unfolding his arms, turning, and following Chicago's police superintendent into the woods.

I scratched at Vira's ears and whispered, "This one's going to be tricky."

Back home, I fed the dogs a late breakfast and then sat at the picnic table in the backyard. I was physically drained from lack of sleep, and from the events of the past twelve hours, but—after Washington Park—I was in no way ready for shuteye. I'd made a stack of toast for myself, but found I had no appetite after all. Eventually, I wound up tossing those slices about the yard for the kids to eat.

And I marveled at Vira's ability for about the tenth time that morning.

It was like in those old black-and-white films my father loves, where a convict escapes from prison and then we see the warden hold the escapee's shirt under a pack of blood-hounds' snouts, and then we're off to the races as the dogs track the fugitive through swamplands and forests and down country roads as they're able to isolate the convict's scent from that of other people. Only in Vira's case, she's able to cut out the middleman—the warden—and figure out the culprit's scent all on her own.

My girl's a prodigy.

With Eddie Clare having thoroughly confessed to Jonny Whiting's murder, it was doubtful my Milwaukee recording would be needed for a trial. Nonetheless, I was grateful that CPD's IT guy had been able to copy the Clare recording off the Voice Memos app so they wouldn't confiscate my iPhone. I took it out, laid it on the table in front of me, and looked at my golden retriever. "What do you think, girl?"

Vira barked once, either to prod me along or at a squirrel that had darted out from beneath a nearby pine tree.

"After last night, you know she's sound asleep," I said and scratched at the top of Vira's head. "You know we're going to wake her."

Vira barked again.

"As you wish." I picked up my phone . . . and tapped in Kippy's number.

PART TWO

CHICAGO

I love a dog. He does nothing for political reasons.

—Will Rogers

CHAPTER 18

Frank Cappelli Sr. sat alone in his home office. He'd hung up the landline, having just confirmed the five-course catering service from Davanti Enoteca as well as the six extra cream cakes from D'Amato's. The Mediterranean cruise packet—first class every step of the way—was hidden away in a bottom desk drawer, awaiting to be wrapped. His wife's birthday was on the horizon and though she'd instructed him, a bit too pretentiously, to throw no surprise party or waste any more of their money on over-the-top gifts—and though he'd nodded along with her pretense, just as he nodded along every year—Cappelli Sr. wondered what would occur were he truly to obey his wife's faux wishes.

Though it wouldn't appear on the thermostat, he assumed the temperature in the household would plummet . . . and not by a mere handful of degrees.

Cappelli Sr. could now add *Event Planner* to the list of things that might have been had birth not dictated his lot in life. That vocation could sit alongside financier, restaurateur, and developer—though Cappelli Sr. was more a behind-the-scenes patron. That vocation could sit on the same *might-have-been* shelf beside race-car driver—though his times at the track, decades earlier, had never been all that swift; the red Lamborghinis were more for appearance. That vocation could sit next to accountant or bookkeeper, which, the more

Cappelli Sr. thought about it, was ultimately what he had
become.

One of the cell phones on his desk began to vibrate.
Cappelli Sr. knew whom the phone indicated, brought it up to
his ear and said, "Yes."

"Phase two is complete."

"Were there any issues?"

"Not unless you sweat a barking dog."

"A what?"

"Nope," the voice said. "There were no issues."

"You know my philosophy on anything that crops up? Anything that threatens the garden?"

"I believe I do."

"Rip it out at the root," Cappelli Sr. said.

"Roger that."

"Tell me about the final piece?"

"Not to worry," Police Superintendent Gerald Callum replied
over Cappelli's burner phone. "That final piece will be like
flicking over a domino."

CHAPTER 19

I'd read somewhere the name "Chicago" comes from the
Frenched-up version of the local Indian word *shikaakwa,*
which stands for *wild onion.* We each had our assigned homework and Kippy's task was to peel back the layers of this wild
onion so we could place our current predicament into some
kind of historical context. Americans everywhere seem to
have at least a foggy awareness of Chicago's checkered past.
We Chicagoans like to wink and joke and guffaw about our
town's *illustrious* history and—knock on wood—pray it all remains in the past. In times gone by, machine politics provided
police protection for prostitution and gambling. In fact, police
corruption had already been a booming industry in Chicago
when the Volstead Act—carrying out the Eighteenth Amend-
ment to prohibit the manufacture, sale, or consumption of
alcoholic beverages—jacked the whole shooting match up on
steroids as bootlegging became big business.

A scar-faced gentleman of Italian descent by the name of
Alphonse Gabriel Capone paid off both police and politicians
on a truly massive scale and, in William Hale Thompson,
Capone had Chicago's compliant mayor in his back pocket.
Chicago's mob—nicknamed the Outfit—rose to power under
the control of both Johnny Torrio and Al Capone, and, since
those halcyon days of speakeasies and Tommy Guns, the
Outfit continued to be involved in extortion, loansharking,

gambling, prostitution, political corruption . . . and, of course, murder. Later yet, Chicago street gangs began controlling the distribution of drugs and, as such, cut dirty deals with dirty cops—drug trafficking with gang members paying several of the boys in blue for protection.

As far as the *apprehended* bad apples in uniform went, in the past fifty years over three hundred Chicago police officers have been convicted of offenses ranging from drug dealing, assault, and protecting mobsters to destroying evidence, theft, and murder. The hefty folder on the kitchen table in front of me included information about a police lieutenant by the name of Jon Burge who ran a torture mill—burning suspects with radiators, electrocuting testicles, you name it. The folder also contained data about a certain chief of detectives and assistant police superintendent named William Hanhardt, who had been convicted of using confidential police data to oversee a mob-connected jewelry theft ring. Moreover, the folder covered an officer by the name of Joseph Miedzianowski. Miedzianowski ran the Chicago Gangs Unit while also running his own private drug gang—evidently multitasking as both cop and drug lord, and was ultimately convicted on ten counts, up to and including racketeering and drug conspiracy.

Unfortunately, the beat goes on and the cluster of acronyms: IAD, IPRA, PB—Internal Affairs Division, Independent Police Review Authority, Police Board, as well as the Mayor's Office and the State's Attorney's Office—have yet to succeed in keeping CPD's corruption completely in check. The blue wall of silence and a bureaucratic indifference has prevented the top brass from eliminating police corruption.

"Wow," I said, after reviewing Kippy's ream of background material. She'd spent quite a bit of time compiling this dossier of macro data on the Windy City's turbulent history in order to frame our discussion. "It's like an FBI agent should be assigned to keep tabs on each one of you."

"Not funny," Officer Wabiszewski replied. "Not funny at all."

By calling in the troops, I realized that any pierced ego

on my part over being *just friends* with Kippy would need to take a back seat now that we strongly suspected that Police Superintendent Gerald Callum, the man who leads the largest law enforcement agency in the city of Chicago, and his chauffeur-slash-henchman—make that two henchmen based on the man's excessive girth—were responsible for the murder of Peter Feist, the head of the Special Prosecutions Bureau in the Cook County State's Attorney's Office.

Vira had caught a whiff of it on one or both of them.

Truth be told, I'd been in more than a trivial state of alarm since yesterday morning's scene at Washington Park, and I damn near dropped ticker tape upon Kippy and Wabiszewski's arrival.

We were scraping pretzels and potato chips through a mildly expired dip I'd found lurking behind a definitely expired carton of milk in the back of the fridge and drinking bottled water—no one had yet to reach for the beer—in my living room as we pored over our homework assignments. Dawn and Maggie May were loafing about outside and, hopefully, keeping tabs on Bill; Sue manned the sofa, while Vira chose to stick with us fogies. My golden retriever had initially appeared interested in our conversation, then her attention turned to begging for pretzels, then in licking Kippy's hand for ten minutes, but now she was sacked out, bored by our discussions, and napping atop Kippy's feet.

"It doesn't help that every other governor in Illinois winds up in prison," Kippy said, and looked at her stack of papers. "Bank fraud, bribery, pay-to-play, lying to the FBI, etcetera."

"It's the Chicago way?" Wabiszewski replied. "You know, like a fish tank that never gets aerated—the water gets all skanky."

When I had shared the news of Vira's having had another *occurrence* after her discovery of Special Prosecutor Peter Feist in a fishpond in Washington Park and her subsequent agitation upon Police Superintendent Gerald Callum or, more likely, his driver's arrival, Kippy took it in stride, but as for her partner—although Wabiszewski had turned over a new leaf in regard to Vira's unique ability—the man remained a tougher sell. But Wabs was a skeptical son of a bitch on most matters under the sun and I planned on taking him along to the dealership next time I bartered for a pickup truck.

Officer Wabiszewski's homework assignment had been more micro in nature. Wabiszewski provided background data on Police Superintendent Gerald "Jerry" Callum. Police superintendent is, of course, the highest rank in the Chicago Police Department, and the position is appointed by the mayor. Ultimately, Superintendent Callum manages the four bureaus—the Bureau of Patrol, the Bureau of Detectives, the Bureau of Organized Crime, and the Bureau of Support Services—with each bureau commanded by a police or bureau chief. Police Superintendent Callum had been strongly recommended by the Chicago City Council—CPD falls under the jurisdiction of the City Council—and had been appointed superintendent four years earlier in one of the prior mayor's concluding acts, with an eye toward addressing the Windy City's soaring homicide rate.

Wabiszewski read from his notes: "There were seven hundred eighty-one murders in Chicago in 2016—one of the deadliest years in decades . . . a bloodbath. The rate dropped to six hundred sixty-four murders in 2017, and then just over five hundred in both 2018 and 2019—which is good news, I guess, but still a goddamned shame." Wabs looked up and added, "Of course we all know how shitty 2020 was, but with nearly three thousand 'shooting incidents' every year, I don't know—maybe we're lucky the homicide rates aren't higher."

I shook my head in response. Depressing numbers.

"And don't get me started on the homicide clearance rates because we're talking percentages in the lower double digits," Wabiszewski continued. "Hell, if we hit twenty percent in a given year, march out the brass band. More realistically, maybe one in six homicides ever gets solved."

Wabiszewski wasn't able to compile much information on

Police Superintendent Callum outside of what was already public knowledge or the bits and pieces from the city's newspapers or the superintendent's curriculum vitae. At age twenty-two, in the late-seventies, Callum joined the Chicago Police Department as a beat cop. Callum then rose through the ranks and was appointed commander of the 12th District in 2004 and became bureau chief of BOC—Bureau of Organized Crime—in 2011.

And it was from BOC that Gerald Callum had made his great leap forward to police superintendent.

Neither Kippy nor Wabiszewski had ever met Superintendent Callum in person, but both had been present at an official CPD event last August where Callum had given a speech. The superintendent's words were mostly praise for the hard work, dedication, and determination of his bureau chiefs in their ongoing efforts to reduce Chicago's unacceptable homicide rate as our most recent fatal shooting levels were five times those of New York City while having a third of NYC's population; hitting the African American community the hardest—more specifically young black males. Superintendent Callum had both outlined his pet program—the implementation of proactive policing—as well as his wish list—advocating the tightening up of sentencing policies, getting smart on bail reform to keep violent felons off the streets, stop handing out probation as though it were Chiclets—and called upon politicians on both sides of the aisle to stay the course and find it in their annual budgets to provide CPD with the required resources. Per the images Wabiszewski had provided from the various press clippings, Superintendent Callum had sharp blue eyes—which I remembered from Washington Park—as well as a lined and weathered face that had seen many a mile.

Until today, Kippy and Wabiszewski had no strong opinion one way or the other regarding Police Superintendent Callum. He was far too removed from their day-to-day functions, too far up the department's totem pole. Both officers got the general sense Callum was respected in his role as the head of the CPD, and certainly wished the superintendent well in reducing the city's murder rate.

Neither Kippy nor Wabiszewski could find anything on the superintendent's driver—the Sasquatch-sized henchman who had stepped from the Lincoln Continental and tripped Vira's trigger in Washington Park. However, Wabiszewski recalled a similar-sized fellow who'd attended Gerald Callum's speech that August afternoon. A mountainous gentleman had hung out in the background, hovering about the periphery of the superintendent's official entourage. The man had loomed large as hell and, as Wabiszewski noted, he might have looked more familiar had he been carrying Fay Wray in one hand while scaling the Sears Tower.

Wabiszewski looked about the room after his quick debrief on Gerald Callum and continued, "We're at that junction once again—you know, with Vira—where we can't go skipping to the mayor or the feebs or the papers and, when they ask how we came by this vital information, tell them we've got us this Mensa dog. 'No shit, Mr. Mayor, really, Vira scored sixteen hundred on the SAT and plans to get a Ph.D. in Biophysics at Stanford—and that's how we figured out Superintendent Callum whacked Peter Feist.'"

We absorbed Wabiszewski's analysis in silence.

Wabiszewski went on, "Listen, I love Vira. If she were taller and brunette, I'd ask for her paw in marriage. And I know what she can do, but describing what Vira *can do* will make us sound like a bunch of fucking nutjobs and we'll get matching bunks in Lakeshore."

Chicago Lakeshore was the city's major psychiatric hospital.

We'd been down the Lakeshore path before.

"Obviously we need hard evidence, Wabs," Kippy replied. "Vira told us whodunit, okay, so now we need to walk back the cat—figure out motive, means, and opportunity—and use them to nail Callum's ass to the wall."

Wabiszewski shrugged. "Piece of cake."

"Piece of cake," Kippy repeated.

Wabiszewski then turned his attention my way. "You got anything, Reid?"

My homework assignment had been easy-peasy. I was to serve treats and drinks, listen and comb through the information Kippy and Wabs had presented, and then do my damnedest to ask intelligent questions . . . of which I had but one.

"What do we do now?"

Wabiszewski tossed a hand in the air. "You know what the safest thing to do would be? Forget all this horseshit. It's Chicago for Christ's sake. Without proof, any anonymous bullshit, like sending a letter or something to the feds or the mayor will be shredded as just some screwball crawling out of the woodwork. And if we start poking about Peter Feist's death on our own, it'll call attention to us . . . and then Vira will have one of her occurrences over our bodies."

Kippy said, "So the bastard gets away with it?"

"Feist flew too close to the sun and got burned. Why should we follow suit? Think about it for a minute. As long as street crime is in steady decline, which is what everyone in Chicago and America is rooting for, why should we give a shit if one of the assholes at the top is on the take?"

"I know you, Wabs," Kippy said. "You don't mean a word of that."

"Unless we're able to cobble together some kind of hard proof, I'm as serious as lung cancer." Wabiszewski tugged absentmindedly on the collar of his shirt and looked my way. "Besides," he said, "I'm a big fan of what you baited Eddie Clare with the other day . . . karma. Superintendent Callum will eventually get his, one way or another."

Kippy didn't buy it. "But what if we're meant to be his karma?"

CHAPTER 20

After another exhausting hour of batting ideas around, Wabiszewski announced, "Those of us with hot dates tonight are heading out." He looked at Kippy. "You coming?"

She checked her watch. "It's still early."

"I think we can all agree I'm a nine, but it takes a little additional time and effort on my part—hair mousse and moisturizers—to achieve that perfect ten," Wabiszewski replied. "I only do it for them."

"You peak at a seven, Wabs," Kippy said. "Get some booze in the poor girl and maybe that'll up the needle to a seven-point-one."

"I could take you home in a bit if you want to keep brainstorming," I blurted out, only to find dead air in need of filling. "I mean Vira and I could run you home whenever you'd like. It's no big deal. Really."

Wabiszewski looked at Kippy as he was donning his jacket and said, "Well, I'll just leave you two lovebirds be, then."

Another hour of dead ends later and we decided I'd make a quick Jimmy John's run for an early dinner while Kippy tossed the Frisbee with Vira and Bill—Maggie and Delta Dawn had grown bored with Frisbee a few years earlier and, based on their temperaments, would rather be quilting or scrapbooking. And Sue had television to watch; it was imperative he not miss a show—the Nielsen Company should rig him up with a box for their TV ratings. Kippy and I thought food might help stimulate the neurons in our brains, help us concoct a plan to—oh, you know—take down CPD's sitting police superintendent and his henchman in the great city of Chicago.

I grabbed my wallet and keys but paused at the door. "The *Tribune* said no one in Feist's office had a clue what he was up to in Washington Park."

Kippy added, "Which means he intentionally kept them in the dark."

I nibbled on that as I stepped across the driveway and almost made it to my pickup when I heard the car engine approach me from behind. A red Miata pulled between my F-150 and the doublewide. Something the size of the Eiffel Tower lodged in my throat when I spotted who sat behind the driver's wheel. I walked over as my ex-wife stepped from the convertible.

"Hey, Mickie," I managed to mutter.

"Hi, Mace."

"You got a new car." I set my fingertips on the hood of the Miata. I'd flunk a polygraph if I didn't admit that Mickie looked great—shorter hair and, of course, a perfect tan.

"Brian felt I should be driving something under warranty."

"Always a good idea."

"I bumped into Kathy at Costco the other day."

"Really?" Kathy is my older sister.

"I asked her how you were doing and she said nobody'd seen much of you lately, that you were *all hermited* up here *with the dogs*."

I cringed internally . . . and possibly outwardly.

Kathy and I would soon be having a conversation and not necessarily a pleasant one. I'd like to believe my brothers would have told Mickie I was dating someone—preferably a

Chicago Bears' cheerleader—but not Big Sis with her never-ending affinity for the truth.

We fidgeted another moment before Mickie plowed ahead. "Look, Mace, we've not spoken since that night you called."

I nodded and began wondering if a person could indeed melt down in a Wicked Witch fashion, figuring I was seconds away from finding out.

"I know my engagement with Brian may have seemed rushed at the time—it was a bit of a whirlwind, I admit—and I apologize if that hurt your feelings." Mickie looked at me. "I care about you, Mace, and I wanted to stop by and make sure you were okay."

At a loss, I continued bobbing my head like one of those dunking birds mounted on an adjustable crosspiece.

"Are you—"

"And pick up some Scrubbing Bubbles, Mason, if you ever want me in that shower again," a voice from behind my screen door interrupted Mickie, and suddenly Kippy stepped outside with Vira hot on her heels. "Oh my god, I didn't know we had company." Kippy's roll-tab shirt was now tucked into her chinos, and a button at the top of her roll-tab had come undone since I'd last seen her. Vira sat upright in the shade of the front awning as Kippy walked over and slid a hand behind my back. "I'm so embarrassed."

I'm not sure who sank deeper into shock at this point, Mickie or me, but my ex-wife recovered first, held out a hand and said, "Hi, I'm Mickie."

Kippy's face lit up. "I've heard so much about you." She introduced herself, ignored Mickie's hand, and leaned in for a hug and cheek kisses. "So when's the big day?"

"Next weekend."

"Where are you guys going on your honeymoon?"

"Cancun."

"Oh, yes, Cancun'll be so much fun," Kippy replied, all rainbows and unicorns. "Mason and I are thinking about spending Christmas in Maui."

I think Mickie may have glanced in my direction before turning back to Kippy, but I couldn't be positive on account of all blood flow in my body having ceased. Vira sat nonchalantly as though a spectator at a tennis match, which perhaps she was. I tried recalling if Dick Weech from up the road had a defibrillator.

"Mace is thinking that?" Mickie asked all incredulously, as though I'd been plotting a trip to the outer ring of Saturn.

"The guy's been pushing it nonstop. My parents own a timeshare there and are always yakking at us to use it."

"I've never been to Hawaii."

"You haven't lived until you've done the islands," Kippy said. "You and Bob have got to go someday."

"Brian."

"What?"

"My fiancé's name is Brian."

"Oh, I'm sorry," Kippy said. "When you and Brian go there, you have to swim with the sea turtles. It's a must. And you won't believe the fish—they're all green and blue and neon and look like they were drawn by Dr. Seuss." Kippy playfully patted my chest. "Mace and I will bring you back some brochures."

"Too much fun." Mickie twirled her car keys. "I would definitely take your parents up on that invite." Mickie retreated a step back toward her convertible. "Anyway, I should probably get a move on."

"Absolutely not," Kippy said. "I didn't mean to interrupt." She gave my bicep a quick squeeze. "I'll go feed the kids and you two get caught up."

On that note, Kippy disappeared back inside the doublewide with Vira again at her heels, leaving Mickie and me to discover newfangled manners in which to fidget.

"Your girlfriend's very pretty," Mickie said.

"Thank you."

"I didn't know you were seeing anyone."

I shrugged. I hadn't known, either.

"And what's up with the shower?" Mickie said, smiling now. "You were always such a neat freak."

"I may have let things slide."

Mickie opened her car door. "I'm happy for you, Mace."

"Mickie?"

"What?"

"Congratulations," I said. "I hope you and Brian have a wonderful wedding."

"I apologize," Kippy said immediately. "I'm paranoid about Feist and Superintendent Callum, so when I heard a car drive up, I peeked outside and . . . I guess I did a bit of eavesdropping." She shook her head. "I should not have done that."

I'd noticed Kippy's holstered Beretta on the end table next to the door when I stepped back inside.

"To be honest, it sounded like your ex showed up to throw a pity party with you as the guest of honor. 'Poor Mace. Poor, sweet, broken Mace.' I'm sorry, but that kind of stuff really pisses me off." Kippy held my eye and continued, "You may have a screw loose, Mace, like the rest of us, but you're not a charity case, you're no one to be pitied . . . and you sure as hell are no one to be condescended to."

All five of my dogs sat quietly on the couch, scrunched close together, and stared my way. I noted that neither Delta Dawn nor Maggie May nor Sue had scampered outside to come see Mickie at the sound of her voice.

It appears I'd truly won custody.

"If you'd like," Kippy said, "I can give Mickie a call and set her straight."

I stepped around the kitchen table, leaned in, and kissed Kippy on the mouth. Her lips were soft and, on my end, sparks flew and fireworks blew holes in the atmosphere, but an instant later there was a hand between us.

I backed away.

"Mace," Kippy said.

"I know," I replied, realizing I had broken our *just-friends* covenant. "You're off guys and all that other BS, but what you did . . . that was the sweetest thing . . . and I didn't feel it should go *unkissed*."

This time the dead air lingered between us for most of a minute before I asked, "Your parents got a timeshare in Hawaii?"

Kippy shook her head. "Of course not."

CHAPTER 21

"Okay, gang," I said, standing in front of my five dogs who were lined up evenly—all comfy and relaxed—across my or, to be more accurate, Sue's living room sofa. "I've been in the backyard scooping up your piles and I saw something I didn't care for." I paused for the words and stern tone to sink in. "Which one of you ate at the dead squirrel?"

I was met with stares and stillness. Omertà—the code of silence.

"So that's how you're going to play it? Quite frankly, I thought I'd raised all of you better than this. I was hoping for a little honesty, but we can do it the hard way. A half cup of pretzels for whoever tells me who gnawed on the squirrel."

Vira caught my eye, hesitated, and then glanced away. "Really, Vira?" I said. "You'd rat out murderers but keep mum on the squirrel-eater among us?" I stared at each of my dogs individually. "Look, if I have to smell your breath, the five of you are going to be in a hell of a lot of hot water. And, by the way, what's all this about me never getting a spot on the couch anymore?" I looked at Sue. "You know none of this shit would have flown before you retired."

My sister collies looked quickly at one another and then back at me. Maggie and Delta were gaslighters from the get-go—it was in their genes—always sharing sideways glances as though they were privy to top-secret information I wasn't. They got their kicks trying to make me feel all crazy and unhinged. The sad thing of it was that I fell for their con game nearly every time, always checking myself in the mirror, wiping my nose, double-checking my wallet and car keys and pockets—trying to noodle out whatever the hell it was I appeared to be overlooking.

If we were around when President Kennedy was assassinated, they'd have had me confessing to being the man on the grassy knoll.

"That won't work today, girls," I told my farm collies. Then I took a long breath and stared at my bloodhound. "We all know it was you, Bill, so don't act like you've gotten away with anything."

Bill smiled in a manner only a bloodhound could, as if to say *don't knock dead squirrels until you've tried one.*

My cell phone vibrated.

"Hello."

"You got a suit?" It was Kippy.

"I do." A few years ago Mickie had me buy a discounted navy blue at a JCPenney factory outlet, back when many of our friends were tying the knot. I knew it was still hiding in a dry-cleaning bag at the rear of the guest room's closet.

"Put it on," Kippy said. "Wabs and I will be at your place in five minutes."

"Why?"

"We're going to a funeral."

"It is with a heavy heart and a tortured soul that I stand before you today. We have lost a beloved husband, a caring father, a precious son, a brilliant colleague, and a dedicated public servant. Peter Feist touched many lives and was a treasured friend to everyone who knew him. How then do we say goodbye to someone who meant so much to so many?"

Mayor Carter Weeks commenced his eulogy as I slid into a back pew of the Holy Name Cathedral, tap-danced between dress shoes, and did my best to cram into a three-inch gap between what was likely a husband and wife. I did so as quietly as possible but still suffered the slings and arrows of irate frowns and annoyed glances. Holy Name Cathedral is one of the largest Roman Catholic dioceses in the United States as well as being the seat of the Archdiocese of Chicago. And today's funeral mass—much like Jonny Whiting's had been—was standing room only except for the occasional dunderhead who, not unlike me, invaded the personal proximities of his fellow parishioners.

Holy Name Cathedral dominates the corner of State and Superior Streets, a half-block south of Chicago Avenue, and the traffic on Chicago had been a bear—stop-and-go the entire way. Wabiszewski dropped Kippy and me off on State Street and then went in search of a spot to stash his car. Once inside the cathedral, I'd lost sight of Kippy as we both swam upstream to find a seat, any seat, for the service that had already begun.

In other words, it was every man for himself.

The chief executive of Chicago looked out over the packed cathedral and continued his tribute, "It's important to remember Peter Feist lives on, not just in the hearts and minds, souls and DNA of his beautiful daughters, but in the good deeds that Peter performed, and in the thoughts and feelings and memories of Peter that we all hold dear. Please forgive me if I get a little misty-eyed as Peter was a dear personal friend, in fact my best friend. To be honest, Peter was the big brother I never had. Frankly, I idolized the man and knew he was what this city needed, what this city required, as head of the Special Prosecutions Bureau inside the Cook County State's Attorney's Office. Peter's was a recommendation I made without a moment's hesitation, and with a great deal of pride. You see, Peter was committed to making a difference for the people of our great city. And make a difference Special Prosecutor Peter Feist did."

Mayor Weeks was young, on the cusp of forty—black hair and thin features—boyishly photogenic like a high school senior voted most likely to succeed, of which I've no doubt

Weeks once was. The mayor had been a well-liked two-and-a-half-term alderman representing Ward 25, a seat on the City Council he'd more or less inherited when a massive heart attack cut short his father's fourth term.

In the mayoral race, Weeks edged out the competition with nearly fifty-one percent of the vote, a razor-thin majority that put him over the top and saved Chicagoans from another pain-in-the-ass runoff election. Weeks's shocking upset came on a populist platform of restoring public trust via reform—the usual suspects, such as education reform, tax reform, police reform; unfortunately, based on recent news coverage, the existing bureaucracy had yet to forgive him.

What I personally believe got Carter Weeks his mayorship was his continual hammering of *The Keepers*.

The Keepers, if I was bright enough to decipher the mayor's rhetoric, was an allegory or metaphor regarding what kept the populace of the Windy City down, what kept all of us worker bees subservient, in our place and forever under their thumb, whether our Keepers be political corruption (aldermen abusing power for their own monetary gain, misusing campaign funds on luxurious lifestyles); or operating in the guise of an overpowering bureaucracy, with us held hostage to an endless and suffocating red tape, a deep state ripe with inefficiency—after all, you can't fight City Hall; or flagrant cronyism (favoritism in awarding jobs or appointments); or even appearing as police corruption—good lord, where to begin. A major part of the mayor's reform platform was to promote integrity and accountability and transparency to a city that's often been dubbed the *Corruption Capital of America*. Mayor Carter Weeks pounded his podium and railed away at the Keepers—at *our* Keepers—in every speech, interview, or campaign event he logged. Weeks couldn't have crushed this theme more if he'd used a jackhammer, and though he'd not been the first candidate to run in such a fashion, evidently enough voters took him at his word and he took office in a squeaker.

Mayor Weeks dabbed at wet eyes with a handkerchief. "Peter Feist was a hero, a shining exemplar of what a special prosecutor should be. Peter was fearless; Peter was methodical, unswerving, relentless, and dedicated. A gentleman of extraordinary intellect, and he was deeply committed in his quest—like a modern-day Galahad of the Round Table. The man never wavered. Peter even looked the part, a handsome Gary Cooper setting about to save the city he so loved. Many question whether ours is a city that can be saved. Others question whether it deserves to be. But never Peter. No . . . never Peter." Weeks took a long breath before continuing, "To Marilyn and David, he was a dearly loved son. To Laura—or Eggs as Peter affectionately and playfully called her—he was a devoted, adoring, and loving husband. To Annika and Kiley, he was a doting father."

Mayor Weeks looked down at the front pew where Feist's parents, widow, and his two little girls sat, all of them weeping. Tears began to stream down his face. "Words fail me—Laura and Annika and Kiley—to tell you how much Peter loved you. Peter loved you with all his heart. You were Peter's world."

The mayor abandoned his damp handkerchief and wiped his eyes with the sleeve of his suit jacket. "To all of Peter's family, we send our thoughts, our prayers, and our deepest sympathies. May God bless you, Peter. And may your memory never leave our thoughts, may your spirit never leave our hearts, and may your commitment to public service inspire all of us. On behalf of the Office of the Mayor, on behalf of the men and women of the State's Attorney's Office, and on behalf of Chicago's law enforcement community, I conclude by saying thank you, Peter—thank you for making a difference . . . thank you for your last full measure of devotion."

I liked Mayor Weeks's eulogy. In fact, I liked Mayor Weeks. I would probably have gotten around to voting for him had I the wherewithal to figure out what precinct I was supposed to show up at, what time I had to be there, and what in hell being *registered* meant. Since it is Chicago, I imagine there were plenty of dead folks vying for my spot in the polling booth.

I know, I know—I should take my civic duty more seriously than I take flossing.

Some attorney that worked for Feist named Marty Kolles stood up next and talked of how Peter had been much more a mentor and dear friend than boss, and that everyone in the Special Prosecutions Bureau was devastated at Peter's death. It looked as if Kolles had more to say, but he began to shudder and stare at his notes on the podium a long moment before his wife stepped up beside him and took his hand. At that point, Kolles cleared his throat, thanked everyone for attending, and the couple returned to their seats in the second row.

The priest then came to his pulpit and spoke of how death brings grief and sorrow, of how God provides hope, and how we receive comfort from each other. I would have enjoyed the priest's sermon more had I not drank coffee all morning and, in my frenzy to shave, gargle, and toss on the only suit I owned, I'd forgotten to relieve myself before darting outside as my associates pulled up in Wabiszewski's spotless Dodge Charger. After my disconcerting arrival, I sat in fear of further riling my pew-mates via a premature exit. I now knew how my dogs felt after I'd left them at home for a twelve-hour stretch with the pet door closed. With minutes left in the funeral service, my discomfort built to such an agonizing nature that, in order to take pressure off my bladder, I loosened my belt a notch and unhitched the top button on my suit pants. The female half of the couple I'd slivered myself between shot dagger eyes my way as though she'd caught me committing a blasphemy.

Since we sat in back, it took another millennium for the ushers to dismiss our row, and then I had to locate a hallway that might lead to one of the cathedral's restrooms. I couldn't spot Kippy in the swarming horde, but I caught Wabiszewski's eye as, evidently, he'd spent the service standing in back. I flashed him five fingers and pointed toward where I was headed. I think he understood.

I quickened my pace, hit the men's room door at a near-jog, palmed it open, took a stride inside and . . . Chicago's handsome young mayor stood, red-faced, by the sink, sideways, not staring into the mirror but into the eyes of Police Superintendent Gerald Callum. Callum, in full-dress uniform, stood stone-faced as the mayor finished shaking a forefinger at his chest as if he'd just recited chapter and verse as to why Callum must now march straight up to his room without dinner. Both heads swiveled in my direction—Mayor Weeks looked steamed; Superintendent Callum expressionless.

I headed immediately to the nearest urinal and unzipped.

"To be continued," Weeks said, and I heard the mayor's footsteps on the tile floor behind me as he exited the restroom.

Next came the sound of hands washing in a sink, long and drawn-out, then a towel dispenser in use, and then silence. After a billion years of being chased by lions and tigers and bears, we Homo sapiens have some sort of evolutionary warning system hardwired into us. A rapid heartbeat began to drum in my chest and the hairs on the back of my neck informed me that Superintendent Callum was watching me, and not in any amiable manner. I faced the wall, too cowardly to twist my head sideways and confront the stillness out of sheer terror of what I might witness. My imagination made a sturdy case I'd behold the superintendent's service revolver aimed at my skull.

Nothing like a massive dose of fight-or-flight at the church urinal.

I nearly wept with joy when a couple more gentlemen entered the lavatory, one heading for a stall, the other stepping to the urinal at the end of the row. A moment later I listened as Superintendent Callum stepped to the door and exited the men's room.

Needless to say, I suffered stage fright and found myself

temporarily unable to accomplish what I'd come there to perform.

Damnit.

It took me thirty seconds of focus, eyes shut, before my bladder relaxed and I finally began to relieve myself. The guy who'd arrived at the row of urinals after me took care of business, cleaned his hands, and left. Other men came and went, several generations passed. I'm not sure if there's a Guinness World Record for taking a leak, but I'm sure I'd at least have made runner-up. Afterward, I washed my hands quickly, dried off, and pulled open the door.

"Well, I'll be goddamned." The mountain-sized man I'd seen at Washington Park towered above me, blocking my way. "If it ain't the dog man."

CHAPTER 22

"That was one hell of a ruckus the other morning." He stuck a hand out; when I reached to shake it, he clasped my forearm with a free hand the size of a baseball mitt and steered me into an alcove adjacent to the men's room. "The barking really woke my ass up."

"Happy Jack gets nervous at crime scenes," I said. "He sometimes gets loud."

"Happy Jack?"

"I name my dogs after songs," I said. "You know, 'Happy Jack'? The Who?"

The man-mountain narrowed his eyes in thought. "'Happy Jack wasn't old, but he was a man. He lived in the sand at the Isle of Man.'"

"That's the one," I said. "Great song."

"But that doesn't make any sense?"

"What?" My neck already ached from craning up at him. His broad features—the lantern jaw and thick nose—looked like something carved out of a hillside.

"The dog I saw you with was a bitch," Man-mountain said. "A golden retriever bitch."

Damn—even across the parking lot he'd been able to see under Vira's hood.

"You're right," I lied through my teeth and looked down at his cowboy boots. "We were waiting there a long time and

by then Jack had curled up in my pickup while I sat with
Bennie."

"So Happy Jack was in the back of your F-150 while you
played with Elton John," Man-mountain said smiling, perhaps letting me know he knew I was full of shit, perhaps
letting me know he knew the model of my truck.

I nodded.

"I heard you had a golden retriever with you when you
helped catch that Eddie Clare prick."

The conversation was going from bad to worse. Kippy, Wabs,
and I had done research on Superintendent Gerald Callum
and his lethal sidekick, and they, in turn, had performed due
diligence on yours truly. While we gazed into the abyss, the
abyss took notes on me.

"We were just trying to help."

"I heard the tape and you did a shitload more than help,"
Man-mountain said. "And your dog started grumbling just
like she did the other day."

"She didn't like being there—you know, city streets at
night." I hoped my eyes weren't as wide open as they felt.

"Them city streets at night can be damned nerve-racking."
Man-mountain nudged his fedora up a half inch. "I listened
to that tape of yours five times, Reid, and after you cooled
Bennie's jets, you started weaseling that drummer boy—
getting all friendly and suck-ass to egg him on—leading Clare
down the garden path until the dumb fuck confessed. Hell, I
thought it was inspiring police work . . . yet you didn't get an
inch of credit, did you?" He stared down at me. "But I knew
what you did, Reid. I knew."

"I didn't know I was so popular," I said, realizing he knew
who I was. The temperature in the cathedral felt like a sauna.
"I'm not sure I got your name."

"I didn't give it."

"But you're part of the superintendent's security detail," I
said. "His driver, right?"

"I drive Callum sometimes . . . and sometimes I do other

things." Man-mountain stood at his full height. "I must confess, Reid. I did some checking on you after that disturbance at the park—yes, I did—and I got kind of fascinated by them sniffer dogs of yours. Finding bombs and drugs and dead folk—a guy'd have to be a fartskull not to like that kinda shit. And damned if it didn't turn out you're more than a dog handler . . . you're a freaking legend. You not only ferreted out drummer boy, but last fall you helped catch that serial killer—the one who filled that pond with all them stiffs. Hell, Reid, they should call you Have Dog—Will Travel."

I felt myself begin to blush, and not from his compliment. I waved a hand as though it were no big deal. "Like I said, we just try to help."

"The one from Washington Park," Man-mountain said. "Bennie—she was the same golden retriever that went for the pond-killer, right?"

A line of sweat formed at my hairline and I nodded slowly, knowing how pathetic my fib about Happy Jack had gone over.

"I'd love to stop by your place in Lansing some time," Man-mountain said. "See how you train them sniffers."

Callum's driver not only knew my name and my truck, but also where I lived.

"You'd be bored."

"Not me."

"Call first," I said, wiping the sweat off my forehead. "I'm training a pack of pit bulls from when they broke up a fight ring. I'd hate to think what could happen if someone showed up unannounced."

"A pack of pit bulls, huh?" Man-mountain smiled again. "I like you, Reid. You got a lot of spunk."

It was then that I caught sight of Kippy standing across the hallway, diagonally from me, monitoring the situation. She must have come searching for me when I didn't show up on the cathedral steps.

"I should probably get going."

"You got friends here?" He looked over a shoulder.

Fortunately, there were still enough attendees buzzing about the church to keep it confusing.

I shook my head, not trusting my voice at this point.

Man-mountain turned back and looked me in the eyes. "Did you know Feist?"

"No," I said, shaking my head again. "I just thought I should come and pay my respects."

"You work for the city, right?"

"A fair amount."

"So they got you by the short and curlies?"

"Huh?"

Man-mountain leaned in again and I saw his nose had been broken a time or two along the way. "If you piss someone off, the contracts go bye-bye. Then what? Shovel shit at PetSmart?"

I shrugged. "I really need to get going."

"Let me give you a ride to your truck," he said. "Least I could do."

"I'm good," I said. I got the distinct feeling if I left with him, eternity would be lonely at the bottom of Lake Michigan, swaying in the undercurrent, feet shrouded in cement.

"You sure?"

"I'm good," I said again, gulping air.

"You're not one to take lightly," he answered back, "are you, Reid?"

I took his query as rhetorical and kept mum.

Then Man-mountain twisted sideways, as though dismissing me. His *aw-shucks* grin returned—spreading broadly across his features—but all I saw were teeth. I began orbiting around his bulk when he spoke again, "Be seeing you."

Without glancing in her direction, I walked past Kippy and headed for Holy Name Cathedral's front entrance hall.

"Wabs went to get the car," Kippy whispered as she followed behind me.

I went outside and spotted Wabiszewski's Dodge Charger sitting curbside. Wabiszewski had to be wondering what the hell was taking us so long. I walked down the steps, crossed the sidewalk, and opened the passenger door for Kippy who was about ten paces in back of me. I opened the rear door and slid into the Charger's back seat. As Wabiszewski pulled away from Holy Name Cathedral, I looked back.

There he stood. Man-mountain positioned at the top of the cathedral steps, watching as we drove away.

CHAPTER 23

It took me three vodkas straight-up and two beer chasers to work my way through the five stages of grief and arrive at acceptance. I waved for the bartender and announced, "I'm moving to Alaska."

"I'm so sorry, Mace," said Kippy. "We should not have dragged you along."

Wabiszewski had driven us to some old-man bar in West Town called Russell's. The place was dark and smelled of cigarettes. A couple of geriatrics, who I assumed were regulars, sat at the bar. Somewhere a jukebox screamed Bob Seeger.

"Then I wouldn't have known they were on to me till I woke to find that big guy wrenching my head around."

"He wants you to keep your mouth shut is all," Wabiszewski said. "That's why the threat about canceling your city contracts."

"He wants me quiet, all right, long enough to figure out the best way to get rid of me."

"Another vodka?" The bartender, possibly Russell the proprietor himself, stood at our booth.

"Have you ever heard of Barrow, Alaska?" I asked. "North of the Arctic Circle—they get night for two months each winter."

The bartender shook his head.

"Barrow it is."

"More vodka?"

"I think we've had enough," Kippy interjected.

"Just coffee," I told the bartender. "I've a long night of packing ahead of me."

Kippy and Wabiszewski shared a long glance.

"What?"

"Tell him," Wabiszewski said.

"Tell me what?"

"About two and a half weeks back—actually, the night before they found Jonny Whiting's body—a real estate investor by the name of David Siskin was murdered in his downtown Chicago office. You might have heard about it, but Whiting's demise blew Siskin's death and just about everything else off the front page. Sure, his homicide made the papers but it was played up as an office burglary gone awry, that Siskin had been working late at night and stumbled onto a team of thieves stealing laptops and petty cash," Kippy said. "What didn't make the papers was the extent of Siskin's injuries. If you interrupt a burglary in progress, maybe you get shot, maybe you get stabbed or smacked in the head with something blunt. That's not what happened here. Siskin got beaten to death; or, more precisely, kicked to death. But it didn't end there. Siskin's killer or killers continued stomping on the poor guy after he'd died. They shattered both bones in each of his forearms—the radius and the ulna—and the tibia and fibula bones in one of his legs."

"These were compound fractures, bones through skin," Wabiszewski added. "That's no small order. And most of the man's ribs were kicked in, too . . . evidently for good measure."

"Much of this *activity*," Kippy continued, "appears to have been postmortem bruising. That means many of the injuries were inflicted promptly after Siskin's death, thank god. Forensics was able to determine that because significant bruising ceases after a person's been dead for several minutes due to the lack of a heartbeat and blood circulation. However, as in Siskin's death, great violence can produce a form of bruising for up to three hours after death. And the homicide detective I spoke with said David Siskin looked as though he'd been hit by a steam locomotive."

"Siskin's death was anything but the result of an interrupted burglary; it was a statement," Wabiszewski cut to the chase. "Now who do we know that looks like a steam locomotive? And who do we know that sports pointed-toed cowboy boots?"

In response, I reached for my vodka glass, wishing it wasn't empty. "Callum's driver."

"Right, and I bet you a nickel that big bastard has them steel-tipped as well."

"We didn't dare poke about Peter Feist's autopsy, didn't want any red flags popping up." Kippy looked at me. "Did you notice anything else beyond Feist's broken neck?"

"The way his head was jerked backward kind of stole the whole show," I said, thinking back to that morning in Washington Park, "but before Vira and I were instructed to vacate the crime scene, they were examining Feist's body, had lifted up his windbreaker and shirt to look for additional injuries, and one of the investigators said it looked as though Feist had been *knocked about.* Not like that investor guy you've been talking about, but enough to take the fight out of him so the perp could do that thing to his neck."

"So they were talking antemortem bruising? Discoloration of the skin before death?"

"They didn't get that far into it before Vira and I were told to leave the area." I shrugged. "Our job was done at that point."

"A kick or two by Callum's driver would take the fight out of Mike Tyson."

"Can they match ante- or postmortem bruising to a guy's boot?" I asked.

"Forensics can pull rabbits out of any hat these days," Kippy said. "I would think pointed-toed cowboy boots, especially steel-tipped ones, would leave a *distinct* mark. It shouldn't be hard for a medical examiner to determine wound patterns."

We remained silent while the bartender set a cup of coffee and small pitcher of cream in front of me.

"So you're thinking Man-mountain may have screwed the pooch by giving Feist a kick or two to take the fight out of him or move him along," I said after the bartender had left, "then maybe Feist becomes linked to Siskin's death via some corresponding injuries as well as the murder weapon—his cowboy boots—and the spotlight then goes to what? Siskin's business ventures?"

"Siskin is from Minneapolis, but he does business in Chicago," Kippy said. "He and some other investors were putting together an upscale Italian restaurant with a nightclub across the street—both of which would feed each other—as well as a nearby parking ramp for all the traffic."

"Okay."

"Remember our homework on police corruption?"

I nodded.

Kippy tossed a forefinger Wabiszewski's way, cuing him. It was now his part of the duet.

"Obviously, we can rule out Superintendent Callum forming an allegiance with street gangs. That's a nonstarter; the man's a dirty cop, not a fucking idiot. And the shift in policy has been to reduce the homicide rate by going after the gangs that cause the bulk of the killing—over drugs, turf battles, initiation kills, drive-bys, you know, the usual bullshit."

Kippy added, "He'd never get in bed with them."

"So that leaves the Chicago mob—remember, the Outfit. New York has their five families, but Chicago has only one. The Cappellis. And the head of the crime syndicate in Chicago—the *capo di tutti capi*, boss of all bosses, or whatever the hell they call him—is Frank Cappelli Senior. Now, it's been whispered, but it's impossible to prove on account of how most folks tend to value their lives and the lives of their loved ones, that Frank Cappelli Senior forces entrepreneurs into doing business deals with him." Wabiszewski thought for a second. "I guess it's trending in the underworld to worm your way into legitimate businesses and properties with big cash flows such as—guess what?—restaurants and nightclubs and parking ramps in order to launder dirty money. They seek to turn their proceeds from their *less savory* ventures—drug trafficking, loan sharking, bid rigging, gambling, and prostitution, whatever piece of the pie they've got their fingers in—into legitimate funds by developing legitimate commerce and establishments."

"And if someone like a David Siskin from Minneapolis says no, or, worse yet, begins working with the State's Attorney's Office," Kippy said, "wouldn't it be sweet to have someone at the highest level of law enforcement in place to cover your back?"

"It's funny how you never hear of any local pressure being put on the Cappelli family. Sometimes the feebs show up and give them the federal equivalent of a jay-walking ticket, but that's about all she wrote." Wabiszewski finished his glass of beer, placed it on the table, and looked at me. "Kippy feels you need to know something else, too. So, in the interest of full disclosure, we're going to tell you about Cappelli's son—Frank Cappelli Junior."

"What about him?"

"Well, for starters—Frank Cappelli Junior is a raging psychopath."

"Of course he is," I said. Any soothing effects from the vodka had worn off. "I would expect no less."

Wabiszewski shrugged. "These are more whispers, gossip from people in the know, although no one's ever come forward and Junior has never been arrested on account of folks valuing their lives and their loved ones, but little Frankie gets his rocks off using a punch knife."

"A punch knife?" I said. "What the hell's a punch knife?"

"You know brass knuckles?"

"Yeah."

"Picture a pair of brass knuckles, only with an inch-long spike sticking out the front."

"Jesus."

Wabiszewski added, "Two years back, the ex-husband of one of Junior's girlfriend's wound up in the morgue with a half-dozen stab wounds to his solar plexus, rib cage, and his throat indicative of a punch knife. And last year a union negotiator wound up in the morgue with similar stab wounds—only more of them, many more. He'd been dumped in a warehouse, and the warehouse had been set on fire. Rumor had it he'd run afoul of the Cappelli family. As a rule, enemies of the Cappellis tend to disappear. So these hits were likely not sanctioned by Frank Senior, as he wouldn't leave a dead union negotiator lying about and he'd certainly not waste his time capping the ex-husband of Junior's girlfriend."

Something tickled in the back of my mind. "Was that warehouse fire with the union guy in the Fulton River District?"

"Yes."

"Last summer, right?"

"Yes."

"Then I've seen his work."

CHAPTER 24

"What are you talking about?"

"That union negotiator was an employment lawyer, right? His name was John something or other?"

Kippy and I watched as Wabiszewski worked Google on his iPhone.

"John Averbeck," he said, looking up. "What are you talking about, Reid?"

"We got called to that warehouse to search for any homeless people who may have died in the fire. Instead, Sue and Delta found Averbeck's body."

If I were I ten, I'd have started to cry. Instead, I beckoned the bartender.

"You don't need more booze, Mace," Kippy said.

"Booze? I'm getting the check," I said, feeling numb. "And then I'm grabbing the dogs and getting the hell out of Dodge. Not only is the head of Chicago PD and his sidekick—Man-mountain—on my ass, but, evidently, the head of the underworld's son is coming for me with a gut knife."

"A punch knife."

"What?"

"It's a punch knife," Wabiszewski corrected, "not a gut knife."

"What's it matter?" I said. "I'll be just as dead."

"It is a lot to take in," Kippy said after a moment, "but you need to consider two points: Mayor Weeks and the feds."

"Mayor Weeks and the feds?"

"If we point Mayor Weeks and the FBI in the right direction, they take down Police Superintendent Callum and Frank Cappelli Senior."

"And if the press catches wind, which I *somehow* know they will," Wabiszewski said, "they'll push a story like this to the ends of the earth; they'll drive it home like there's no tomorrow."

"The mayor, the FBI, and the media?"

"Yes," Wabiszewski replied, nodding. "Marinate in that for a while."

I marinated in that for several moments and then said, "That could work, but how do we suck in the mayor and the FBI?"

"My aunt volunteered on the mayor's campaign, not only because she believes in Carter Weeks, but because her best friend and old college roommate, Becca Drake, was a major fundraiser for him. She took a leave from her ad agency to lead his direct-mail campaign. Becca's a political animal, and she's known Carter Weeks for years," Kippy said. "I even spent a weekend canvassing for him during the campaign."

"You did?" Wabiszewski gave his partner a crooked stare.

"My aunt's a hard woman to say no to," Kippy replied. "Anyway, between Becca and my aunt, I should be able to parlay a sit-down with Mayor Weeks. He'll probably think I've got some sexism beef—rampant harassment throughout the department or something like that."

"He's going to wish it were something like that when you tell him what you're really there for," Wabiszewski said. "Sadly, the meeting will only last another half second after you inform him that our evidence stems from a golden retriever."

Kippy shrugged. "I'll start with Mace and Vira at Washington Park, but I'll fudge a little. I'll make it sound like you two were a lot closer to Superintendent Callum and his chauffeur, maybe just a few yards away when they pulled into the lot. I don't know—within sniffing distance—and Vira caught some kind of scent off Callum's driver that, we believe, tied him to the Peter Feist murder scene that Vira had just discovered a few minutes earlier. You get threatened on the spot by Gerald Callum himself, and then, at Feist's funeral, you get a bag full of veiled threats from Callum's chauffeur who suddenly knows everything about you. Highly suspicious, red flags fly up the mast. Then I'll segue into David Siskin's murder, you know, and talk about the chauffeur's pointed cowboy boots and of possibly comparing both Feist's and Siskin's autopsies for similar wounds."

"And about the superintendent's change-up in investigators."

"What change-up?" I asked.

Wabiszewski said, "The Peter Feist murder investigation naturally falls to Jim Hartwick, a homicide investigator out of the Second District who's got a clearance rate higher than Dick Tracy. But Superintendent Callum yanks Detective Hartwick off the case and assigns it to some pencil pusher— Callum's pencil pusher—under the guise of his office taking direct control of the investigation."

"So Callum can deep-six the case?"

"To manipulate it is more likely."

"The mayor wasn't too happy with Callum in their conversation in the restroom," I said. "I think Weeks is pissed at the lack of progress in the investigation."

"Well, don't hold your breath—I don't see the superintendent arresting himself anytime soon," Wabiszewski replied. "No doubt in a week or two, one of the usual suspects will get hauled in—probably some half-assed thief with a long list of priors or a mid-level drug dealer. He'll be dead, of course. After a shootout with Callum's men, of course . . . since dead men tell no tales. And they'll find some bullshit evidence to feed the press, of course, something from Feist—a notebook or journal or, hell, I don't know, a lock of his hair—hidden in a box of steaks in the dead guy's freezer."

"Case closed," said Kippy.

I thought for a second. "But what if you strike out?"

"What?"

"What if Mayor Weeks listens, but then laughs in your face and tells you to hit the road?"

"Then we'll have to take it to the feds ourselves, but I'm praying Weeks doesn't laugh in my face because I want him to be the one bringing in the FBI."

"And what do we know about the FBI in Chicago?"

"The SAC—special agent in charge—of the Chicago Division is Len Squires. From everything I hear, Squires is a straight shooter, a boy scout," Kippy said and glanced at her notebook. "Another plus is he's an outsider who's only been in Chicago for one year. Before that he was the SAC of the New Orleans Division. Another huge bonus is Squires previously served in a supervisory special agent position in the Public Corruption Unit of the Criminal Investigative Division, which means Squires has personally worked investigations involving law enforcement corruption. So, if we get Mayor Carter Weeks, and Weeks brings in SAC Len Squires, Superintendent Callum's in a box and our job is done. We sit back and watch the inevitable take place."

"And if the dam breaks," Wabiszewski added, "maybe other businessmen who've been extorted—forced into these silent partnerships with Frank Cappelli—will step forward and all of this *Outfit* crap will get washed away for good."

A glimmer of light appeared at the end of the tunnel. Our back-of-the-napkin conspiring might pay dividends after all, but then a thought occurred to me. "This is going to take some time, and I'm not thinking Man-mountain has a great deal of patience," I said. "I really don't want to move to Alaska, but Hulk knows where I live."

"Okay already, you big baby," Wabiszewski said. "You

can stay with me in the interim, but you buy your own food and you clean up all the dog crap immediately. Seriously. I don't want to see it and, if I step in any piles, you're getting pistol-whipped."

I nodded my agreement. "You got cable?"

CHAPTER 25

Kippy entered Beatrix—the River North location—at 7:30 a.m. sharp, as she'd been instructed to do per her aunt in last night's phone call. Although she wasn't on duty, Kippy wore her uniform, hoping it might tip the scales in any suspension of disbelief on the mayor's part. Beatrix was a favorite dining spot of Mayor Weeks, Kippy's aunt had informed her. He loved their quinoa cakes—whatever the hell those were. Kippy's aunt had first chatted with Becca Drake and came back to Kippy with three conditions: be there at 7:30, don't make the mayor wait; you've got five minutes with the man; and, foremost, don't be a flake.

Kippy mentally rehearsed the message she intended to deliver to Mayor Weeks and figured she'd at least be able to live up to the first two terms.

Kippy looked at the line for coffee and then she scanned the room. A flurry of motion at a back booth caught her eye and she recognized Becca Drake waving her over. Kippy crossed the restaurant as Drake stood, slung a Louis Vuitton handbag over a shoulder of her dark wool blazer, and grabbed her coffee-to-go cup with a free hand—Drake's mane of red hair flowed perfectly in an invisible breeze.

"Hi, Becca."

"Good to see you again, Kip," Drake said and air-kissed a cheek. "I don't think you need an introduction."

"Good morning, Mayor Weeks," Kippy said while standing at attention.

"Have a seat, Officer Gimm," Weeks said, motioning to the seat across from him.

"Thank you, sir." Kippy slid into the booth.

"Okay, kiddo, you've got five minutes," Drake said, looking Kippy in the eye. "And remember, don't be a flake."

And with that, Becca Drake made her exit, undoubtedly off to conquer new worlds.

"You should have the chai latte with a pinch of cayenne, if you're not yet awake," Weeks said.

"I'm good."

Kippy noted how the mayor was more than halfway through his breakfast, finishing what looked like an interesting take on poached eggs with a few bites of pancakes littered about his plate. She realized his offer of coffee and the fact that he was concluding his meal was another indication that their meeting would be short and sweet. Kippy glanced about the restaurant and spotted a gentleman in a blue sport jacket sipping a cup of joe several tables away—out of earshot—and staring their way. She pegged him as being with Mayor Weeks, some part of his security detail.

"You sure?" Weeks asked. "Best in the city."

Kippy nodded.

"I've nothing but good to say about your aunt, and I certainly wouldn't have won without Becca."

"Becca's a genius."

"That she is," Weeks replied. "She told me you volunteered as well, canvassed for me."

"I did."

"How many doors got slammed in your face?"

Kippy smiled. "More than one."

"Becca said this meeting was all hush-hush . . . and I hate hush-hush." Mayor Weeks poked at a poached egg with his fork, and then looked up at her. "What exactly did you want to see me about, Officer Gimm?"

Kippy had memorized her talking points and, considering the clock was already ticking on her allotted five minutes, she dove right in. "We need to talk about Peter Feist."

CHAPTER 26

"Where the hell are you guys?"

"What?" I said into my cell phone.

"You two are late. I called Kippy, but she's not picking up," Wabiszewski replied. "I'm at the guard's desk in the lobby, standing here with my dick in my hand."

"Kippy's probably in her car with the phone in drive mode, and you'd better zip up Little Wabs before you meet with the mayor," I said. "I got a call from the man himself an hour ago. It blew me away—the freaking mayor of Chicago calling me up. He said he wants to have a few minutes alone with each of us."

"Why?"

"I think he wants to look us in the eye and feel us out. Gauge us, I guess, see how we come across. Mayor Weeks is taking a hell of a leap of faith bringing in the feds and, like Kippy keeps saying, we can't be flakes. He wants to make sure we're on the up-and-up before we meet with Special Agent Squires."

"When the hell do you show up?"

"In half an hour. I'm at Daley Plaza sucking down a Coke and killing time with Vira." I sat alone on a park bench. I had poured some of the soda pop over my fingertips and was letting Vira lick them clean.

Chicago City Hall is an eleven-story leviathan on North

LaSalle and sits imposingly next to the Richard J. Daley and James R. Thompson Centers. As well as housing the Office of the Mayor, City Hall is also home to the offices of the City Clerk and City Treasurer, a hodgepodge of city departments, aldermen of the city's various wards, with the City Council Chambers anchoring the building's west side, and assorted offices of Cook County anchoring the east.

"Ah shit," Wabs said. "I didn't know it was going to be a fucking job interview. I was hoping to sit back and chew gum—let Kippy do all the talking. I've got nothing to add that she's not already told the guy. Come early, dude."

"Weeks sounded like a good guy on the phone," I said. "I'll be there soon enough, Wabs. And remember, don't let him know you're a flake."

Sue, Bill, the girls, and I had been living the life of Riley in Officer Dave Wabiszewski's surprisingly tidy townhome in Albany Park for the past five days. I'd planned my getaway to Wabiszewski's as though the kids and I were breaking out of East Germany at the height of the Cold War. I'd parked the pickup in the yard on the far side of my trailer—making it difficult for any prying eyes, real or imagined—and chucked a couple bags of dog food and a duffel full of clothes and shower gear into the cargo bed before returning the F-150 to its natural perch in my driveway.

That took all of five minutes.

Then, hours later and under the cover of darkness, I slipped the dogs into the cab of the pickup. All but Sue appeared elated at our new adventure; however, my German shepherd shuffled out of my trailer home at a slow gait and sporting a sneer—no doubt angered at the breach in our nightly protocol. I took a right on the road leading into downtown Lansing before flipping my lights on.

That took all of four minutes.

I darted in and out of parking lots and alleyways as I worked my way toward the highway. Then I cruised to Albany

Park—changing lanes, increasing and decreasing speeds at random, veering off the freeway and then back on—as though I were Burt Reynolds or the cast of *The Fast and the Furious*. I wish I really knew what I was doing or could tell if I'd been followed, but the headlights behind me all looked the same. I figured if anyone was truly tailing me, I'd have at least served to piss them off.

That took all of seventy minutes.

Fortunately, Officer Wabiszewski had just gotten home after his shift and I didn't bother sharing with him the depth of my madness lest he get the wrong idea.

At Wabiszewski's townhome I scored the guest room— shared it with my convalescing German shepherd—while Vira, Delta Dawn, Maggie May, and Bill got to romp about the unfinished basement. So far Wabiszewski hadn't stepped in any piles of waste, I hadn't been pistol-whipped, and no neighbors had complained about the dogs. Wabiszewski and I bonded over cheap beer, cheaper tacos, and watching mixed martial arts on TV. Somewhere along the line, I started calling him "Wabs" and he hadn't batted an eye or taken undue umbrage.

All good cheer and male bonding aside, it'd been five days full of apprehension and lost sleep. I placed the odds at fifty-fifty that Man-mountain had caught Wabiszewski's plate number off his Dodge Charger as we pulled away from Holy Name Cathedral. If so, that would mean *they* now knew about Wabs—that he was a cop—and that the female I'd opened the Charger door for was his cop-partner, Kippy Gimm. Of course, all of that was likely a moot point; since they'd done their homework on me, they'd damn sure know about my cop friends—the same cop friends that had recently solved the Jonny Whiting murder case and brought Eddie Clare to justice.

Yes, Kippy and Wabs were police officers, but what about Gerald Callum? Christ, he was Chicago's police superintendent—the top of the freaking totem pole, miles above them. So, with Dirty Cop Callum and Man-mountain well aware the three of us had been hip-deep in unraveling Jonny Whiting's death, what exactly would that amount to from their point of view?

Would we be dismissed as paper tigers? As some kind of half-assed tomato can—you know, the crappy, over-the-hill boxer they drag out to pad the record of an up-and-comer?

Or would it put a scare into them? Would it force them into taking action?

Ultimately, what really caused me to toss and turn these past several nights was the question: Were the three of us perceived as an *immediate* threat?

We'd not come at them . . . yet . . . certainly not in the manner Peter Feist had come after them. And, hopefully, that would give them pause, at least a long enough pause for when we did come after them because by then, per Kippy's plan, we'd come at them in full force with the cavalry—the Mayor's Office, the FBI, and the media—on our side.

So when Kippy had returned from her meeting with Mayor Weeks full of smiles and excitement, thoughts of rental igloos and Barrow, Alaska, began to fade away. Her five-minute get-together with the mayor had stretched into nearly an hour. The mayor took in what she had to say, turned various lighter shades of pale, and began whispering back in response. Evidently, he had a dozen questions about cadaver dogs and their special abilities, which Kippy parried as best she could without any references to séances or Ouija boards. He recalled an odd look flash through Superintendent Callum's eyes when I walked into the restroom at the Cathedral. He also found it strange that Callum had switched up investigators in the Peter Feist murder case.

And the mayor had shared with Kippy the personal observation that he trusted Police Superintendent Gerald Callum about as far as he could physically throw the man.

Mayor Weeks had asked for a second meeting with Kippy the very next morning—same time, same table at Beatrix—where Weeks informed her that his going near or requesting the two autopsies would tip his cards and clue in Superintendent Callum that someone was on to him; instead, the mayor wanted Kippy, Wabs, me, and Vira to attend a meeting in his office with Special Agent in Charge Len Squires. The Office of the Mayor takes up City Hall's fifth floor. We were to tell no one, and there'd be no record of the meeting for Superintendent Callum or any of his people to stumble across. Our names would be added to the visitor list in the main lobby as attendees for a retirement party of some geezer in the City Clerk's office. The mayor would dismiss his immediate staff for a lengthy lunch and personally meet us at the elevator and usher us into his private office to avoid anybody hovering about the main reception area.

Mayor Weeks felt that SAC Squires brought four things to the table. First, he could get authorization of surveillance, electronic and otherwise, of Superintendent Callum and the same for the superintendent's chauffeur. Second, Squires could swoop in and compare both autopsy reports using the Bureau's own medical examiner. Third, Squires could protect yours truly and our gang from any head twists, kick marks from steel-tipped cowboy boots, or puncture wounds. And, finally, Squires could hit Callum like gangbusters if and when more solid evidence turned up. Those items were off the top of his head, Weeks had told Kippy, and that it would be of great interest for us to hear what other goodies Agent Squires could bring to the party.

The mayor also told Kippy that—even though David Siskin's death sent a terrifying and cartel-like message—with the FBI and his office involved, perhaps other investors having their arms bent by the powers that be might be willing to step forward.

We were moving ahead at lightning speed.

I'd been so energized and relieved to hear this great news that I once again trampled our *just-friends* covenant—much like I'd done in my trailer home after Mickie's visit—and bounced up from Wabs's sofa and gave Kippy a hug.

It lasted all of a second . . . but she didn't pull away or reach for her Taser.

CHAPTER 27

"Officer Wabiszewski?" Mayor Weeks said as the elevator doors chimed open.

Wabs nodded, stepped into the atrium, and shook the outstretched hand of the city's chief executive. "It's an honor to meet you in person, sir."

"Wish it could be under other circumstances," Weeks replied, motioning for Wabiszewski to follow him down a hallway. "Any other circumstances, I'd have to say. Was it all good at the lobby desk?"

Wabs pointed at the visitor badge clipped to the front of his shirt. "Some city planner is retiring this week. Guess I've known him for years. Party's on the eighth floor. Maybe I'll stop in for cake on the way out."

"I hope you're not insulted I'm bringing you in the back way," Weeks said, "but I don't want to parade you past our main reception. Trying to avoid any prying eyes. I had my personal staff take a hike, go grab a bite to eat for a few hours." Weeks shrugged. "I'm sure they think I'm having an affair, which, compared to this insanity—I wish I were."

Wabiszewski smiled.

"Based on how it goes with Special Agent Squires, we may migrate over to his field office on Roosevelt." The mayor shook his head. "I should have planned this powwow there to begin with, but all this has been ad hoc and by the seat of my pants."

Wabiszewski empathized with the mayor's uncertainty. "We struggled with how best to bring it to your attention, sir. The entire situation breaks reality, but several things were said that Mace Reid took as direct threats against his well-being."

"Reid is the dog handler I spoke to, right?"

Wabiszewski nodded as the mayor steered him down another hallway in the maze that was City Hall's fifth floor.

"Tell me about him?"

"Mace is a good guy—scared shitless, of course—but solid, honest, and wants to do the right thing."

Weeks came to a stop in front of a door with no label or number on it and began bumbling with keys on a chain. "This serves as a back entrance to my office suite. It's what I take when I sneak out early or come back after a liquid lunch."

The mayor led Wabiszewski down a short hallway, past a closet, a coffee station, a microwave and fridge, and then into an empty reception area the size of a basketball court. Brown leather couches and chairs lined the walls, with coffee and end tables peppered about. A couple of magazine racks that would make the Harold Washington Library green with envy stood at opposite ends of the room, likely for antsy visitors to peruse whenever the mayor ran late. A nameplate on the solid oak desk centered in front of the windows read *Shelly Talcott*.

"This is Shelly's domain—my executive admin. I told her to get lost till two. Don't touch anything on her desk, don't drop a wrapper on the floor, because, god knows, I'll hear about it."

"I think I'm dating Shelly's sister," Wabiszewski said.

Weeks chuckled and opened the door adjacent to Talcott's desk. "This is my inner chamber, I guess they call it."

Wabiszewski glanced about another room the size of a basketball court. Weeks's office had dark mahogany walls, a plush cherry carpet Wabs took as Berber, an L-shaped oak desk that made the one in Talcott's reception area look like a newborn, and a couple of partially open doors along a far wall. The mayor's desk faced inward, a wall behind his throne displayed several family portraits. On each side of the portrait wall stood palatial floor-to-ceiling windows, allowing the chief executive officer to watch over his fiefdom. Expensive uprights stood in front of the desk for visiting dignitaries, of which Wabs found it difficult to believe he was one.

"Bigger than my first home, but this is where the sausage gets made. There's a bathroom," Weeks pointed at one of the doors across the room, "if you need to take a leak. That other door's a bedroom in case I need to nap or stay overnight for emergencies. To be honest, I'm thinking of subletting and pocketing the cash." The mayor placed a hand on Wabiszewski's shoulder. "Please have a seat."

As Wabs took a chair in front of the desk, the mayor continued, "I wanted to talk to each one of you separately, just in case you have anything to tell me—anything at all—that might be easier to voice without Officer Gimm or the dog handler in the room."

Wabiszewski looked sideways at the mayor, who'd remained standing in the doorway. "Yeah, about that, we hammered out exactly what we wanted Kippy to pass on to you, something that would fit in less than five minutes. I know the two of you talked at greater length about the situation, but I'm with Officer Gimm on this—a hundred percent. Kippy and I see eye-to-eye."

"Then I guess it'll be a pretty short conversation," Weeks replied. "Can I get you some coffee?"

"No thanks."

"For today's discussion, I'm going to need a fresh pot. I'll grab you a bottled water—don't say no," Weeks said. "And make yourself at home."

The mayor disappeared in his quest for caffeine, and the door shut quietly of its own weight. *Great,* thought Wabs, *taking down a crooked cop at the highest level of city government and all I get is a bottle of water out of the deal. I should have held out for a case of Heine.* Wabiszewski looked again around the room. He wished he was good at math so he could calculate the square footage of the mayor's office.

He glanced at the portraits on the wall behind the mayor's desk. The largest frame was a picture of Weeks's family—a pretty blond wife and a boy and a girl who both looked to be about ten years of age. Another portrait was of the mayor's father, obviously in healthier years, before the heart attack had cut his life short.

There were a couple of glass picture frames on the mayor's desk with their backs to him. Wabiszewski nudged one around with a forefinger. It was a picture of the kids, both in white gym shorts and shirts, holding tennis rackets—perhaps at tennis camp. Wabs remembered Kippy's background brief, something about Carter Weeks having been a hotshot tennis player in high school or college or both.

On a good day, were he feeling generous, Wabs might consider tennis a real sport.

Wabiszewski turned the picture back around and nudged the second glass frame toward him. It answered his question as there stood a younger Carter Weeks, late teens or thereabout, clutching a giant trophy that sported crossed tennis rackets at the top. Wabs figured young Weeks had taken a state tourney or something. On one side of him stood his proud father, grinning from ear to ear at his son's athletic achievement. On the other side, also smiling broadly, was . . . *oh, fuck!* . . . a decades-younger Gerald Callum.

Wabiszewski grabbed the picture in both hands, swallowed the lump in his throat, but there was no confusion. None at all. He recognized Police Superintendent Gerald Callum. A thought flashed through his mind—he had to warn Kippy. Then he spotted something reflected in the glass frame . . . some kind of movement behind him . . . Callum's driver.

A strap looped around Wabiszewski's neck. He then shot up from his seat like a fish pulled to dock, his feet no longer touching the floor, the picture frame dropping to the carpet.

Wabs's elbows shot backward, jackhammering at the big man's ribs.

Gasping for air that refused to arrive, Wabs shot his elbows back again . . . and again, but it was like hitting a tree. Both hands then shot to his throat, clawing at the strap as it tightened, and tightened more. Wabs felt the strap sink into his flesh, crushing his throat and cutting off blood to his brain; his eyes began to bulge, and Wabs grabbed at his revolver, but by then he had no juice, and Callum's driver slapped his hand away with the kick of a knee as though batting away a fly.

In Wabs's final seconds, his legs jerked outward, one hitting the mayor's executive desk—*where the sausage gets made*—and his other kicking over the frame of Weeks's kids at tennis camp.

CHAPTER 28

"Do we have to do the girl, Uncle Cal?"

Police Superintendent Gerald Callum, a man Carter Weeks considered his uncle in every shape, manner, and form excluding blood, stood a step inside the mayor's office while Weeks was a step outside, remaining in Shelly Talcott's domain. Both had been watching Cordov Woods as he'd loaded an IKEA box the size of a dishwasher on the far end of the room, next to the door leading into the mayor's private quarters.

Two empty IKEA boxes waited inside the mayor's side room. Cord Woods had generously strapped down the top lid with packing tape and was now using up the roll by strapping tape across the sides and top and bottom. Nothing would be left to chance when the three boxes were carted back to the freight elevator, brought down to the underground parking lot, loaded into a van, and taken to a place from which none of the cartons' inhabitants would ever be seen from again. Jethro, their computer savant, would scrub any security video of Woods wheeling a pushcart through back hallways as well as any images of Woods in the elevator or of Woods loading the boxes into the van in the basement garage. Officers Gimm, Wabiszewski, and the dog man's names would also be expunged from the retirement party list posted on the lobby guard's PC.

There would be no record of the three of them ever having

set foot inside City Hall. Later that evening, Cord Woods and Jethro would pay a visit to each of the trio's residences, which would then be sanitized. All in all it was a perfect plan, considering it had been organized on such short notice.

"Officer Gimm is the brains of the operation," Callum told the man he considered his nephew. "We got rid of the brawn; it was a smart move to do Wabiszewski first. In a few minutes we'll be saying au revoir to Gomer and Lassie. Gomer's a joke, but this little gem," Callum held a tranquilizer gun up for the mayor to see, "is for his dog and contains a dose that would put a rhino into a coma." Callum shook his head slowly. "I'm sorry, Carter, but Gimm's the real threat here. She ran that Jonny Whiting thing; she's the one that could sink us."

"Becca Drake's going to press me."

"Why?" Callum said. "Officer Gimm wanted to discuss gender pay disparities. You told her you thought the wages were equitable, but you'd have your bean counters crunch the numbers and get back to her . . . and then you never heard from her again."

Mayor Weeks took a deep breath. "It just seems so . . . wrong."

"It is wrong, son," Callum said, nodding agreement. "I'll never try to talk you out of that notion. But in a way it's good you see it firsthand—up close and personal. Generals aren't on the front lines—they're not involved in the hand-to-hand combat, but they see the aftermath. They see the bodies strewn across the battlefield. Ike wasn't storming the beaches himself on D-Day, but you can be goddamned certain he knew the consequences . . . and you can be goddamned certain he took them to heart."

Weeks thought a moment and replied, "I think you're comparing apples and oranges."

"*Comparing apples and oranges.* For the love of Christ, don't get Cordov started on idioms—the man'll never shut up," Callum said. "Look, we've talked about this before. Here's what we're attempting to achieve," Callum said, holding the tranquilizer gun above his head. "And here's our starting point." Callum then lowered the gun to below his waist. "If we hope to achieve our objectives, we're going to get dirt under our fingernails. That's a given. You don't think the Daleys tossed a few in the volcano for the greater good? You're not the first man to sit in that chair and get dirt under his nails . . . and you sure as hell won't be the last."

Mayor Weeks stared down at his dress shoes and said nothing.

"This is a minor blip on the radar; a hiccup. For fuck's sake, Carter, you know our policies are working. We're taking out the trash—getting guns and gangbangers and turf wars and all that other shit off the street—which is what the voters want anyway, and you can't put a number on the lives we'll save. Even in the short run, it'll far outweigh whatever happens here today." Callum added, "We get the kill rate down to three hundred—hell, anything below four—and we're talking dynasty, Carter . . . we could even be talking a presidential run."

Weeks said nothing.

"Your father—God bless him—could explain it much better, but I've been around since the dinosaurs and, ultimately, it comes down to this—you either run Chicago . . . or Chicago runs you." Superintendent Callum glanced down at his watch. "We're going to have to deal with your pangs of conscience later, son. It's time for you to get the dog man."

CHAPTER 29

"So, you're the little yipper that started this great war?"

Mayor Weeks had met us in the elevator atrium, crouched down, and held a couple fingers under Vira's nose for her to sniff.

"Not so much started as she's trying to end it," I said of my golden retriever.

"Just paraphrasing something a local boy who'd made good once said."

"Lincoln to Harriet Beecher Stowe, right?"

"Impressive, Mr. Reid. Our canine trainer knows his history," Weeks said as we shook hands.

I shrugged. "We studied Harriet in high school. I think I got a C."

"Sounds like you excel in other avenues," the mayor said, pointing at Vira.

"It came naturally," I replied. "How was your meeting with Dave?"

"Dave?"

"Officer Wabiszewski."

"Oh, yeah," he said. "Dave's a good guy."

"Not a flake?"

"Not even a small one."

The mayor led Vira and me down a corridor away from the main reception lobby, mumbling something about a back entrance to his office and sending his staff away to secure some privacy for our undisclosed meeting with Chicago's leading G-Man. Weeks seemed a bit distracted. I could only imagine what had been bouncing about in his brain since his initial morning meeting with Kippy a few days earlier.

"So, when did you first realize you wanted to be mayor of Chicago?" I asked as we took one more turn into another back hallway. I wanted to break the awkward silence that had engulfed us, but, instead, I'd likely stuck my foot in my mouth.

Weeks paused and turned toward me. "Truth is, I wanted to be a tennis pro."

I recalled the background discussions I'd had with Kippy and Wabs. "Didn't you take state?"

"I was great in high school and pretty darned good in college," Weeks replied. "But light-years away from good enough to take it to the next level. I'd be lucky to return any serve from one of those tour boys." Weeks looked at me. "Do you play?"

"I can hold my own in ping-pong."

"Sacrilege," the mayor said and, whether he was joking or not, we walked the remainder of the way to his office in silence.

"This is my outer reception area."

"Wow—you could land a helicopter in here."

"I'm not sure Shelly would approve of that."

Apparently, someone named Shelly Talcott was the mayor's secretary or administrative assistant or personal bouncer or some combination of the above. Evidently, she ruled this cavernous room with an iron fist. Ms. Talcott and the others on the mayor's immediate staff had been sent away for a long lunch with instructions not to return until after two o'clock or work the remainder of the day from home like so many employees are wired in to do these days.

Weeks swung open his office door. I was busy looking out

of Talcott's floor-to-ceiling windows at the traffic below and didn't become aware of Vira's *occurrence* until I heard a singular whine—a soft cry, like a breaking heart must sound, if it *had* a sound—and glanced down. My dog stared straight into the mayor's office, shivering as though we stood naked in the freezing cold, but then her spasm was over. Vira looked up at me with alarm in her gaze and released another soft cry.

The mayor and I locked eyes.

Vira didn't budge. She stood frozen to the carpet, but her leash allowed me room to maneuver from my perch at Talcott's window to stand in front of Weeks. And it allowed me to stare beyond him, to peek into his empty office.

"Where's Wabs?" I asked.

"He went to the bathroom."

I spotted two partially open doors on the far side of Weeks's office.

"Wabs?" I called out loud; and then, louder still, "Wabs?"

"Keep it down," Weeks said. "He's using the hallway restroom, for Christ's sake. He's giving us some time to get acquainted."

Vira began growling behind me, low and steady. Her warning mode.

"How's he supposed to get back in?" I said. "You've got the keys?"

"He'll knock on the door."

Vira continued growling, same low pitch.

"From way back there?" I motioned with my arm beyond Talcott's reception area, to the hallway leading to the back door.

"Look, calm down, would you?" the mayor said, pointing inside his chambers. "Officer Wabiszewski will wait until you and I are done, so just take your dog and have a seat for crying out loud. I'll get us some coffee."

Vira stayed in high alert, cautioning me, still glued to the floor—her every muscle taut as she continued staring inside Weeks's office.

I peeked beyond the mayor again; I looked at the chairs across from his desk, where Weeks still pointed, and then glanced about the rest of the room. The hair on the back of my neck stood. No lights were on in either of the side rooms, and the two half-open doors gave off an ominous sensation, the jaws of a crocodile in search of prey . . . and a single IKEA box sat in a far corner of the room.

Vira's snarl stayed in warning mode; her eyes glued to the IKEA box.

I looked at the mayor. His face was pale, a line of sweat across his forehead, and he stared back at me with alarm in both eyes. Vira's snarl continued, but she now stood at my feet. Weeks stepped backward into his office; Vira and I stood in the doorframe.

"What's in the box?" I asked in a whisper though I suspected I already knew.

"Just have a seat," the mayor said, his voice trembling.

"What's in the box?" I asked again.

We stared at each other a long moment.

"Take a seat for Christ's sake." The mayor's voice was now stern. He'd reverted back into a man accustomed to getting his way. He grabbed at my forearm in an attempt to guide me toward a guest chair.

Not smart for Weeks to lay a hand on me under these circumstances.

Vira leaped.

And Weeks stumbled backward into his office, Vira's jaws appended to the wrist of the hand that had touched me. Weeks backed into his window as Vira dropped off him. She kept him cornered—like a raccoon—barking and snapping in front of him as Weeks held his bleeding wrist with his other hand, his face a mask of terror.

A flash of movement in my periphery and I spun my head. One of the open doors now filled with Police Superintendent Gerald Callum aiming some kind of gun our way. Filling the other doorway was Callum's driver—Man-mountain—dangling a length of cord.

"Vira!" I screamed as Callum pulled the trigger.

She was at my side in a flash. I thought the gun must have misfired, a dud, as there'd been no explosion. Callum's mouth dropped open and I snuck a glance at the mayor. A thick dart stuck out from Mayor Weeks's lower thigh, just above his kneecap, where Vira had been a heartbeat earlier. Weeks's eyelids drooped as he leaned back against the window and then slumped to the floor.

The room came alive. Vira a fury of barks and snarls, pulling at the leash, fearless, in attack mode. Callum fussing with his dart gun, apparently reloading. And Man-mountain marched into the room—giant steps—heading in our direction.

That's all it took.

"Vira!" I screamed again, and the two of us were at full sprint, bats out of hell, racing down Talcott's corridor, past the coffee station and refrigerators, Vira a full leash ahead on the way toward the mayor's back exit. I hit the doorway with a shoulder, twisted the knob, and suddenly we were in the hall-way, running full-bore, retracing the steps where Weeks had led us to slaughter, where I knew in my heart he'd led Wabs.

Vira cut left ahead of me. I spun the corner, top speed, and bounced off the wall like a bowling pin. I stayed on my feet as we kept moving. We flew about a final turn, fleeing to the elevator vestibule as the door to one car dinged open and out stepped Officer Kippy Gimm. Hearing the commotion, Kippy's hand dropped to her holster as she turned to face us.

"Hold the door," I shouted. "Hold the door."

Confused, bewildered—both understatements—Kippy stepped toward us as the elevator door behind her slid shut. I dropped Vira's leash as she sailed for Kippy, twisted myself past the two of them, and jabbed fingertips at the elevator buttons, both up and down arrows.

"It's a trap, Kip," I said, sucking air. "It's a trap."

Kippy backed away from Vira, her eyes wide. "Where's Wabs?"

"Callum and that big fucker were there, in Weeks's office," I choked out the words, lunging for Vira's leash. "Where are the stairs?" I pressed at the elevator buttons again as if that would make them open faster and glanced about. "Where are the goddamned stairs?"

"Where's Wabs?" Kippy repeated, searching my eyes and not liking what she saw. "Oh, no. Oh my god."

Vira's leash stretched tight, a low snarl emanated from her chest. I faced the corridor from which my golden retriever and I had just fled. Like Vira, I sensed his presence before he turned the final corner, a lone figure filling the hallway, a hundred feet away, now staring back at us.

Man-mountain's right arm swung out from a fold in his long jacket; that's when I caught sight of the firearm in his hand—black and deadly—and pointed at the floor. Our eyes met and he stepped forward, another long step, turning to strides—heading our way down the corridor and breaking into a sprint.

Vira was on fire, barking, howling, snapping, and demanding to be set free. The elevator chimed open beside me. I jammed a heel in the door, grabbed fistfuls of leash, and wrenched my golden retriever into the elevator car.

"Kippy," I shouted, grasping a clump of uniform and shoulder flesh, pulling her into the elevator with us, pressing floor buttons at random with my leash hand. Tears dripped down Kippy's face, and I pulled her deeper into the car, knocking her off balance as she struggled for her sidearm.

My last image of Man-mountain as I stumbled and yanked the crew backward into the elevator car was that he'd covered more than half the hallway, racing toward us, his pistol up, beginning to sweep in our direction. The doors began sliding shut as I continued stabbing the close button with a forefinger. I could hear his footsteps—felt them, too, as though he were a T. rex after prey—right on up until the doors squeezed shut and we began our descent.

"Why'd you stop me?" Kippy said, facing straight ahead.

"What?"

"I was going to kill that son of a bitch."

"Kippy," I said, trying to control the wave of panic that had flooded over me, knowing there could be no upside in a fire-fight outside the mayor's office. "We need to get the hell out of here."

As the elevator door opened, we stumbled onto the third floor—Vira quiet now, body taut as a drawn bowstring. We brushed past a small horde of business suits, Vira running point with me towing Kippy by her forearm. I figured the floor layouts were similar on each level and we rushed down the hallway looking for what I'd spotted in our mad dash across the fifth floor. And suddenly there it was. I hit the brakes at the red alarm mounted on the wall.

I smashed the glass with my elbow and pulled the alarm. A siren went off, piercing and intermixed with a prerecorded voice instructing people to stay calm as they exited the building. Seconds later we were in the south stairwell with an expanding hive of employees and visitors, politicians and aides, many expressing frustration, others wondering if this were yet another drill timed to screw up their lunch hour . . . or the real deal.

By the time we hit the lobby and the crush of wall-to-wall foot traffic, the security guards were active. They were in fire evacuation mode, holding open doors and ushering hundreds of people out onto the plaza. Sirens were louder yet outside City Hall as the fire engines began to arrive.

Five minutes later, we were in my F-150.

CHAPTER 30

"There is no goddamned fire," Police Superintendent Callum barked at the security guard. They both stood inside the entryway to the mayor's office.

"Sir," the guard replied, "with all due respect, *everyone* must evacuate the building until we're allowed back in."

"It's a false alarm—there's no smoke, there're no flames."

"The chief fire officer makes that call. My job is to clear this floor ASAP."

"Do you know who I am?"

The guard nodded but repeated, "My job is to clear this floor ASAP."

The two had been going at it for over a minute, Callum and the broad-shouldered cop-wannabe who worked for building security. The glorified crossing guard clung to his crackling walkie-talkie as though it were the nuclear football.

"Sir, I can get into big trouble if I don't do my job." The guard walked over and peeked in the bathroom, and then he took a glance in Weeks's side room. "Are you the only one up here, Superintendent?"

Callum's eyes flicked toward the two IKEA boxes along the far wall. One contained the mortal remains of Officer Dave Wabiszewski. That box would not be an issue. At least not until two or three days passed and the odor became all-encompassing—something that could not be ignored, mayor's office or not. But Callum had no fear of three days passing, much less another hour. It was the other IKEA box that was problematic. He and Cordov Woods had worked quickly to place the comatose Carter Weeks as gently as possible inside this second carton, and they were able to curve him into a fetal position at the container's bottom.

Callum realized it was past time to get this unyielding security guard the hell out of here. It would be most inopportune for the sedative to wear off only to have Weeks shrieking and popping up from the second IKEA container like some deranged jack-in-the-box. Callum assumed the mayor would be unconscious for hours—hell, considering the dose of the sedative, perhaps until the following morning—but, if an early awakening did occur, Woods would soon be packing the third IKEA box with the remains of an expired building security guard.

"The mayor left with the others as soon as the alarm went off," Callum said. "Sorry to be such a pain in the ass, son. Let me head out with you."

Callum also wanted to draw the cop-wannabe away from the mayor's side room. If the guard got a wild hair up his ass about inspecting the room's closet, he'd be most unhappy with what he'd find in there . . . most unhappy, indeed . . . and the third IKEA box would be filled.

Cordov Woods was to stay behind with the mayor no matter what. Woods was also to make certain no one—no firemen, no security guards, no random dipshits—laid one finger on any of those two boxes. Callum would have a quick chat with the chief fire officer and, unless he'd lost his touch, he'd be back up in the mayor's office inside of ten minutes. They'd then get Carter Weeks laid out on the side room's bed and tend to his wrist, which was really just a series of puncture marks and broken skin from that mutt's teeth.

The mayor would be just fine.

Police Superintendent Callum, however, was consumed with silent fury. He'd cautioned Carter Weeks against appointing Peter Feist to head the Special Prosecutions Bureau. Feist was a boy scout and *deeply committed in his quest* and all that other happy horseshit the mayor had flung far and wide during his eulogy at Holy Name Cathedral. But that made Feist uncontrollable, and—subsequently—a force to be reckoned with. Carter, of course, hadn't taken his warning seriously and, sure as shit . . . Feist began poking about in things best left alone.

It was Chicago, after all.

Eliminating Feist's real estate investor source had been difficult enough, but eliminating Feist was not a decision Superintendent Gerald Callum made lightly. Quite the opposite. It tore at his guts. But Feist's actions forced his hand . . . and a decision had to be made.

Callum kept underestimating the dog handler, including earlier today when he'd assumed the girl was the only one with any real brains. He'd wondered if Reid's sniffer dog had placed Cord Woods at the scene of Feist's demise that first morning at Washington Park. He'd even asked Woods to check up on the dog trainer. Woods had come back with some stories—interesting stories—about a couple of the dog man's more recent cases. But he'd waved away pursuing any action as their plate was full and, quite frankly, it made no sense to chase after a fart in the wind. Callum changed his mind when he spotted Reid in the cathedral's restroom. Sure, Reid was likely intimidated by Police Superintendent Callum—he had that effect on people—but the dog man was squirming in his dress shoes.

Squirming as though he held a secret.

Callum had sent Woods to throw a scare into the dog handler, to introduce him to his proper role in the universe. And, perhaps down the road, something of a more permanent nature could be undertaken.

But then—out of the clear blue fucking sky—this female cop shows up and forces a meeting with Carter Weeks. And at the top and center of her agenda is . . . the fucking dog man.

Callum's anger burned with the intensity of a collapsing star. The plan, a good plan—*his plan, for Christ's sake*—had turned to shit, and there were now pieces scattered about the board that required his immediate attention. What should have been a quick fix would now go extra innings . . . and all because of that fucking dog trainer and his golden retriever.

Even though it had only lasted a handful of seconds in Mayor Weeks's office, he'd seen the look in Reid's eyes. Sure, there was the initial shock, but then something more. *Disdain*. Reid had glared at him with great disdain, something the police superintendent was not used to in all his years on the force. *No one stares at me like that*, Callum seethed, and—as he headed down the stairwell with the overgrown security guard—he thought of what he'd told Cordov Woods before he'd shut the closet door.

"It turns out that goddamned mutt is special. Kill it quickly. But when you catch the dog man," Callum had instructed his driver, deadly serious, "and before he takes his final breath . . . cut out his eyes."

PART THREE

ROCK LAKE

Here, Gentlemen, a dog teaches us a lesson in humanity.

—Napoleon Bonaparte

CHAPTER 31

I broke speed limits getting from City Hall to Wabiszewski's townhome in Albany Park. I figured we had a minor head start before Police Superintendent Callum—and all the power at his disposal—came hunting. Kippy and I toyed briefly with making a run for it in her vehicle, but then we quickly realized her squad car could too easily be tracked. We were at Wabs's home for two minutes; just long enough for me to stuff some clothes, dirty and clean, into my gym bag, hoist a bag of dog food onto my shoulder, and grab Maggie, Delta, Bill, and my napping German shepherd.

Kippy spent her hundred twenty seconds liberating a few of Dave's sweatshirts from a top drawer as well as a couple of sweatpants and a short stack of his Cubbies hats. She spent her final ten seconds in her partner's office, tucking Wabiszewski's *homework* packet under her arm—Wabs's ever-expanding research, thoughts, and ideas about the mess we'd found ourselves in.

The mess that had reached out and claimed his life.

Soon, we were in front of an ATM machine at a nearby strip mall, both of us withdrawing as much as our accounts would allow in a single transaction. I withdrew four hundred dollars, which pretty much cleaned me out. Fortunately, Kippy was able to hit her daily limit at an even grand.

A half-hour later we were standing in Paul Lewis's office at Chicago Animal Care and Control.

"You can't just show up here out of the blue, act as though you've been diagnosed with stage-four lung cancer, request a favor, and then not tell me what this is all about."

"The less you know, Paul, the safer," I said. "Believe me."

Paul took a moment to sit down in his chair. "Whatever's going on, I'd recommend calling the police." He looked from his closed office door to me, then to Vira, before his eyes settled on Kippy. After a moment he added, "But then you are the police."

Kippy stared at Paul and said nothing. Except for a logistical yay or nay or short-phrase ambiguities on any requested information or queries on my part, Kippy had kept silent, withdrawn—she was with us in the flesh, but her thoughts had checked out. Vira had noticed this, too, had placed her head on Kippy's lap on the ride over to CACC, and even now nuzzled at her fingertips.

Paul looked my way. "Is this a *Vira* thing?"

I nodded my head.

"And you need to borrow one of my trucks—no questions asked?"

I nodded again. Chicago Animal Care and Control was a fifty-four-thousand-square-foot facility on South Western Avenue. CACC acts as a shelter and can house over five hundred animals in separate kennels at any given time. It's also the command center for Paul's squadron of animal control officers, with a fleet of eighteen animal control trucks and an extended van equipped for off-site adoptions and vaccine clinics. With eighteen CACC trucks in play, I figured they could get by on seventeen for however many days we might need one.

"Lenny will notice it missing and come tell me."

Lenny Blakeman, one of Paul's animal control officers, had worked at CACC for decades.

"Tell him it's with a mechanic, getting some work done."

"Lenny's the one in charge of getting the trucks repaired."

I shrugged. "Just stave him off, okay? Buy us a few days—that's all I'm asking."

"A few days? And after that you'll let me know what the hell's going on?"

"God, I hope so," I said. "But listen, Paul, in four days—or three if Lenny keeps pushing at you—you need to call the police and report the truck missing. Okay?"

"Call the police?" Paul stared at me as though I'd sprouted a second head. "Why can't you just bring it back?"

"I will if I can, but if I can't, you need to call the police and report it missing." I took a deep breath; now for the hard part. "One more thing, Paul. If my name comes up in any conversation with any cop or detective, in any way, tell them how I've volunteered here for years—which is true—and how I know where everything is kept, which is also true, and how I could easily have grabbed the truck."

He began shaking his head.

"I know, Paul, but if any cop starts asking about me, sell my ass down the river. Tell them you can't believe I'd ever do such a thing but if, for some reason, I wanted to get my hands on one of your trucks . . . it'd be real easy for me to pull off. And I'm just a volunteer here—you only know me on a superficial level, just enough to say 'Hi' and bitch about the weather. Keep your answers short, Paul. All you know is some prick stole one of your trucks and you want it back, pronto. That's all you know."

"You're starting to scare me, Mace."

I began to reply but realized I had no idea what to say.

CHAPTER 32

We transferred our gear from my pickup into one of Paul's CACC trucks. Kippy hopped behind the driver's seat and headed out. She was chauffeuring Vira, Maggie May, and Delta Dawn to the O'Hare Inn and Suites, which was just a couple miles from O'Hare International Airport.

After they left, I turned to Paul. "Can I beg a final favor?"

"Name it."

"Take care of Sue and Bill for me, okay? Sue's still recovering, he can't move fast, and this excitement could be too much for him to handle." I glanced at my bloodhound. "And Bill is Bill—he's just a puppy."

"You got it," the head of CACC replied. "Knowing Sue—he'll want a penthouse suite with showgirls feeding him grapes."

"Something like that," I mumbled, handing both leashes off to Paul and kneeling in front of my two boys. I scratched at the back of my German shepherd's neck. "I sure wish you could come, Sue—you know I do—but you're still healing. And you gotta keep healing, buddy."

Sue sensed something in my tone—in my mood—and licked at my cheek, attempting to cheer me up in his own manner. It was the first time my shepherd had done that in eons.

I then gave one of Bill's ears a gentle yank so he wouldn't feel left out. "Be good, Bill. And try not to roll in anything."

Paul stood next to my F-150 as I got ready to leave. He

said, "Jesus Christ, Mace, one hell of a first date you've got yourself on."

I looked at my friend a long moment, hoping my features didn't betray how frightened I was. I patted him twice on the shoulder and jumped into the cab of my pickup.

I drove to the airport, dumped my F-150 in long-term parking, put on one of Wabiszewski's Cubs caps, and took the free shuttle to the Inn and Suites where Kippy and the girls were waiting.

After two hours in cruise control, I pulled the CACC truck into a motel on the outskirts of Rockford, Illinois. The lodge had lots of dark wood and seemed as though it'd been serving the needs of travelers since Truman roamed the White House. The motel's marquee screamed *FREE HBO* in large font and, below that, *Pets Welcome* in substantially smaller letters. I unbuckled my seat belt and reached for the door when Kippy spoke for the first time in over an hour.

"I'll check us in." Her words were slow, a firm command.

"I got this."

"Mace," she said, shaking her head, "you're a horrible liar. Everyone in the lobby will remember the jittery guy with no ID who insisted on paying in cash. I'll be the friendly ditz in town for some animal convention who left her purse on the kitchen table back home in Chicago."

"Okay," I said, thankful just to hear Kippy speaking in complete sentences and gladder yet to see her back in the here and now and engaged in our predicament. My only thought since the City Hall disaster had been to flee. I'd exhausted all ideas that came from my years parked in front of detective shows on cable TV.

Switch vehicles to something clean and untraceable. Check. Turn off mobile phones and pop out the batteries. Check. In fact, our disassembled smartphones sat in the glove compartment in the F-150 I'd stashed at O'Hare. Check. Wear baseball caps and sunglasses. Check. Pay for everything only in cash. Check. Find someplace safe to hunker down—well, hopefully, that's what Kippy—all decked out in Wabiszewski's baggy sweats and Cubs cap—was now scoring for us. Check.

After that . . . I had nothing.

I looked at Vira, sitting in the passenger seat Kippy had recently vacated. "What do you think, girl?"

My golden retriever looked at me a second and then returned her gaze back to the side window. "Oh, great." I glanced in the back seat at Delta Dawn and Maggie May. "Either of you got any ideas?" My sister collies returned my look but remained silent. "Yeah," I said, "me neither."

Kippy did have a valid point about my being a horrible liar as there'd been an occasion when we'd first met—when I didn't know Kippy, when I saw only the uniform she wore—that I'd massaged and stretched and fudged the truth in order to keep some close friends out of legal jeopardy as well as save Vira from being put to sleep at CACC. Per Kippy, not unlike some sexual harasser in the workplace, any and all bearing witness to my untruths are rendered uncomfortable. While being dishonest I tend to avoid eye contact, turn red, and then fidget and squirm like some grade school kid in urgent need of a bathroom pass.

Pathetic—a preschooler can tell when I'm full of shit . . . and, evidently, it's now something I need to work on.

A minute later Kippy returned to the car and opened the passenger door.

"Room one-twenty," she said and pointed. "The last room on the end."

I tended my girls. First, we went for an extended walk. Then I fed them each a cup and a half of dry cereal and, afterward, rinsed their bowls and set them up as water dishes. Kippy had retreated back into her shell, silent again, seated at the room's only table and sorting through Wabiszewski's documentation.

"You hungry?"

Kippy shook her head and continued staring at her

partner's paperwork, though I wondered how much of it she was actually absorbing. Vira was curled up at her feet. Delta and Maggie had hijacked the bed, while the local TV news droned on in the background. The two collies kept glancing toward the window every time a car door slammed.

"I'm going to grab us some takeout and something to drink."

Kippy flipped pages but said nothing. I slipped out quietly, alone, leaving Kippy to watch the girls or, perhaps, for the girls to keep an eye on Kippy. I thought maybe Kippy needed some alone time and that I'd drive around a bit, but I changed my mind once I hopped in the CACC truck. It'd be safer for all of us to stick together.

I returned after twenty minutes with a bag of cheeseburgers and a six-pack of bottled water.

I managed to choke down a burger that was likely quite tasty, but, tonight, it went down like soggy cardboard. I also drank two bottles of water while sitting on the bed and working the TV clicker. Most of the local news dealt with events in Rockford—car accidents, a pawn shop robbery, some guy had been arrested for his eighth DUI, sports, weather, and on and on it went. I'm not sure what I was expecting. Luckily, no one cut in with a newsflash about Chicago's mayor having been assaulted. There were no breaking headlines about the tragic death of a Chicago police officer named Dave Wabiszewski. I continued working the clicker, flipping from local news to cable and eventually tripped over a news station out of Chicago.

I sat glued to the screen for forty minutes but they had nothing to report concerning today's events at City Hall, not even a quick blurb regarding the fire alarm.

I took the dogs out for a short walk—long enough for them to make peace with their bladders for the long night ahead of us. I shook off a series of yawns, suddenly realizing how drained I had become. Upon my return, I sat at the table in the chair across from Kippy. I was glad to see she'd nearly finished one of the water bottles.

"You should eat something."

"I can't, Mace."

I leaned back in my chair, closed my eyes, and listened to the station out of Chicago in case there were any late-breaking headlines we should know about. My head bobbed. I was exhausted, physically and mentally. I went to the bathroom and brushed my teeth with a forefinger and some toothpaste I squeezed out of an all-but-empty tube of Crest I'd found floating about the bottom of my gym bag. I dumped the pumpkin-colored bedspread along with a couple of extra pillows I'd taken from the closet onto the floor in front of the TV, and then turned the volume down.

I glanced over at Kippy. "You should try to get some sleep."

I wasn't sure she heard me but ultimately she replied. "I don't think I can," she said. "I keep thinking about . . . Wabs."

"I know, Kip," I said. "I know."

"It was my plan. I'm the genius that walked us into an ambush," she said. "I'm the genius that got Wabs killed."

"There's no way you could have known."

"It's like whenever something crazy happens in that god-damned town, we all shrug and roll our eyes and say, 'That's Chicago for you.' I was naïve, Mace. And stupid. I should have guessed the mayor was part of the same stink—that Weeks was worse than any of those *Keepers* he railed about in the campaign."

The tenor of her voice, her thousand-yard stare—Kippy was shattered, her remaining pieces being devoured by guilt and shame. "You're not clairvoyant, Kip. Of course Callum and Weeks knew each other, but none of us—Wabs included—could have guessed they *really* knew each other."

I wished to God I'd never gone downtown to attend Eddie Clare's interrogation; that made me Johnny-on-the-spot for CPD to grab and send off to Washington Park in search of Peter Feist. If I'd not already been at police headquarters in the middle of the night, I knew of at least two dog handlers that lived closer and would likely have been contacted first.

And then we'd never have been sucked into this nightmare.

Kippy continued sitting at the table, motionless. I could tell my attempt at lifting her spirits had fallen flat. I spent a minute contemplating ways to string words into phrases into sentences that might somehow lessen her grief before realizing that silence would be best. I lay down on the bedspread and pillows and stared up at the ceiling.

I was floating off to sleep when Kippy spoke again.

"When they come, Mace, they won't be coming to arrest us," she said softly. "They'll be coming to kill us."

I chewed on that until my eyelids grew heavy and, soon after, I was dead to the world. When I woke in the late hours of the night, my cheek was wet. I'd been so zonked out that saliva had drooled from the corner of my mouth, soaking my pillow. Half asleep, I stumbled to the bathroom, shut the door, and relieved myself. When I emerged, in the light of the quietly droning television, I made out Kippy on the bed, lying on her back and snoring lightly. Vira had snuggled up on one side while the collies nested on the other. Her Beretta sat on the night table beside the bed. I lay back down on my bundled bedspread, felt my eyes moisten as I reflected on what had proven to be the worst day of my life.

An hour or two later I drifted back into unconsciousness.

CHAPTER 33

Arturo Solos freebased cocaine for personal use, extracting impurities with diethyl ether. It was a dangerous fucking process, as ether is a highly volatile and flammable liquid, but it leaves you with damn near one hundred percent pure cocaine—not like shit-ass crack, which contains baking soda and water. You pipe it to produce vapors for inhalation. The cocaine is then absorbed via the membranes in your lungs, thus hitting your bloodstream and brain within ten or fifteen seconds . . . and that's when Arturo Solos's voyage deep into the universe commenced.

Solos was alone, shirtless, and lying in boxer shorts on the king size. He was also halfway through his trip about the cosmos when his cell phone buzzed. At first Solos thought the sound was coming from the soft-core on Cinemax, and it took him ten seconds to realize he'd set the flat-screen on mute some time ago. Solos picked up his buzzing phone and glanced at the caller ID. It was Sebastian, or Bastardo as Sebastian was more commonly referred to.

Fuck.

Bastardo was his right hand, and his calling at this time of night spelled trouble.

"Bastardo," Solos said into the cell phone.

"Run, Arturo! Run!" Bastardo screamed through the line. *"Corre ahora!"*

"Fuck you saying?"

"La Raza's coming for you. Made up as SWAT—*policía* and shit. Run fucking now, *mi amigo! Muévete rápido!*"

Solos dropped the phone, bounced off the bed, ran to the condo's balcony, peeled back a drape, and looked down on Forty-Fifth Street. From his angle, he spotted a dark van parked in the center of the street in front of his building and what appeared to be the rear bumper of another dark vehicle in front of the van. Solos glanced down the street and noted the shadow of another vehicle—more car than van—parked diagonally across Forty-Fifth, blocking traffic. He began sliding the glass door open, thinking he could drop to the balcony below him, and from there to the first-floor terrace, but then he spotted a lone figure in black on the sidewalk.

And the figure was staring up at him.

Solos jerked back, slid the door shut, and flicked down the latch. This made no fucking sense. Solos had paid La Raza their cut. And he paid their cut on time, each and every month, without so much as saying boo. The side-selling then flashed through his mind, deals made in other parts of the city that didn't get declared to La Raza. A limited number of small-ass sales that were left off-book. But that was fucking pocket money . . . something everyone did . . . it was how the world worked. And how the fuck would news of those small-ass sales get back to La Raza?

Unless, he thought . . . unless someone on his crew had stuck the knife in his back.

Is that what Bastardo had tripped over and called to warn him about?

And this setup—La Raza making it appear as though SWAT and the cops had come for his sorry ass. Bona fide investigators looking into the incident would receive looks of incomprehension from neighbors and witnesses, who would wonder why CPD was there asking them questions when it was CPD's own damned SWAT unit that came for Solos.

It was brilliant in a certain manner.

Well, fuck this, and fuck La Raza. They want to come for him, they want to go down this road, then Arturo Solos would take them all the way down to where the street dead-ends. Solos ran back to his bedroom and grabbed his AR-15 off the side table. Buying the assault rifle from that bug-eyed dealer out of Indiana was going to be worth every fucking penny the black-market asshole had gouged him for it, and these La Raza motherfuckers were going to rue the day they decided to come to his casa—to violate his crib—and take him down over some chump fucking change.

He wished he had time to pipe more vapors. Maybe later—after he got away. And he wished fucking Bastardo had given him a bigger head start. But it is what it is. When this was over, he and Bastardo would ferret out the rat—*la rata*—in the crew that had fucked him over.

Solos ran to the condo door and stared through the peep-hole, then jumped backward as though like a marionette on a string. He'd been hoping to book it down the hallway, dive for the far-side stairwell, get down to first, and creep out the back . . . but there was a man in black directly outside his door, giving hand signals to others who were out of view. Solos's throat went dry and he wondered again about the balcony, but the guy on the walk could easily pop a cap in his ass as he tried to spiderman his way down the side of the building.

Goddamn fuck.

Arturo Solos stood in the center of his living room, aimed the AR-15 chest-level at his door, and began squeezing the trigger. He heard voices, some kind of scramble in the hallway.

"Yeah, motherfuckers!" he shouted, and pulled again at the trigger; only nothing happened this time, and he tried again. Nothing. He held the AR-15 sideways, confused, and stared down at it.

At that moment, his front door blew inward, followed by a deafening noise and piercing white light.

Solos was now somehow on his back, his bare chest a cascade of crimson. He stared up at the faces and handguns.

But not for long.

CHAPTER 34

I found myself jogging down a dark path for what seemed an eternity, twisting and turning in the shadows, tree branches reaching ever closer as though to embrace me. There was a hint of water in the background—I could hear it trickling, I could smell it—and I slowly came to realize I was back at Washington Park . . . where it all began. And with that knowledge came panic, terror—an ice pick to the heart—and I sprinted faster, and faster yet. I dared not peek left, toward the fish pond because, if the trees thinned out, I knew I'd see him again . . . Peter Feist . . . only now he'd be sitting up in the blackish water, face still in that impossible position, watching me as I flew past, his mouth open in a gurgle of regret. I heard nothing but my breathing, and then my footsteps pounding on the pathway, but I somehow knew *he* was right behind me on this never-ending trail on this never-ending night.

What started as a lucid dream turned nightmarish . . . and I ran for all I was worth. I ran for my life. I dashed about a curve, nearly fell but pulled myself to a halt. In the sliver of light before me I spotted a figure—Police Superintendent Gerald Callum aiming what might be a dart gun my way. And suddenly I was ensnared, lifted as though by tentacles, and pulled backward in an ever-tightening grip. I felt Man-mountain's breath on my neck, hot like steam, followed by a dank whisper in my ear, "I've got a special box to put you in, dog man. A very special *death box* just for you."

I tried to struggle, but it was pointless. My arms and legs now a thousand pounds each . . . and Man-mountain began to cackle.

"Mace." Someone called my name from miles away.

"Mace." Someone rubbed at my shoulder. "Mace—wake up." My eyes flipped open. Kippy knelt over me.

"You were trembling," she said. "Starting to scream."

I shook my head to clear it. "Bad dream."

She squeezed my arm. "You've got to get up now."

I lifted my head an inch. "What's going on?"

"We have to get out of here, Mace," Kippy said. "You and I—we're all over the news."

We crossed into Wisconsin before pulling into an I-90 rest area to feed the dogs. The sun had yet to rise, but the rest stop was well lit, awash in overhead lights. Apart from an eighteen-wheeler parked in the opposite truck lot, the place was deserted. Kippy and I dined out of a vending machine. We sat at a picnic table on the far end of the wayside, Cubs caps shrouding our features while we let the girls roam free on the grass. In the meantime, we nibbled on overpriced crackers, chips, and cookies, washing them down with bad coffee.

I'd leaped from the floor at Kippy's warning, hit the bathroom at a jog, splashed cold water on my face to verify the past day hadn't all been a nightmare, and listened as talking heads on the news channel out of Chicago told how CPD had raided the home of a minor gangbanger and dealer with suspected ties to Los Zetas—one of the more bad-assy of the bad-asses making up the various Mexican drug cartels. The dealer was named Arturo Solos. The police had been tipped off by a CI—a criminal informant—as to Solos's involvement in the murder of Special Prosecutor Peter Feist.

A SWAT team had gone to Solos's home on Forty-Fifth Street

where Solos proceeded to open fire on them with an assault rifle. When all was said and done, one door was destroyed, no SWAT officers were hurt, and Arturo Solos had taken four to the chest. The station showed a quick clip of a body bag being hauled out the front of an apartment complex.

The news said Peter Feist had been busy investigating gang ties tracing back to any of the south-of-the-border cartels, and, evidently, Arturo Solos decided to nip that investigation in the bud. A logbook on Solos's laptop implicated two Chicago police officers on the drug dealer's payroll—Officer Dave Wabiszewski and Officer Kippy Gimm.

As Kippy navigated us toward Wisconsin, we caught the rest of the story on the dog mobile's radio. Authorities received a search warrant for the residences of the two CPD officers and, though Dave Wabiszewski was not home, investigators discovered thirty street packs of black tar heroin and twelve grand in hundred-dollar bills stuffed behind an air vent cover in an office wall. And though Officer Gimm was not home, either, they found fourteen grand in like-size bills also hidden behind an air vent in her apartment. Somehow the police discovered Kippy Gimm had "recently been shacking up with"—no shit, "shacking up" is how the newsreader phrased it—a guy named Mason Reid, who ran cadaver dogs for the Chicago Police Department. CPD hit Reid's trailer house soon after 2:00 a.m. It appeared empty—evidently abandoned—and investigators initially surmised the three must have heard about the shootout with Arturo Solos through police channels and hightailed it for the hills. However, two things were quickly discovered in Mason Reid's trailer home. First, a Kahr CM9 registered to the late Peter Feist was retrieved from a silverware drawer in Reid's kitchen. Much more alarming, police then discovered the body of Officer Dave Wabiszewski in Reid's bathtub, covered in blankets and pillows, with the shower curtain drawn shut. Officer Wabiszewski had been strangled to death. Authorities believed a falling out among the band of thieves occurred after receiving the news of Arturo Solos's death. The newscaster then went on to inform listeners to be on the lookout for Mason Reid and Kippy Gimm, both thought to be armed and dangerous and may be riding in a black Ford F-150, and then he read my pickup's plate number several times before repeating a phone number to call in case any listeners had any information regarding the whereabouts of Mason Reid or Kippy Gimm.

The only saving grace, apparently, was that they'd not found my F-150 at the airport . . . not yet, anyway.

"Jesus, Kippy," I had said in the CACC truck, "we are so screwed."

"That number they keep giving for anyone who's spotted us," Kippy had replied, "I bet it links back to Superintendent Callum so he can send his hit team."

"If I were drug trafficking for this Arturo Solos fellow, I think I'd have a newer truck. And I might not live in a trailer home." I sat at the rest stop table, shook the remaining crumbs from a cookie bag down my throat, and thought of how Wabs had nailed it on the head at Russell's bar in West Town—how Callum would pin Feist's murder on some patsy drug dealer or thief. It just never occurred to me that we'd be part of that picture. "When he hears all this, Paul's going to freak."

"Will he call in the truck?"

"No, I don't think Paul will do that right away, although I couldn't blame the guy."

Kippy thought for a second, and then spun the manila folder on the rest stop table so it faced my way. Officer Wabiszewski's packet of information. "You know Dave kept at it, don't you?"

"He'd sometimes grab a beer at night, tell me he was going to *chip away,* and then shut himself in his office for a couple hours," I replied. "I just assumed he was surfing porn."

"I imagine there was a fair amount of that, but as an investigator Wabs was meticulous. He'd gotten burned early on at a trial, made to look like a buffoon in front of a jury by some defense attorney. Wabs took it to heart and every incident report he wrote from that day forward overflowed with every single minute detail. I used to give him shit about it, told him we weren't getting paid by the word." Kippy blinked back tears. "Anyway, check out the article on top."

I flipped open the file and saw a picture of a smiling Peter Feist and a headline: *Mayor Appoints Peter Feist to Head Special Prosecutions Bureau.* It was an article from *Chicago* magazine dated last year, soon after Carter Weeks took office. Wabs must have printed it from the magazine's website. I looked across the picnic table at Kippy.

"Give it a read," she said. "It's just a one-page puff piece."

The profile began with Peter Feist's background—where he'd grown up, Lincoln Park; the law school he'd attended, Loyola University School of Law; his wife and daughters, Laura and Annika and Kiley; then segued into the positions he'd held leading up to his current posting; four years as Cook County State's Attorney and six previous years serving as an assistant state's attorney; and it concluded with a short interview. Kippy was right, the article was a pure puff piece like something you'd find in *People* magazine. Feist spouted platitudes about how fortunate he was to lead the brilliant legal team in the Special Prosecutions Bureau and how he promised to work twenty-four/seven for the great citizens of Chicago. In the final paragraph, Feist talked about how he'd promised his wife he'd take a sabbatical from the weekends he spent at the family's old cabin on Rock Lake, near Lake Mills in lower Wisconsin. Evidently, Feist lived to fish—odd, since every photograph I'd seen of the man had him city-boyed up in expensive suits—and the special prosecutor mentioned a certain honey hole only he knew about where the rock bass literally jumped into your boat. But Feist had sworn to his wife that he'd grant the bass and walleye and pike in Rock Lake a reprieve as—between his new role leading the Special Prosecutions Bureau and his fishing weekends at the cabin—his wife would never see him again . . . and soon forget what he looked like . . . and possibly start dating again.

Ergo, the fishing trips were dispensable—they had to go.

That's how the article ended, but Wabs had drawn a line from the reference to the *family's old cabin on Rock Lake* to the margin in pencil. In the margins Wabs had jotted down an address in Lake Mills, presumably that of the Feist family cabin.

"What are you thinking?" I asked.

"Two things. First, you find yourself working on something huge—a case that's a game-changer—so big it could take down some very powerful men, right?"

"Right."

"If I were Feist, I'd be so damned paranoid that I'd squirrel away a thing or two—I don't know, a flash drive or photocopies of documents or images in a Ziploc bag—in a place only I knew about as an insurance policy, right? For safekeeping?"

"But at the family cabin?"

"Why not?"

"You'd hide things where your children play? Where the extended family or friends hang out?"

"The cabin sounds more like a getaway that only Feist used for fishing, or maybe for a little solitude and downtime."

"Well, these days you can get invited to somebody's *cabin* for a weekend," I said, "and you're thinking it'll be rustic and small—Ma-and-Pa-Kettle like—but when you show up, it's like a freaking first-class resort."

"Feist referred to it as the *family's old cabin* in the article. And it's probably been in his family multiple generations. Maybe the only renovation it's ever seen was when they got rid of the outhouse in the eighties or whenever. It sounds like Feist didn't bring his wife and kids along when he went fishing, so I'm thinking something more Ma and Pa Kettle than five-star lake resort," Kippy said. "Feist was an only child, right? And remember his parents at the funeral?"

"What about them?"

"They're both in their seventies and his dad was using a

walker." Kippy tapped a finger on the *Chicago* magazine article. "I think Feist had this place all to himself. Perfect for stashing something away."

I thought for a moment. "What's the second thing?"

"What?"

"You said you thought of two things."

"Peter Feist's fishing cabin," Kippy replied. "No one would think to look for us there."

CHAPTER 35

CPD superintendent Gerald Callum hung up the phone, splashed a heavy wave of Baileys into his mug of steaming black coffee, shoved the bottle back into the lower drawer, grabbed the cup, leaned back in his chair, put his feet up on his desk, and glanced about his empty office. He'd not had a drop of caffeine after midmorning in a couple of decades; it fucked with his circadian rhythm, but since he'd been up all last night he didn't think he'd have a problem when his head finally hit the pillow this evening. It was nearly eleven in the morning and, quite frankly, Callum knew he'd be lucky to make it to five o'clock.

No doubt about it—yesterday had been a goat-fuck . . . a goat-fuck of epic proportions.

As soon as he'd gotten back to the mayor's office, he'd tasked Cordov Woods with getting their hacker, Jethro or Bumbo or Dumbo or whatever the hell the computer guy's nickname was, into erasing all evidence that the two police officers and the dog handler were ever in attendance at City Hall—deleting any security footage of the three of them and, most certainly, any proof of Officer Kippy Gimm or the goddamned dog man having yanked the fire alarm.

Then Cordov Woods hauled the recently departed Dave Wabiszewski over to the dog man's piece of crap trailer and dumped the deceased officer into Mason Reid's bathroom tub.

It had also been a stroke of fucking genius on Cordov Woods's part to wipe down Feist's handgun—Feist's *registered* Kahr CM9—which Woods had lifted from the prosecutor's windbreaker on the night of Feist's demise in Washington Park, and drop it into one of Reid's kitchen drawers. Woods then planted props—cash and street drugs—in the homes of both Officer Wabiszewski and Officer Gimm.

And once the authorities had been pointed in the *right* direction—well, hell—nature would take its course. In fact, nature had already begun to take its course. Callum had just received a report indicating that fingerprints lifted from Reid's trailer placed both Officer Wabiszewski and Officer Gimm at Reid's home, and that Mason Reid's fingerprints were all over Wabiszewski's domicile.

Superintendent Callum took a long sip of his spiked coffee.

The Arturo Solos scenario had been initially set in place when it became clear that Special Prosecutor Peter Feist had to go, and would have occurred days earlier had Officer Kippy Gimm not shown up on Mayor Weeks's doorstep with a tale that, at face value, sounded preposterous, but, for the most part, happened to be spot-on. Superintendent Callum personally directed the SWAT team—his handpicked squad of *no-shit* shooters that no one in their right mind would ever wish to run afoul of—from his office phone. Who knows? These hardasses from SWAT might well have shot Arturo Solos on their own accord—as payback for Peter Feist—had Callum and Cordov Woods not stacked the deck for them.

Truth be told, Solos was a major-league fuck-up with zero ties to Los Zetas, was hooked on the snow himself, and would likely never have made it through another Chicago winter without managing to punch his own one-way ticket to the morgue. About a minute before SWAT was going to cave in his door, Solos got a call from his chief soldier or lieutenant, or however in hell these low-grade chucklefucks rank themselves, screaming that another street gang—La Raza—was coming for him dressed up as pigs and SWAT and whatnot.

And though the call from Solos's lieutenant had been quite convincing and full of passion—it had been staged.

It had been complete bullshit.

And why had Solos's lieutenant's call been so convincing, so Academy Award winning? Because during the call Cordov Woods had an arm around the lieutenant's throat and a knife stuck in his ear. Solos's lieutenant had the mistaken expectation that he'd be let go and sent on his merry way with a bag of cash once this small favor had been performed. Not only would Solos's lieutenant never be heard from or seen again, but he'd also go down in the police report as having been the criminal informant that dimed Arturo Solos in the first place. And Solos's reaction to his lieutenant's call could be spotted coming from miles away. The junked-up spic did what his junked-up spic genes told him to do—he grabbed an assault rifle and began firing at the entry door. That is, until the incompetent twat had jammed his own fucking gun.

Superintendent Callum's team then blinded him with a flash-bang and put him down for the count.

Ain't life grand?

The way it went down was the equivalent of a signed confession. And it would place the entire Peter Feist murder case in the rearview mirror. As for Arturo Solos—no great loss there—just another coke head in a sea of coke heads whose premature extinction would spell victory for the common good and for the great city of Chicago.

Callum took another long hit from his coffee mug.

The superintendent's concern now lay with the media. He figured Officer Gimm would attempt to make her case to the press and—even though her story was so far-fetched and unbelievable, and no hard evidence existed—Callum would just as soon Officer Gimm's *allegations* never make the light of day. Even if they were chuckled at as *Gimm's Fairy Tales* and quickly dismissed. So Callum had been playing the media preemptively—leaking the story in real time, creating the narrative—and morphing the couple into a modern-day

Bonnie and Clyde, both armed and dangerous; only, in this particular case, be sure to hide the women and children as these two psychopaths kept a kennel full of junkyard dogs to boot. He had the media singing in one-hundred-part harmony that Gimm and Reid were not only on the loose, but on a rampage. And though that image of Mason Reid fed to the *Chicago Tribune* had been taken at some goddamned dog show or another, and though it had been taken of Reid barking commands at his dogs, in today's context the picture made him look like a young Charles Manson . . . rabid and obsessed.

Yup, Callum had been leaking more than a litter of week-old puppies.

And the special phone number provided for anyone who'd seen fugitive Kippy Gimm or fugitive Mason Reid ultimately led back to Superintendent Callum's office, thereby giving Cordov Woods a head start on any incoming tips from concerned citizens.

They had the pair on the run, but they needed a knockout punch before Officer Gimm tried connecting with the media or, worse yet, those worthless glory hounds at the FBI. In Callum's book, the feebs were a bunch of sugar-tit pussies, always had been. As crime fighters, they did none of the hard work but insisted on taking all of the credit. He'd met a time or two with the FBI's new special agent in charge, Len Squires, and the undersized stump of a man seemed like all the rest—another pompous egghead with a stick stuck up his ass sideways. Were he in Gimm and Reid's predicament—ill-fated and on the lam—Callum would try to broker some kind of surrender to SAC Squires, to be able to live long enough to tell his tale. Of course, in their case, without any evidence, Callum's prompt reply would be a resounding denial—never met you, don't know you, you killed my good friend Peter Feist—and then leave the rest of the chattering to the attorneys. But, again, Superintendent Callum did not want Gimm and Reid's allegations released into the public sphere, which was why the call he'd just ended with Cordov Woods brought a smile to his face and a song to his heart. It was the reason he'd celebrated with two shots of Baileys in his java instead of just the one.

"Jethro got a hit from Wabiszewski's history," Woods said.

"His home PC?" Callum asked.

"Yup. It shows an interest in a cabin Feist's parents own in Wisconsin. He did an address search. Some fucking place on Rock Lake. Wabiszewski even did a Google Earth search on the address."

Callum thought for a moment. "Remember Feist's threat of having backups of his backups?"

"Yes."

"Take the psycho and the nerd along," Callum ordered.

"The psycho makes me nervous," Woods replied.

"Psychos tend to do that." Callum felt the Cappellis should have some skin in the game; especially since Cappelli Sr. and that big-shot friend of his had created this mess to begin with, and then the two pricks dumped it in his lap for cleanup. "But we can't have anyone slipping through the cracks this time. And turn the nerd loose if you find any PCs or smartphones."

"Can do," Woods said.

"And Cordov."

"What?"

"About Feist's cabin, burn that fucker down," Callum replied. "After you kill Gimm and Reid and the dog, of course."

CHAPTER 36

I pulled the CACC truck into a Walmart on the outskirts of Beloit and ventured in on a quick supply run while Kippy stayed with the girls. With one of Wabiszewski's Cubs caps down around my eyebrows, I did ten minutes of tossing cases of water, a loaf of bread, peanut butter, a couple pounds of trail mix, popcorn, and a half-dozen bags of beef jerky into the cart. Then I hit Electronics and grabbed a prepaid cell phone off the rack.

I headed for the checkout lanes, but then veered toward the Garden Center. Five seconds later I came to a halt and turned the cart around. I was in serious need of having my head examined. We're on the run, Wabs is dead—murdered in the mayor's office—our lives are turned upside down and, depending on who gets to us first, we may not have lives—turned upside down or not—and here I am thinking of picking up some flowers for Kippy.

Crazy couple of days, huh, Kip? I got you some tulips.

Mom must have dropped me when I was young.

At the self-checkout, I ran the prepaid cell phone package over the scanner. It didn't take. I tried several more times. No luck. I lowered my cap as far as it would go—just a nose peeking out—glanced sideways and saw that the checkout attendant was busy with another customer. I looked behind me. The line was now several customers deep, all of them staring back at me.

I felt my face begin to redden.

I scanned and bagged the groceries at an Olympic pace, and then tried the phone package again. Still no cigar.

Damnit.

The attendant was free and I flagged her over.

"This won't scan," I said, urgently handing her the phone package, and then realized I shouldn't be acting all urgent-like and panicky and tried turning it around. "Isn't that just the darndest thing? The other stuff scanned perfectly, but it keeps getting stuck on this one item."

She smiled noncommittally and tried running the barcode over the scanner.

"I bet you get this all day long," I said, lump in throat, and with what I hoped was an amiable smile.

The attendant had yet to say a word but poked at the screen until some fields came up where she could tap in numbers. Her tapping took and she looked my way. "You're good to go."

"Thank you so much." I got it in my noggin that no one would think I was the fugitive from the news headlines if I were super polite. "That was very kind of you."

Twenty seconds later I had to flag her down again.

"It doesn't like my twenties." At this point—deep down inside—I believed the scanner had read my anxiety level and was intentionally stalling me out until security arrived.

Of course the attendant was able to feed each of my twenties into the slot on her first try.

"Thank you so much," I repeated. "Very nice."

She continued smiling noncommittally, but I got the gist of how my worth had been appraised and found wanting.

"Jeez, Mace," Kippy said when I made it back to the CACC truck, "what took you so long?"

I got behind the wheel and shut the door. "I don't want to talk about it."

Sure, the Maps app on my iPhone would have led us the hour-plus jaunt from Rockford to Lake Mills, I thought, but

I doubted it would have been able to steer us all the way to the Feist family cabin. Of course, this was a moot point as our smartphones lay disassembled in the glove compartment of my F-150, which I prayed still rested in undisturbed peace in a parking space at O'Hare International. The road had switched from blacktop to gravel as we weaved the CACC truck past the winding lanes leading down to the cabins on the western shores of Rock Lake, of which Feist's cabin was one. Fortunately, there were address signs on metal posts, or nailed at waist-level to trees, proclaiming the family summer abodes that lay at the foot of the descending driveways.

I spent the trip thinking about my parents, and how by now this nightmare had to have splashed all over them. Hell, they'd probably already been served with a search warrant. Investigators were no doubt in the family room smashing apart my old pine wood derby cars in search of the meth. My brothers—normally jovial spirits—would fail to see any humor in this situation and might even believe that somewhere in the mental wreckage of my divorce and its aftermath, a hot brunette could lead me down a perilous path. I couldn't believe Mom or Dad or Big Sis Kathy would ever buy into my working for some Mexican drug cartel or, good god, having gone on a killing spree. Of course they knew how bad I'd taken Mickie's departure from my life—how bad I'd taken her engagement—and how I'd spent much of the past two years in a less-than-pleasant place, stumbling about on autopilot like a zombie in a piss-poor horror movie, and downing a bit too much booze at night.

Mickie would likely connect with Mom and Dad and offer her two cents' worth on how chummy Kippy and I had appeared when she'd stopped by the other week. My parents also knew my chosen profession hadn't set me on any kind of fast-track toward becoming a millionaire. And, as they read about their son in the newspaper, maybe they'd start thinking of Kippy Gimm as some sort of twenty-first-century femme fatale . . . leading their poor boy down a lethal pathway and beyond the point of no return.

Plus, Detective Ames—sphincter that he is—would likely seize the opportunity to stick a knife in both our backs. I could picture him trashing Kippy in the press, saying there'd always been something dubious about her, about the two of us . . . and call for our scalps.

We were so screwed.

A thought occurred to me. "This didn't begin with Feist, but with that Siskin guy that got stomped to death at that downtown firm, right?"

Kippy nodded. "David Siskin was a real estate investor from Minneapolis who had some ventures with the Michael J. Mc-Carron Investment Group in Chicago."

"And McCarron leads the firm, right?"

Another nod.

"Well, after all that's happened, McCarron's got to be shitting bricks," I said. "Maybe he can help."

"From what I read in the newspaper, McCarron was shocked and horrified at Siskin's death." She shrugged. "He probably knows or suspects something but doesn't want to die or put his family in danger."

We drove awhile farther until another thought occurred to me, and I don't know if it was frayed nerves or if I'd finally lost my marbles, but I started cackling like a toddler on helium.

"What's so funny?"

"We're making our *getaway* in a dog catcher truck." I glanced Kippy's way. "There's something inherently absurd in that."

She looked glum but said, "I wish it were an ice cream truck . . . I'd kill for butter pecan."

"Then we'd have a bunch of kids on our ass as well."

Kippy had become a vigorous navigator since my numerical skills had proven subpar; I'd incorrectly veered off at a fork in the road and cost us ten minutes in backtracking. She'd even dug about the cages and nets, tongs and gloves, snare poles and leashes in the back of the truck, and when she finally returned to the shotgun seat, she had a pair of binoculars hanging from a strap about her neck. She also handed me a bite stick—which is basically a police baton—as our only other weapon on hand was Kippy's Beretta.

"I wonder if the snare pole could be used," I said. A snare or catch pole is a long rod with a wire loop at one end to capture rowdy animals around the throat and then hold them off at a safe distance.

"If you feel the need to chase Callum's driver around the block with that damned thing, have at it," Kippy replied. "I plan to blow his head off."

We drove in silence after that, each of us lost in thought, until—at eleven-thirty sharp—Kippy pointed at a numbered sign screwed to a green post. "That's it."

I kept driving, unhurried, curving around a bend in the gravel road, and eased to a stop at the top of the neighbor's driveway.

"Take Vira," I said.

Kippy nodded, and she and my golden retriever were quickly in the woods, slanting downhill, diagonally toward Feist's cabin, toward the basin of Rock Lake. I'd taken a quick peek down Feist's dirt path as we'd maneuvered past his entrance. I couldn't spot his cabin from the access road; therefore, no one kicking about the lake home could glance up and spot us. Seclusion. Beloved seclusion. It had been that way for most of the homes on this side of the water. And, like the other cabins, Feist's driveway curved downward as it worked its way slowly toward Rock Lake. Ice fishermen would need four-wheel drive to pilot most of these driveways in the winter months or pray a gracious neighbor wouldn't mind towing them up from their lake lots.

Another plus was the acre or two of dense woodland between cabins. No one this side of the lake lived atop another—a short nature hike, laterally, in order to borrow a cup of sugar or coffee, and longer still if you were herding toddlers. This being a weekday, I was rooting for added seclusion. A final checkmark in the plus column was the nice weather. A sunny day in mid-May; warm. What we were attempting to accomplish would be difficult under the best of conditions but rendered shit-like had it been rainy and forty degrees.

It had been decided—Kippy vetoed my request to carry out recon duties—that it would be her task to cut through the pine and birch, cedar and poplar, ash and evergreens, and perhaps even some willow as she worked her way downhill to inspect Feist's cabin for any signs of life. If no signs of life, we'd park the CACC truck in an inconspicuous spot, possibly hidden behind the tree line, where it wouldn't be seen from above or, just as importantly, spotted from the lake. Then we'd had a short discussion about our preferred method of B and E—breaking and entering—but, considering the bind we found ourselves in, a smashed window here or a kicked-open door over there wouldn't tack much more time onto our prison sentences.

My immediate task was far simpler than Kippy's. I was to turn the truck around—hang a u-ey—without, god forbid, getting a tire stuck in the soft ditch of weeds beyond the gravel. I worked the wheel, swooped wide left at the mouth of the neighbor's driveway, pulled forward slowly, making sure the front tires were never close to running out of gravel, backed up, and then turned left, heading back to Peter Feist's driveway. I took the fifty-yard bend at a crawl, giving Kippy the time she needed without providing any potential passersby cause for concern at the sight of a parked vehicle. By the time I pulled even with the driveway, Kippy and Vira were next to Feist's address sign, both staring at me as though I'd been away since Easter.

Kippy walked to my window and said, "It's empty."

CHAPTER 37

Cordov Woods drove past an intimidating set of wrought-iron gates and steered the Lincoln Continental another half mile on the paved road that wound itself toward the Cappelli estate. Frank Cappelli Sr. and family lived in Winnetka, a tony, high-end village in Cook County, about fifteen or so miles north of downtown Chicago. Not only is Winnetka one of the richest and most exclusive suburbs in Illinois but in the entire country. The Cappellis lived on a forty-acre compound, their mansion of light stone and curved roof tiles was shrouded by a discouragingly tall security fence along with numerous high-res, night-vision cameras as well as motion sensors powerful enough to detect anyone stupid enough to be lurking about in the bushes. Woods even imagined some kind of patrol marched the perimeter at odd hours during both the day and night.

In other words, no one got in unless Frank Cappelli Sr. wanted them in.

Woods was greeted by a man in a dark suit—a man with something bulky beneath his left breast pocket—and flagged to park the Lincoln on one side of a roundabout that surrounded a two-story fountain of some Roman god spitting water. Woods had been here on a handful of occasions before as a go-between for Superintendent Callum, in situations where something physical needed to be exchanged with Cappelli Sr.

"Jethro," Woods said to the young man in glasses beside him, "you're going to want to move into the back seat because I guarantee he'll want the front. I know you've not the gift for gab and, in this case, that's a good thing because he's volatile, like handling nitroglycerin."

As Jethro grabbed his gear and scrambled around to the rear of the sedan, Woods joined the man in the dark suit and headed up a front stoop that would look more natural in a coliseum. Woods was led through a lengthy foyer and deposited in a surprisingly modest den.

Frank Cappelli Sr. stood from an armchair beneath a window, dropped his *Wall Street Journal* onto the ottoman in front of him, and crossed the room.

"Good to see you again, Cordov." Cappelli Sr. reached out a hand.

Woods took it. "Always an honor, sir."

Cappelli Sr. had a thin face, thin arms, and thin legs that contrasted awkwardly against his burgeoning paunch, as though the head of the Chicago Mob had affixed a half-deflated basketball to his midsection. He eats well, Woods thought. Although approaching sixty, Cappelli's hair and mustache remained as black as a raven's feather. A dye job, Woods figured.

Cappelli Sr. motioned for Woods to sit in the chair across the ottoman from where he'd been perched. "Would you like some coffee?"

"God yes," Woods said, and sat down. "It was a long night."

"So I heard." Cappelli shut the twin doors leading into his office, went behind a bar that took up the south side of the room, and began working a French press. "My son will be down in a few minutes, but I wanted a chance to talk to you first."

"He's all well, I trust."

"As right as rain," Cappelli Sr. said and looked up. "Does that count?"

"It does, sir. And thanks for remembering."

Cappelli brought Woods his coffee in a china cup and saucer. "Never could get that. How is something considered *as right as rain*?"

Woods shrugged. "It originated in England, where rain is part of their daily life."

"I guess that makes sense," Cappelli said; he sat back down in his armchair and focused his attention on Woods. "Have you given any thought to my offer?"

"I have," Woods replied, gingerly. "The way I see it, sir—in a manner—I already work for you."

Cappelli Sr. nodded, perhaps appeased. "The reason I keep pushing is on account of my son," he said. "You know he thinks the world of you."

"I'm awfully fond of the kid myself." Woods was startled and hoped it didn't show. He could barely stand Cappelli Sr.—he had to—but Cappelli Jr. was a demented little shit.

"The work I do," Cappelli Sr. said, "has kept me away from home during most of my boy's *formative* years. To be honest, I'd not been there when he needed an authoritarian figure, when he needed guidance . . . when he needed me."

Woods sipped at his coffee and said nothing.

Cappelli Sr. continued, "I'm ashamed to say that Frank Junior has not had the greatest of male role models in his life, if you know what I mean."

Woods put his cup and saucer down on a side table. He found it odd that Cappelli Sr. was waxing on as though his freak of a son were twelve instead of twenty-five. "It's hard raising children in this day and age, sir. Especially for a man in your position."

"That it is," Cappelli Sr. said. "That it is."

Woods read between the lines. The offer on the table was more to provide daycare for Frank Cappelli Jr., to mentor him on the *acceptable* manner in which things should be done, and to keep him out of trouble with the authorities. On some level Cappelli Sr. had to know what kind of shitshow he'd sired, and now he wanted someone else to reel the kid back in, to keep him from spinning off the rails. Quite frankly, Woods thought, the kid was already off the rails, and had been for years. Woods would never accept Cappelli's offer of employment, not in this life or any other. And if Cappelli Sr. wanted Cordov Woods's honest advice—advice Woods was far too bright to ever share with the head of the Chicago Mob—it would be to snap the kid's spine, toss him in a shallow hole in the middle of nowhere, get a trophy wife, and start anew instead of trying to pawn his Frankenstein monster off on someone else.

"We're having a gathering for my wife's birthday tomorrow evening," Cappelli said.

"Is that so?" Woods replied. "A pivotal one?"

"She won't allow me to mention any numbers but, by all means, come if you can."

"It would be an honor," Woods said. He'd rather twist corkscrews into his temples than come back here tomorrow night, but when Frank Cappelli Sr. invites you to a party . . . you go to the goddamned party. Woods hoped it'd be crowded and busy—something he could slip out of early—and that there'd be no more talk of job offers or wayward sons.

The twin doors to the office opened and there stood Frank Cappelli Jr. in a brown suit that likely cost more than Woods's entire wardrobe.

"A fucking road trip with Cordov," Frank Cappelli Jr. said. "I call shotgun."

CHAPTER 38

Feist's cabin turned out to be more Ma and Pa Kettle than Ritz-Carlton. I backed the CACC truck onto the clumps of grass behind the cabin, in a spot clearly meant for stashing battered boat trailers. The truck could not be seen from above until you were nearly to the cabin itself, and Feist's cabin blocked the dog mobile from being spotted from the lake. We didn't want any fishermen or canoeists or other boaters— potential acquaintances of the Feist family, neighbors who were most certainly aware of recent events—coming to investigate or phoning the authorities.

Feist had been serious in his interview with *Chicago* magazine about conceding his once-frequent Rock Lake fishing weekends as his dock was out and had likely not been put in for the past season or two. Vira and I stood in the tree line near shore, while Maggie and Delta scouted about the woods. Kippy and I realized voices had the potential to carry so my new assignment was to stand hidden among the trees with a right arm in the air. I had a clear view of the lake and my raised hand indicated the coast was clear—no fishermen trolling nearby, no kids farting about in their Sunfish sailboats, and, despite the warm temperature, no water-skiers or inner-tubists zipping past.

Kippy, of course, had the more difficult task. The front door faced lakeside. We'd discussed breaking a pane, reaching in and unlocking the door, but we discounted that approach as anyone pontooning past might notice the broken or missing pane and recognize what that signified. It's unlikely that Feist's cabin would be the first on Rock Lake to be broken into, and neighbors tend to keep an eye out for each other. So it was decided that Kippy would attack a side window, the one above the kitchen sink, which no one looking in from the lake could spot as being broken. Kippy would break the lower pane of the top window as gently as possible with the bite stick, if something like that was possible, then twist the latch, slide the window up, and slither through the opening. She was going to attempt this as quickly as possible due to potential lake traffic—potential witnesses to the break-in, potential phone calls to the local authorities.

But there were obstacles.

First, she'd have to pull herself up, position a forearm on the outer windowsill for balance, as well as brace the soles of her shoes against the cabin's siding for added support. Second, all of this would leave only her right hand free to wield the bite stick, flip the latch, slide up the window, brush aside any shards of glass, and pull herself inside. Third, she had to accomplish all of this while continually peeking my way in case my arm dropped. A dropped arm meant she had to immediately hit the dirt, scoot behind the cabin, and hide by the truck. We figured the task might take Kippy two or three bites at the apple; that she'd need time to shake out her joints and take five before completing this particular gymnastic routine.

My eyes were glued to a couple of fishermen—geezers in a fiberglass Lund to my left—about sixty yards away and anchored in a bay of weeds. Perhaps they'd discovered Peter Feist's honey hole. I shot a glance about the lake; a few other boats, all fishermen, but no one else close enough to cause concern. I glanced back at Kippy. She'd already made short order of the outer screen. It took her all of five seconds to pop that puppy off and toss it behind the cabin. Now she was in an awkward perch, spidermanned against the side of Feist's shack, bite stick in her right hand as she studied the window as though it were a final exam. I looked back at the geezers. The chubbier of the two was working the anchor while the thinner guy reeled in his line.

Shit.

Evidently, they'd not discovered Feist's honey hole.

The tink of breaking glass took all of a second. It wasn't loud but I heard it, and so did the thinner of the two fishermen. His head jutted my way. I jerked down even though I was already hidden in the brush. But chubs said something and thinner turned to his friend and pointed across the lake. I dropped my arm as thinner set his fishing pole in the Lund and chubs began working the engine, flagging Kippy to drop and hide.

Vira and I spun around. A lump stuck in my throat.

Kippy had gone for it in one gymnastic routine instead of breaking it into separate chunks. Her lower half—from the rump down—hung out of the now-open kitchen window. No one boating past could misinterpret that implication. Vira and I raced across the dirt and weeds, a Doppler of boat motor in the background. Kippy, tipped-off by the outboard, scampered like hell, her butt now inside, her legs sticking out. I shoved the bottom of her shoes inward as hard as I could before diving behind the cabin with Vira. I scurried to the other side, peeked about the corner, staring out at Rock Lake.

Both chubs and thinner were out of the tree line, both boat and fishermen now in clear view. Thinner was chuckling at something chubs must have said. Both faced inland, gazing indifferently at Feist's stacked dock. And then they were gone . . . seemingly on their way to a hopefully more prosperous fishing hole.

CHAPTER 39

"Are you okay?" I stepped quickly over a rotting front step and through the front door Kippy had opened for me, closing it once inside.

"No worries," she said. "My forehead broke the fall."

"Oh, god—I am so sorry."

"The alternative is I ice it at county lockup while we wait for Callum's men to come for us."

I circled the room. Though Feist's shack was hardly the Ritz-Carlton on the outside, the inside was even worse. The refrigerator must have come over on the Mayflower. The kitchen sink had seen more utility gutting fish than scrubbing dishes. And a dead stench wafted up from the drain. Kippy should get a tetanus shot for sliding over it on her flight in, I thought. The kitchen table looked decent enough, top-of-the-line Goodwill circa 1965. The sofa was clearly salvaged from the Hindenburg, post-explosion. Even the finest vacuum that Kirby had to offer could never make the carpet look as though it should not immediately be set ablaze. Mold and mildew ran a dead heat as to which could cause more nausea.

Of course we didn't have to worry about Feist having the place rigged with an alarm system. The system itself would cost more than anything worth stealing.

"I may know why the wife and kids don't bother coming."

I flicked a light switch on and off several times. "There's no power."

Kippy opened the fridge door and shut it rapidly. "Evidently not."

"Excellent."

"We need to air this place out." Kippy began opening windows, the ones opposite the kitchen and above the couch, ones that also couldn't be spotted from the lake.

I leaned against the sink and gave a quick whistle. I peeled the front door curtain back a half-inch and peeked out. The coast was clear, so I opened the door ten inches and let Vira and the girls squeeze in. I checked the cupboards, realized Feist was my kind of guy, and retrieved three paper bowls. I set them in a line on the floor and emptied a bottle of water equally among the three dishes.

Kippy had disappeared into the single bedroom and now returned. "A couple of bunk beds and pillows, no sheets. And a fossilized mouse in a trap, so I don't think he's been here on any overnights in quite a while." She pointed at the only other room that made up Feist's lake home. "There's a toilet, a shower, and a sink, but the water's turned off."

"I'll try and rustle up some light."

On the far wall near the corner of the room, at face-level, was a wooden cabinet, maybe five inches wide, with a copper latch. I opened it and found what I was looking for. The small cabinet acted as a shell for the electrical service panel—the fuse box. I opened the hinged cover. Considering the size of Feist's cabin, it was a basic unit. I flipped the main breaker.

"Try now."

Kippy flicked the light switch on and off, shook her head, and said, "We don't need it, Mace. With the side curtains open, there's enough natural light coming in."

I picked up a cardboard box from the bottom ledge of the cabinet. The box contained enough fuses to replace any blown ones a dozen times over.

"We don't need to fix his electrical, Mace. Remember, come

night, the last thing we need is for neighbors to notice that lights are on."

I put the box of fuses back where I'd found it, shut the cabinet, and then pulled the sofa away from the wall. My unearthing included an old pack of Bicycle playing cards and another dead mouse in a trap—just fur and bone—fossilized, like the one Kippy had found in the bedroom. I tossed the mouse, trap and all, in the bin under the sink—so the dogs couldn't get at it—and did the same with the trapped remains from the bedroom. These forgotten mousetraps didn't bode well for the special prosecutor having been here any time in the recent past.

Then I tackled what I'd been putting off, flipped the cushions off the couch, grimaced—focused my mind on Kippy's banging about the bathroom, removing tank lids and opening medicine cabinets—and stuck my hand deep inside the crease and slid my fingers across the inner crevice of Feist's sofa, the back and both sides.

All I came away with was a long string of fish line and what I hoped were only coagulated cough drops. I wasn't even able to scrape together loose change for my trouble.

Kippy came into the room holding a broom she'd found somewhere and stared up at the ceiling. I followed suit. The cabin's ceiling ran parallel to the eaves—a flat surface of rustic pine, possibly the original tongue-and-groove boarding. Kippy used the tip of the broom shaft to tap the ceiling boards in case any were unfastened or contained some kind of hidden compartment that Feist may have utilized.

I pulled a kitchen chair to the center of the room, under the singular light fixture—realizing we were quickly running out of places to search—when the idea occurred to me. I walked back, opened the wall cabinet, and grabbed the cardboard box containing the fuses.

"Really, Mace," Kippy said, "it's not as though we're going to cook a Thanksgiving dinner or anything."

Considering the supplies I'd picked up at the Beloit

Walmart—trail mix and beef jerky—a Thanksgiving dinner it would most certainly not be.

"I know," I said, turning her way and running a hand through the various fuses. Flipping the main breaker had pretty much exhausted the extent of my electrical knowledge, but if Kippy thought I was bright enough to be an electrician, who was I to contradict her.

Besides, I had something else in mind.

"I'll check the light fixtures and the kitchen, and you rip apart the bedroom, okay?"

"Sure," I replied, still peering inside the box. I noticed a fleck of purple at the bottom of the fuse carton. I shook the container, like panning for gold, until I saw more purple. It was relatively thin, maybe a couple inches long, with a black cap.

"You okay, Mace?"

I reached inside, pulled out the item—which was definitely not a fuse—and held it in front of my face.

"What's that?"

I looked at Kippy and we both spoke as one.

"Flash drive."

CHAPTER 40

"No shit? Callum wants the dog-fucker's eyes?"

"The man was not pleased with how things went down at City Hall," Cordov Woods replied to Frank Cappelli Jr., keeping his eyes focused on I-94 west. Young Cappelli indeed rode shotgun in the Lincoln Continental while Jethro chewed a bushel of Twizzlers in the back seat.

"So he's sending a message, huh?"

"Not really, since we're disappearing them. You know, the crematorium." There was a cremation service they used in Skokie. In fact, it was a service Cappelli's father, Frank Sr., once brought to their attention, and it was where the three IKEA boxes were intended to be sent had recent events not gone south. "He's just big-time pissed off."

"And you want me to do the job, right?" Cappelli Jr. asked. "Cut the fucker's eyes out?"

Woods nodded. "I've a weak constitution."

"What's that mean? Like bill of rights and shit?"

"I think it means he's got a weak stomach," Jethro piped in through red teeth, the first words he'd spoken since young Cappelli had joined them for the road trip.

"Fuck you, geek," Cappelli Jr. said over a shoulder and looked at Woods. "I call bullshit. I know stuff about you, Cordov, and you ain't got no weak stomach. I bet your ancestors wore black hoods and lobbed off heads. It's in your blood."

"You won't do it?"

"Hell yeah I'll do it. You assholes made my day by showing up."

Woods nodded again.

"Can't wait to see how Goldy'll work on eyeballs."

Goldy was Cappelli's pet name for the pair of brass knuckles he sometimes used; knuckles with a razor-sharp spearhead in front. Woods knew he himself had issues shrinks would have a field day deciphering, but Frank Cappelli Jr.—Jesus Christ—the man got his rocks off inflicting pain on others. Cappelli Jr. not only embraced his sadistic streak but rolled about and frolicked in the meadow with it. Cordov Woods took care of Superintendent Callum's *dirty work,* had done so for years, but left to his own devices Woods went for the quick kill except on those occasions, like today, when Callum demanded extra.

And Callum had been demanding *extra* more and more of late.

Woods looked sideways at Cappelli Jr. Frankly, he detested the spoiled little shit, but daddy's name was Frank Cappelli Sr., so Woods placated the kid, tried to reason with him, hoping against hope some semblance of rational thought might rub off on him. And Woods did consider how he'd won a minor victory some months back in the battle over leaving punctured corpses strewn about Chicago for medical examiners to comb over, because if Cappelli Jr. were ever arrested with Goldy on his person, the spiked brass knuckles would tie him to a fistful of Windy City killings up to and including that union negotiator the kid had been dumb enough to torch, thinking a warehouse fire would cover up a killing. Dead men do tell tales after all, but the disappeared dead— the cremated dead—do not. Woods recalled the conversation he'd had with young Cappelli, where he spoke in the most basic of terms he'd hoped the young psychopath would comprehend.

"Remember the movie *Home Alone*?" Woods asked him over beers.

"I fucking love that movie," Cappelli Jr. had replied.

"Remember how one of the burglars left the water running in all the homes they robbed?"

"Yeah—they called themselves the Wet Bandits."

"Remember when they got caught, how the police were able to tie all the flooded-home burglaries to them?"

Woods thought he spotted a spark of understanding in young Cappelli's eyes.

"Oh . . . fuck," Cappelli Jr. had said.

Since then, the crematorium in Skokie had received repeat business.

Woods figured Cappelli Jr. was a good-enough-looking kid—black hair slicked back, medium height, muscular, a snazzy dresser. Yup, the kid could probably have been a men's clothing model except for one distinguishing factor: young Cappelli had a cleft lip or, more insultingly labeled, a harelip. There'd been surgery when the kid was an infant, but a light scar remained visible. However, the overriding rule of hanging out with young Cappelli, and he'd stressed this with Jethro on their ride over to pick up Cappelli Jr., was don't acknowledge the harelip in any manner, shape, or form. Don't look at the harelip, don't talk about the harelip, and, if you're fond of your time spent cavorting about on planet Earth, never ever joke about the harelip. Woods had heard tell that Cappelli Jr. once used his precious Goldy to carve a harelip into some numbskull who'd made an offhand and unflattering remark concerning young Cappelli's most-dominant facial characteristic before stuffing said numbskull—still alive and kicking—into the Skokie crematorium.

Woods's cell phone buzzed. He drove with a knee and checked the text message. *Security found Reid's truck at O'Hare.*

"Looks like the dog man dumped his Ford at the airport," he announced to the car.

"What's he driving now?" young Cappelli asked.

"They don't know yet," Woods said. "Guess we'll find out at Rock Lake."

CHAPTER 41

"You look more pregnant than fat."

"Thanks," Kippy replied. "I guess."

We'd squished and molded and duct-taped a pillow from one of the bunk beds to Kippy's midsection. It took a while to get it just right before she slid on one of Wabiszewski's sweatshirts. Before that, Kippy had me cut her hair with a pair of rusty scissors we'd found in a kitchen drawer where Feist kept his fillet knives. I gently held the dark locks in the back and cut them at middle-of-the-neck level. I could never moonlight at a hair salon, but Kippy seemed to think I'd done a passable job. She then used half a case of bottled water to wash her hair, accompanying the aqua with little bottles of shampoo and conditioner that she'd liberated from our motel in Rockford. After that she pushed everything back with her fingertips and let it dry.

"You don't look anything like yourself."

"No one should look twice at a woman in her third tri-mester," Kippy said, "and think it's the fugitive lady from the news."

After discovering the flash drive, we'd gotten reenergized and continued ransacking the rest of Feist's shack. It didn't take long. Kippy took apart the kitchen and rechecked the main room while I tackled the bedroom and double-checked the bathroom. When we were done—and nothing had been found—we switched areas and I knocked about the kitchen and main room while Kippy tore apart the rest of the cabin.

Nothing additional had been discovered and we called it quits.

Kippy asked, "Do you think Paul's called the truck in yet?"

I had given this a lot of thought. Paul would know my working for a Mexican drug cartel was a joke—complete bullshit—as was my killing of Officer Dave Wabiszewski. Plus, Paul knew all about Vira, about her special ability. "I think he's going to buy us as much time as possible without sinking himself."

"You know they're drilling through our colleagues, friends, and family," Kippy said. "They've probably already talked to him."

"Paul will tell them he doesn't buy the news reports—that there's no way I'm running around Chicago like some kind of crazed fiend—but they can knock themselves out looking around CACC. Hopefully, they don't know enough yet to brace him on the vehicles."

The last we'd heard on the CACC truck's radio, they were still reporting the plates off my F-150. And Paul was cagey; I pictured him covering himself, leaving messages on my answering service, begging me to get a lawyer and turn myself in. Perhaps tomorrow he'd call the local police about the missing truck. If he did, hopefully it'd take another day for Callum's forces to catch wind and realize exactly what the missing truck meant.

"You know we stick out like a sore thumb in that dog mobile."

"When you get near the frontage road, pull over and check the radio," I said. "If they're jumping up and down about the CACC truck, come right back and we'll figure out something else."

The something we'd already figured out was that a pregnant, short-haired Kippy would walk into the Lake Mills Public Library, feed the librarian whatever line of BS it'd take to use one of their computers without an ID or library card, find out what Peter Feist had on the flash drive, and then come right back so we could plot our next move. If Feist had something good on the flash drive—something to lawfully kick Callum and Weeks in the nuts—our next move would basically be noodling out the smartest method in which to share Feist's content with the media and the FBI.

Of course, if the flash drive contained only images of the various walleyes and largemouth bass Peter Feist had pulled out of Rock Lake . . . then we were shit out of luck.

CHAPTER 42

"The library?" the gas station clerk stared at Kippy as though she'd asked him which aisle contained gold bullion. "Can't you bring that up on your cell phone?"

Kippy had done as Mace had suggested, parked and listened to news reports on the CACC truck's radio before turning onto the paved road that both circled the lake and connected with the highway leading back to town. The latest update repeated that Mason Reid's Ford F-150 pickup had been discovered by security in long-term parking at O'Hare International Airport, but, fortunately, there was still no all-points bulletin regarding the two of them making good on their escape in a glorified dog-catching mobile . . . thank you Paul Lewis.

"I left it at home," Kippy lied. Cheap burner phones tend not to come with a wide assortment of applications.

"Ardith," the clerk called to his coworker who manned the neighboring cash register, "do you know where the library is?"

Since it hadn't appeared the authorities were yet on the lookout for the CACC truck, Kippy had topped off the tank as she didn't know when the opportunity might arise again should that status change. She figured the twenty bucks in premium would score her a quick set of directions from one of the townies.

Evidently, Ardith didn't give two shits about Kippy's purchase of premium gasoline as she shook her head as though brushing away a cloud of gnats and continued ringing up her current customer's box of donuts, bag of chips, and large Slurpee. It didn't appear either gas station clerk was willing to take out their own smartphone in order to assist in her quest . . . certainly not Ardith. So much for the notion that people will bend over backward to help those with child.

Kippy would have pressed the point were she not wanted for murder.

As it turned out, the hardest part of the trip to Lake Mills Public Library was finding the damned place to begin with.

"Try Maggie at the café," the proud new owner of gas station donuts, overpriced chips, and a Slurpee informed her. "She always reads books on breaks or whenever it's dead."

"The café?" Kippy said.

"Café on the Park," Large Slurpee replied, holding his treats and motioning at the street outside with his chin. "Just down Main, you can't miss it."

It turned out Large Slurpee was right. The staff at Café on the Park was a bit more literary than those at the gas station.

"Of course I do," Maggie the waitress-slash-bookworm replied to Kippy's request for directions and began jotting the street-by-street route down on a napkin.

Kippy left Café on the Park with Maggie's napkin as well as a couple of iced-coffees and a bag of cornbread muffins to go with tonight's dinner of trail mix and jerky.

Though the library parking lot was only a quarter full— about what you'd expect for midafternoon on a school day in a small town—Kippy backed the animal control truck into an open spot in the far back and hiked in. She figured this would give her a clear view of the vehicle when the time came to exit the library, in order to make sure it wasn't receiving any *undue* attention. Kippy glanced about in every direction.

No sirens and no signs of any local constables.

So far, so good.

The Lake Mills Public Library itself was two stories of rustic stone and steep roofs. It looked more like a villa you'd see in Switzerland than the main public building in a sleepy fishing town in southern Wisconsin. She might have even enjoyed poking about in there for an hour or two were it under other circumstances . . . any other circumstances.

"Good afternoon," a petite woman in a skirt and blouse said after opening the door for Kippy.

"Thank you," Kippy replied.

"Is it a boy or a girl?" the woman asked.

"Huh?"

"Your baby? Do you know if it's a boy or a girl?"

"Oh, yeah—my husband and I decided to wait and be surprised."

It turned out the woman, who introduced herself as Donna, worked at the library.

"I forgot my purse at home, so idiot me didn't bring my card," Kippy lied through her teeth. "I just need to verify that my current assignment is on here and not the one from last week." Kippy had held up Feist's flash drive as though it were an airtight alibi. "Can I use one of your computers to double-check?"

"Of course." Donna the librarian led Kippy past the reference desk and over to a row of computers.

"Class keeps me jumping," Kippy said. She was all set to blather on about homework assignments and strict professors but decided to leave it at that.

"This is read only." Donna had fumbled with the login a second or two and then pulled a chair out for Kippy to sit in. "You won't be able to write or save changes to your memory stick."

"That's okay," Kippy said and did her best imitation of a pregnant woman lowering herself into a chair. "Thank you for all your help."

Kippy continued smiling at Donna until the librarian took the hint and strolled away. She then looked about the room. As expected, just a handful of library patrons, none of whom were staring in her direction or casting off weird vibes.

Kippy then plugged the flash drive into the USB port, brought up Windows Explorer, and then clicked the removable drive to find out exactly what Special Prosecutor Peter Feist had ferreted away. There was only one folder . . . and the folder was titled SISKIN.

After thirty seconds of review, Kippy could barely wait to get back to the cabin and share the news of what she'd discovered with Mace, to let him know they weren't shit out of luck.

Instead, they'd hit pay dirt.

The flash drive was pay dirt.

CHAPTER 43

Two hours in the same car and he could barely stomach the little fucker. Can't stomach . . . Woods mentally checked off another idiom.

There certainly was a lost art of conversation—Woods had been railing about it for years—social events chewed up by small-talk dullards and gossiping hens. That said, Woods would rather have the most somnolent-inducing bore or cloyingest of gossipmongers riding shotgun with him than spend another five minutes with young Cappelli. In the world according to Cappelli Jr., everything revolved around cutting or stabbing, punching or gouging, slicing or burning, and—of course—the endless tales of all the hot babes he'd screwed as well as the various positions in which he'd screwed them.

"So I pop the dog-fucker's eyes out and we watch him run around the yard like a chicken with its head cut off," Cappelli Jr. said.

Cordov Woods shook his head. *Never again*, he thought. Woods also considered how easy it would be to reach across the seat, grab the psychotic little shit by the throat, and squeeze the undeserved life out of him. The world would be a much sunnier place without Frank Cappelli Jr. wasting perfectly good oxygen. Woods was willing to bet he could do it without even swerving out of his lane. Hell, he'd done it once before. But how would that play out? Three bodies at the Skokie crematorium instead of two? Then use Cappelli Jr.'s own cell phone to make a few late-night calls to casinos in Las Vegas, bullshit with whoever answers about reservations and weather forecasts and upcoming concert events long enough to make it appear as though Junior had held several actual conversations before he vanished, and then bust up and toss Cappelli's phone into Lake Michigan.

Alas, Frank Cappelli Sr., unlike his offspring, wasn't a fucking idiot. Woods could keep a straight face and might be able to pull it off—but Jethro?—those fuckers would shake Jethro's ass a little bit, show him a branch pruner, and find out everything Jethro knew in about six seconds flat—and then the two of them would be taking a horizontal drive out to the Skokie crematorium. No, Woods thought, if he ever got serious about capping this little Cappelli shit, his best move— after he'd done the deed—would be to drive over to Frank Cappelli Sr.'s Winnetka compound and take him out along with about ten other Cappelli soldiers.

However, even with the skill set Cordov Woods brought to the table, that might prove a bridge too far.

Mobsters . . . what are ya gonna do?

"But it's not like he could get away," Cappelli Jr. said, disappointed.

Woods shook his head again. "We don't need him screaming."

"I could cut his tongue out."

"I think he might still be able to scream," Jethro offered from the back seat.

"Without a tongue?"

"Well, he certainly wouldn't be able to say much," Woods replied, "but I guarantee he'd scream up a blue storm."

Yup, Woods thought. After today, he would never again

work with Junior the infantile psychopath, nevermore . . . no matter what Callum ordered or Cappelli Sr. offered.

Woods spotted the address on a post—Feist's cabin number—and shot a glance to his right as they passed by. "Either of you see a car or truck down there?"

"I couldn't even see the fucking cabin," Cappelli said. "Why aren't we driving down?"

"The girl's got a gun," Woods said. "Maybe Reid does, too."

He pulled their Continental into the next driveway, backed up, and turned around. Woods drove past the entrance to Feist's driveway again, much slower this time, but still couldn't spot any vehicle or the cabin itself. This was of no surprise as, on this side of the lake, owners had to navigate some steep and twisty hills to get down to their lakefront dwellings. Woods kept on driving—one, two, three driveways away before pulling in and parking on a flat spot between trees. Woods figured this was where the cabin owner had any visitors park who showed up in vehicles lacking four-wheel drive.

"Why so far away?" Cappelli asked.

"I don't want to spook Reid's dogs or let them spot us in the neighbor's driveway," Woods said and looked back at Jethro. "You're staying put, kid. If anyone comes knocking on the window, show them that badge I gave you and request they return to their cabin until further notice."

Woods then looked Frank Cappelli Jr. in the eyes. "Okay, city boy, we're going to see what's going on at Feist's cabin. Stay forty yards behind me unless I wave you over, okay? And stick to the grass and dirt. Don't be stepping on sticks or busting branches."

"I'm not a fucking idiot."

"I know you're not," Woods lied, "but we need to be as silent as possible so we don't spook the dogs."

"I fucking hate dogs."

"If we see any," Woods said, fitting the silencer onto his SIG Sauer P226, "it's proof they're here. But don't worry;

these aren't pit bulls or German shepherds, like the cops use. They're cadaver dogs. Sniffers, not fighters."

Cordov Woods slipped through the brush, eyes on the ground in front of him, his P226 hanging loosely from his right hand. It was hot for May and he should have lost the long coat, but his tools of the trade were in different pockets and you never knew what might come in handy. He worked his way down the hill as quietly as possible and—grudgingly—had to hand it to Cappelli Jr., who appeared to be doing the same.

Woods squatted fifty yards up from the Feist cabin; glanced back to make sure young Cappelli had stopped as well. Then he settled in and stared down at the little shack. His first thought was *goddamnit*. No car; likely meant nobody was home. Woods rolled onto his stomach and crawled forward a few more yards until he got a better angle. From here he could see into the side window, which meant nothing. Feist could have left the curtains open to show teenage vandals there was nothing to steal and not much to bust up, either. But then Woods realized the window itself was open.

Feist would have been a damn fool to leave a window open and let the elements in.

Feist may have been a fool, but he wasn't a damned one.

Woods motioned Cappelli Jr. over with a wave of his gun hand.

The young thug tiptoed over like some kind of conscientious burglar not wanting to wake a sleeping household and mouthed, "What?"

"I've got a plan," Woods whispered.

PART FOUR

CADAVER DOGS

You beat me like a dog, yet were surprised when I bit back.

—Jonny Whiting and The U-Turns, "Chainsaw"

CHAPTER 44

Vira began to snarl.

I cut her off with a gesture. Maggie and Delta joined her in facing the side window above the dilapidated sofa. A branch snapped and I leaped off my seat at the kitchen table where I'd been flipping cards at solitaire, rushed to the drapes, and yanked them shut. I twisted sideways, back now against the wall, reminding myself to breathe. At first I thought Vira had been notifying me of Kippy's arrival in the truck, but whatever was outside was something else.

All three dogs began to growl.

"Shh," I whispered, a finger at my lips.

I heard approaching footsteps now, heading downhill toward the cabin, toward us, and nudged the drape an inch to peek outside. A young guy in a fancy brown suit was traipsing our way.

That's when he began calling out to the cabin.

"Laura," he shouted, sliding around the corner, approaching the front stoop. "Laura, are you in there?"

I watched the suited figure through the thin, flowery curtain covering the windowpanes. He began rapping lightly on the cabin door.

"Laura, it's Rick from next door. Anna said she heard a car and thought you might be here with the little ones."

I held my finger to my lips and stared hard from Delta to Maggie to Vira.

"I know somebody's in there." The figure rapped harder on the door. "I saw you shut the drapes."

Hair stood on the back of my neck. This was exactly what we'd been worried about, some Rock Lake busybody popping by to check in. I stayed glued to the carpet.

"This isn't funny," the figure continued speaking. "Not with all that's happened."

The figure jiggled the doorknob, and then jiggled it harder. Thank god I'd locked it after Kippy's departure. The figure now put a shoulder into the door; it shook in its frame.

Vira spun a slow three-sixty. Paying no heed to my warnings of caution, she began a low growl. I stepped into the center of the room and placed a palm on top of her head. The figure working the door ceased his knob-jiggling and we all stood in silence.

"I heard that," the figure said, breaking the stillness. "I'm done fooling around out here. I'm going to call the cops." The figure held up what appeared to be a smartphone.

"I'm Laura's brother," I said, surprised at how calm the words resonated. "I just stepped out of the shower for Christ's sake."

After a beat, the figure said, "Laura's brother?"

"Yes," I replied.

"I didn't know Laura had any brothers."

"Laura has two," I said, getting better at deceit, improving my game. "Weren't you at the funeral?"

There was another pause, this time longer, and we watched the figure through the thin drapes as he shifted about on the rotting front stoop.

"We sent flowers," he finally said. "It was a horrible thing that happened to Peter."

"Yes," I said. "It was."

"Are you going to open the door?"

"I'm dripping wet."

"Look, I don't know you," the figure said, "so I'm going to have to see some identification to prove you're *really* Laura's brother."

"I'm dripping wet," I repeated.

"What, you haven't been drying off while we've been talking?" the figure said. "Fuck are you? A faggot?"

Feist's Rock Lake neighbor had taken an unusual conversation in a most-unusual direction. I squinted at the cabin door and tried to think. "Give me ten minutes and I'll come over with my ID and a six-pack of beer."

A plan was forming in my head. Get this lake-neighbor guy the hell out of here, grab the dogs, hustle up to the access road, hide in the brush until Kippy returns, flag her down, and vamoose as far from here as humanly possible.

"No, I don't think I want to drink a six-pack with a faggot," the figure said, still holding up his phone. "And I sure as hell don't think you're Laura's brother."

"What's the matter with you, pal?" I replied, apprehensive now, grasping at straws. "Laura wanted me to check on the cabin, make sure it's still standing."

"I'm not your fucking pal, and I could knock this door down if I wanted to."

The figure was getting seriously bent out of shape; all tenor of neighborly love had long since evaporated.

"Don't do that," I said in my best high school principal tone. "Laura's selling the place and she'll be angry if you bust it down."

"Open this goddamn door, faggot."

Jesus, what the hell was the matter with this guy? "I've got dogs in here, sir . . . and you don't want to get them pissed off at you."

The figure took a step backward. "Ain't you been watching TV? There's a manhunt for the guy and lady that helped kill Feist. And I heard they got them a pack of dogs."

Both the figure at the door and I stood motionless a long moment.

"Holy shit," the figure finally said, stumbling off the rotted stoop. "Holy shit—you're that guy."

And, with a final *holy shit*, the man in the brown suit took off running, this time kitchen side. I watched him through the open window as he scampered up the driveway, phone held in front of him, likely in search of that elusive bar he needed to dial 911.

I shot for the front door, fumbled with the lock. The girls and I needed to get the hell out of here ASAP. The kids raised a chorus of barks and snarls, trying to warn me of something, but I was moving way too quickly. I began opening the door right as I noticed the bulk of humanity now standing outside. A hand clasped my shirt. A split-second later, I was flying ass-over-teakettle, tumbling onto the dirt and sand as the door slammed shut . . . trapping my dogs inside.

CHAPTER 45

Kippy was going too fast on the gravel road and was lucky to catch the glare off a bumper as she sped past a lake home access road several doors down from Feist's cabin. A jerk of her head confirmed a good-sized car was now parked amid the trees at the neck of the neighbor's driveway. She didn't recall seeing a car parked there earlier that morning on their first approach to Feist's shack, back when she'd been in the passenger seat. And she'd been in cop mode at the time. She also hadn't seen it sitting there on her way out to the library, while also in cop mode.

Kippy curved a bend and eased the dog mobile to the side of the road, pocketed her handcuffs, and slipped into the woods. The Beretta had always been with her, holstered inside the folded pillow of her pregnancy which she now tore out from under the sweatshirt to get at her firearm. She jogged back a couple dozen yards and dropped to her knees.

She cursed under her breath.

A Lincoln Continental . . . Illinois plates . . . and the vehicle was still running.

Kippy cursed again. She did not feel good about this. She should have had Mace sit out in the woods with the dogs, a half mile away from the cabin. She closed her eyes and listened. No sound, no dogs yapping, nothing busting up the tranquility of a late afternoon at Rock Lake. Half the lot owners were probably from Illinois. But a Lincoln Continental left idling—who was she kidding? This meant Police Superintendent Callum's driver. Sure, the plates were civilian, but with the shit that Callum's driver had pulled—or planned on pulling—he'd not be bopping about the Midwest sporting government plates.

Then something moved in the back seat and Kippy nearly jumped from her skin.

She kept low, cutting wide left for a better angle. She got behind a tree no more than thirty feet from the sedan and stood up. She realized why the car was running, air-conditioning; someone's head bobbed up and down as though to music. Kippy checked her six and stepped toward the back of the Continental, Beretta in a two-handed grip. She was able to sneak up, curve around the stern of the sedan, and come even with the rear side window without being spotted.

Kippy saw the reason her stealth activity had gone undetected. A young male, mid-twenties, with thick glasses and inch-long hair that stuck up like a paintbrush was shooting at winged dragons on an Xbox or PlayStation or whatever. He had headphones plugged into the computer game and was either jamming to tunes or to the slaying of computer-generated medieval beasts.

Kippy exhaled and lowered her pistol. Just some nerd who'd rather dick around with his toy instead of visit with mother and Gladys at the lake home. But then two things happened in rapid succession. First, Kippy spotted a picture of herself sitting atop a file folder on the seat next to the young man. It was turned his way and looked like an eight-by-ten of her current driver's license photo. The second thing that occurred— the young man turned her way.

Kippy yanked open the door, Beretta in the gamer's face. "Get your ass out of the goddamned car."

The kid's mouth dropped to his navel. Suddenly, the afternoon calm shattered, dogs began to bark and howl. Several of them. Kippy had no time to mess around. She pulled the young guy by his shirt front until he dropped onto the ground, his Xbox and headphones falling to the dirt beside him.

"How many?"

No answer, so she kicked him in the chest. "How many?"

"Two."

"Where?"

The kid motioned in the direction of Feist's cabin.

"Who the hell are you?"

"The computer guy."

She kicked him in the chest again.

"Jesse Aarestad," he said, spraying saliva. "They call me Jethro."

Mace's dogs continued their wild rant, loud and fierce. Kippy wanted to scream. Instead she said, "You move, you die."

She whipped open the driver's door. Turned off the sedan, popped the keys from the ignition, and dropped them in her pocket. Then she flipped the trunk latch.

"Get your ass up."

Callum's computer guy stood, his face white. The dogs continued howling. She felt ill.

"Wallet and phone," Kippy yelled. "On the ground."

Jesse "Jethro" Aarestad bumbled the objects from his pockets, and Kippy slapped them to the dirt. She took a second to frisk him; the computer guy was clean. There was no more need to gab, and Kippy shoved him to the rear bumper of the Continental. She thought for a moment, then grabbed his coke-bottle glasses and tossed them into the woods behind her before ramming him in the spine with a palm, knocking him into the luggage compartment, then slamming the trunk. If the kid was somehow able to Houdini himself out from the car, he'd be blind as a bat as he attempted his getaway.

Besides, by that time this thing would be over . . . one way or another.

Kippy turned but noticed something missing.

The yowling had ceased.

Kippy started to run.

CHAPTER 46

A hand grasped the back of my collar and belt buckle, and I was airborne again, dwarf-tossed across the yard, landing on the hard dirt of Feist's lower driveway. I struggled to my knees, but Man-mountain grabbed me by the throat, lifting me like a rag doll, legs dangling, and marched me to the back side of the fishing shack. As we turned the corner, I caught a quick glance at the lake. No witnesses to my murder. And then the view was gone. I was thrown against the wood siding of Feist's cabin.

I bounced hard; fell to my knees in the spot where I'd nose-dived to hide from that fishing boat only hours earlier. My girls were going insane, barking mad in the shack's bedroom behind me. I looked up. Man-mountain stood where the CACC truck had been parked, a gun with some kind of bar on its end pointed at my face.

"I like you, dog man," Callum's driver said. "You blew me away at Weeks's office, you really did. And making us chase your ass out here of all places. Like I said before, you got spunk. Hell, I'm proud of you, kiddo, but all good things must come to an end . . . which may be more proverb than idiom." He appeared lost in thought for a second before his attention returned to me. "Where's the girl?"

I looked up at the tower of a man. "We went our separate ways in Chicago."

Man-mountain struck in a flash. The tip of his cowboy boot smashed into my gut. Hard. I snapped backward into the wall again, and then dropped to my hands and knees, sucking air. The dogs barked louder. The man in the fancy brown suit—Feist's fake neighbor and the figure formerly behind the door—strolled back down the driveway, a smirk on his face, with something glinting in his right hand . . . and I suddenly realized who he was.

I'd seen some of his work in a burned-out warehouse in the Fulton River District last summer.

A wave of nausea washed over me, and I began to throw up.

CHAPTER 47

"Don't get puke on me or I'll stab you in the fucking heart."

I leaned backward against the cabin wall at an awkward tilt, pinned by Cappelli Jr.'s forearm against my chest. Man-mountain stood yards away, where the ground jutted upward as the hill rose above the lake, his gun held at his side, pointed down. Cappelli Jr. twisted his special pair of brass knuckles in front of my face, showing me the sharpened center spike.

"I call these fuckers Goldy because they're gold-plated, except the spear tip is silver."

I gulped air, hoping the nausea would pass, hoping not to be sick again, wishing to be anywhere but here, any time but now. The chorus of barks and snarls continued uninterrupted.

Cappelli's face was inches from mine—so close as to be out of focus—but there was something off, something about his expression, his mouth. He caught me staring, his features grew dark . . . and he chopped at my chin with the bottom brass of his deadly knuckles.

Shards of pain spiked through my skull. When it cleared, seconds later, he was still there, still inches away . . . smiling.

"Now the big guy asked you a question, and a pretty important one considering our current circumstances, but you thought you'd be cute," the young mobster said, a glint in his eye, and I realized how much he was enjoying himself. "So

I'm going to ask the big guy's question one more time, and the last thing you want to be with me is *cute*." He stared at me. "Where's the girl?"

"She dropped me here to look for evidence, and then took off for Madison," I said. It sounded plausible and, in my shaken state, it might come across as truth. "She knows an agent in the field office there."

Cappelli Jr. stared at me another second, uncertain of my admission. He pressed harder against my chest, pressed the tip of his knuckle-spike against my neck, and turned to look at Man-mountain.

Man-mountain shook his head.

Cappelli's head snapped back, a broad grin on his face. "You dumb motherfucker," he said. "Now I get me an eye."

I blinked uncontrollably as he brought the spike tip closer and closer to my left eye. When it came within a millimeter, I squeezed both eyes shut as though that could somehow save me. I felt the cutting begin. I opened my mouth to scream, but a hand cupped against it. The pressure against my chest released. I raised my arms, but Cappelli hit me, a hard left hook to my ear, and I sank back into the wall.

"Don't you fucking scream and don't you fucking puke." Cappelli Jr. was an inch from my face. "That was just a trial run, motherfucker."

My head rang. I blinked open my eyes, still had vision in both. Cappelli had cut me, all right, but a half-inch slash below my left socket. I felt the blood dripping down my face.

"You may need a few stitches there, *pal*." Cappelli Jr. turned toward Man-mountain for validation, and then turned back. "Last time, motherfucker. You going to be cute?"

I shook my head.

"Any more of your bullshit and I'll pop your eyeball like a grape," he said, his eyebrows raised. "Where's the fucking girl?"

"I came here to find evidence," I said, half-heartedly. "Officer

Gimm never left Chicago. She's trying to connect with Special Agent Squires."

The words rang hollow. Not even the squirrels or rabbits or earthworms about Peter Feist's cabin believed me, but Cappelli Jr. twisted about to look at Callum's driver.

"Take his eyes," Man-mountain said.

CHAPTER 48

Vira scampered from the bedroom, circled the main cabin room, and backed toward Feist's old sofa. She stared at the kitchen's open window above the linoleum countertop; the one Kippy had earlier slipped through. Vira dashed the short width of the cabin and threw herself into the air, landed on the linoleum counter, skidding, nails scratching metal as both front paws slid into the sink. She steadied herself, backed onto the countertop, and let go with a staccato of barks and yaps. It was then that Delta Dawn and Maggie May ran into the main room and stared up at her.

Vira flew through the kitchen window.

"I'm in uncharted territory here, motherfucker," Cappelli Jr. said, swirling the knuckle-spike in front of my eyes. "Let's see, do I come in from the side or underneath."

He'd kicked my feet out from beneath me, dropped on my chest, his knees pinning my arms. My head lay in the dirt against the cabin wall. I tried wiggling, kneeing him in the back, but he slammed another left hook against my ear.

"Has the patient any preference for his procedure today?" Cappelli Jr. asked. The man was insane, clearly enjoying this, savoring every last detail.

"Cut the shit," Man-mountain said. He'd moved toward the

cabin corner, still near the incline, staring off at the water, gun still in his hand, still aimed at the ground. It didn't appear he cared to witness my upcoming surgery. "Let's get this fucker done."

Then Man-mountain's demeanor changed—a jolt in expression as though he'd just seen Nessie emerge from Rock Lake. His gun began to rise. Immediately, Vira was between me and Cappelli, her paws dancing about my chest, her jaws clamping on Cappelli's right wrist, the one holding his gold-plated brass knuckles.

Cappelli Jr. screeched as though his face were on fire, leaped to his feet, nearly sixty pounds of Vira hanging off his wrist. He jerked his arm and Vira tumbled to the ground. Cappelli took off running—shrieking for all the world to hear—with Vira hot on his tail, nipping at his ass as they both disappeared into the woods. A second later Maggie May bounded over me, joining in on the hunt.

I propped up on my elbows, and Delta Dawn was by my side, snarling at Man-mountain, baring her teeth. Man-mountain's gun was back in play, this time aimed at Delta.

"If that dog moves an inch, I'll kill it."

I put a hand on my collie's neck. "Easy, girl, easy."

"How 'bout Cappelli Junior?" Man-mountain said and began to laugh. He touched a knuckle to the corner of an eye as though wiping a tear. "Folded like limp foreskin. More Fredo Corleone than James Caan."

Unsure what to say, I pulled myself to my knees.

"How bad is that going to be?" he asked, motioning where Cappelli Jr. and my dogs had bolted.

"They're protecting me from him," I replied, "but they're not killers."

"I'm going to let the dickbag think he needs rabies shots—the ones they give in the navel," Man-mountain said. "Look, Reid, you never asked for any of this shit. It's not your fault Cappelli's pal fumbled the ball."

Cappelli's pal?

The big man continued, "You were just doing your job, a working stiff like the rest of us, and you happened to fall in the outhouse. But it's blindfold and cigarette time. I'll make this quick."

"You don't care where Officer Gimm is?"

"You already told me. By trying to send us away, it means she's coming back, probably with a bucket of chicken," he said. "And, who knows, we may not even get to her if I have to rush Boy Dillinger to the hospital."

I stared up at him. "Please don't hurt my dogs. Delta here is fifteen and nearly blind. I have no idea how she made it through that window."

"Once you're gone, frankly, I don't give a shit about the golden. And your collies mean nothing to me," he said as he leveled the gun my way. "You ready?"

"Can I send her away?" I looked at Delta Dawn, who stood frozen next to me, growling softly at Callum's driver.

An imperceptible nod. "If I like someone, kiddo, I'll give them a few seconds to get good with God. And since dog's a reverse palindrome—you got five."

I burned a moment wondering what the hell that meant, and then sat on a foot and knee next to my farm collie.

"Delta girl," I said, choking up. I ran a forearm across my face. It came back covered with blood and snot. My collie looked sideways at me, still growling. "Delta honey." I reached to touch the back of her neck but dove forward instead. "Sic!"

CHAPTER 49

The dogs barking frightened Kippy.

The dogs no longer barking terrified her.

Kippy'd heard no gunshots and she intuited they'd have to use guns on the dogs. She hoped the girls had given Mace enough warning to slam the windows and maybe upend the kitchen table against the front door. She hoped the dogs would throw Callum's driver and the second attacker for a loop, giving her enough time to get back to the cabin.

Kippy jogged through the woods, a swift pace, doing her best to keep quiet. A lot of good she'd be if Callum's driver heard her coming and took her out before she even made it to Feist's property.

Then a scream stopped her in her tracks—an ungodly bloodcurdler she prayed didn't belong to Mace. Kippy began sprinting, Beretta in both hands, scanning the forest path in front of her, hoping no unknowns waited in the brush. The scream didn't stop, not right away, and suddenly it sounded closer. She ducked behind an evergreen. The shriek stopped, but now a commotion, someone was coming her way . . . someone bat-out-of-helling it back to the perceived safety of the Lincoln Continental. Kippy peeked from behind the tree. Some dark-haired male in a brown suit was flying toward her at an Olympic pace, abject terror smeared across his features, with Vira and Maggie hot on his heels.

Kippy broke from her concealment, slanting downward to meet him. The man never saw her coming, not even as the side of the Beretta smashed into his mouth, shattering teeth and tissue. He dropped to the forest floor like a sack of cement.

Kippy looked at Vira and swore the golden retriever read her mind. Vira veered on a dime, doubling back to the cabin, back to help Mace. Maggie May circled the prone figure, snarling. It was then that Kippy realized who lay at her feet.

"Get it away," Cappelli Jr. said through busted teeth and blood. "Get that thing the fuck away from me."

She kicked him in the ass. "Get your arms around that goddamned tree or she'll chew your nuts off."

Kippy had never seen anyone move as fast as the young mobster; he bellied forward and wrapped his arms around the base of a cedar tree. His broken mouth seemed to be the least of his concerns. Kippy handcuffed Cappelli as Maggie sat growling nearby. She yanked the cuffs tight to make sure Cappelli Jr. wouldn't be going anywhere, not caring that her action caused more blood to ooze from his dripping wrist.

Kippy looked at Maggie May and said, "Mace."

Maggie lunged forward, bit Cappelli in the armpit, and then turned and followed in Vira's footsteps back to Feist's cabin.

"Oh, god," Cappelli Jr. sobbed, blood and saliva hanging from his mouth, tears streaming. "Oh, god—I'm bleeding. I'm bleeding."

Kippy held the Beretta against the back of his head. His whining ceased immediately.

"If Mace is hurt," Kippy said, "you're a dead man."

Her finger lingered on the trigger, and then she pulled herself away from the impulse, turned, and headed toward Feist's cabin.

CHAPTER 50

I was becoming an accomplished liar.

Delta Dawn is not fifteen years old. She's eight. And Delta is anything but blind; my farm collie has eyesight like an eagle. Delta had attended a thousand training sessions with me, was often my show dog . . . and she knew each and every command by heart.

Delta blasted off the ground like a rocket ship, sinking her teeth into the flesh under Man-mountain's thumb and the back of his gun hand, clamping down with a vise-like grip. I don't care how big an ass-kicker you are, when a fifty-pound farm collie goes for you in attack mode, it'll throw off your A game. Two shots from Man-mountain's pistol spit into the dirt where Delta and I had been an instant before.

I kept rolling and grabbed the bite-stick-slash-police-baton Kippy had dropped by the cabin corner after smashing in the kitchen windowpane. I twisted about, flicking up the baton, causing the two additional shafts to expand and lock in place. It was now twenty-six inches of high-carbon steel. Delta clung to Man-mountain's hand, her legs in perpetual motion, claws whipping against the towering man's long coat as he shook his arm in some frenzied tempo only he could hear.

"Run!" I screamed, holding the baton above my head like a crazed samurai.

Delta dropped to the ground, scrambled backward as

Man-mountain whipped his head sideways at the new peril. With all my might I brought the baton down hard on his gun hand—on the backside of his palm. His pistol and silencer dropped to the dirt, his left hand cupping his injury. I drew back the baton, a batter at the plate, and swung for Man-mountain's head, wanting to knock it into the bleachers. But the big man was lightning. He caught the top section in his left hand, wrenched it from my grip, brought it across his chest, and backhanded me in the temple.

I was on my ass, against the cabin wall again; legs sprawled out in front of me, wondering how I'd gotten there. My ears rang. I felt like I should rise but had forgotten how. The only reason my skull hadn't cracked open like Humpty Dumpty was that Man-mountain had let me have it with the baton's foam handle . . . and I sat there staring up at him, oddly disengaged, as the circumstance was remedied. Man-mountain flipped the baton into the air, caught it by its foam grip, and stepped my way. My bell had been thoroughly rung and—like an injured player on the field watching as concerned faces rushed to help—I watched my impending extinction with a remote detachment. In some through-the-looking-glass manner, I fully understood how this was the part where I get beaten to death; but, like a bird crashing into a plate-glass window, I had a stunned lack of involvement, and my overriding reflection was *I'll be damned, he's ambidextrous.*

Man-mountain lifted the baton and suddenly Delta Dawn was attached to his inner thigh. My girl had disobeyed a direct command and returned to save my life. Man-mountain brought the base of the baton down on her head—once, twice—like picking at a block of ice, before she dropped with a yelp. Delta twisted about, prepping another attack, when the baton swung sideways, smashing across my dog's shoulder, and sending her tumbling. The bastard turned, and though my farm collie was barely moving, he headed her way to finish the job.

I struggled to my knees. Cappelli's brass knuckles, Goldy,

lay within reach and I scooped them into my right hand. Tears streamed down my face and I willed myself to rise, but I couldn't. Somehow I managed to fling Cappelli's evil little weapon at Man-mountain as hard as I could, which wasn't much at this point, but the knuckles bounced off the back of Man-mountain's head. This didn't do much except return his ire toward me.

And there lay Delta Dawn on the ground, somehow still wiggling. My poor beautiful little collie was a scarlet mess.

Bile flowed from my mouth, but I stayed on my knees, facing the son of a bitch. He held up the baton for me to see—drops of Delta's blood dripping at the base—and again he stepped my way. I was functioning at maybe twenty percent so I didn't hear the snarl until Man-mountain snapped his head backward.

Vira flew off the hill like something out of a Jack London novel, connecting with the big man's face a heartbeat before landing, twisting about like an F5 tornado, suddenly leaping, his left forearm between her jaws. The baton tumbled to the dirt, and Man-mountain punched at the whirlwind attacking him with his injured right fist. Man-mountain's cheek, where Vira had nicked him in mid-flight, was shredded, dripping blood. His fedora had been knocked to the ground.

And I spotted something out of character in the big man's eyes.

Fear.

I realized at that moment something I suspected Vira already knew—what with her being two steps ahead of anyone else in the room. Something Delta had also known, something that had brought her back into the fray. This was not a win-win situation. And there could be no happy middle ground.

Either Man-mountain dies . . . or we do.

I pushed myself to my feet, maybe now at thirty percent. Man-mountain switched tactics, grabbed a fistful of fur at the back of Vira's neck, yanked her off his forearm in a spray of crimson, and slammed her to the ground. Vira cried out in pain, bounced up, and circled behind him.

I marched in, throwing fists, pounding his stomach with every ounce of energy left inside me because no one fucks with my dogs. No one. But it was like hitting a brick wall. And suddenly he had me by the throat again, lifting me up, cutting off oxygen, choking me to death, and I stared into Man-mountain's eyes.

He had crossed over—was pure animal now—feral, a wild beast . . . like my dogs . . . like me.

Then a flash of movement between us, his mouth turned a distorted *O* in a silent scream, and he flung me against the cabin wall. I ricocheted off, smashed to the hard ground; my chin now throbbing in pain. There wasn't a square inch that didn't screech in agony.

I looked up.

Maggie May had locked her jaws below Man-mountain's navel and, a blur later, Vira found his most-vulnerable spot. She'd attached herself to the back of Man-mountain's neck. Callum's enforcer spun about in a demented danse macabre, striking at Vira futilely, trying to smash her down. He swung wide; my golden's body a helicopter blade, and then dropping. Man-mountain's hands shot to Maggie May as she refused to let go of her hold on his abdomen. A left hand felt its way to her right paw, and he snapped it outward. Maggie dropped to three legs with a cry that broke my heart.

She hobbled for safety. Man-mountain raised a boot to stomp her life away, but abruptly he froze, staring my way. I'd made it to my feet and realized I'd been screaming at the top of my lungs. I came at him in a fighter's stance, fists held high, as Maggie stumbled to the cabin wall and collapsed in pain. I was at five percent, maybe, but this was all for show anyhow. I had nothing left. But I'd seen something Man-mountain hadn't—Vira again mounting the hill behind him. Man-mountain threw a roundhouse, but I was already backing away. It glanced off my forehead, and I went down on my ass, mostly from the breeze.

Vira leaped and connected, riding the back of his neck again, a swing ride at the state fair, and as Man-mountain spun frantically to shake her off him, I saw his neck and the top of his long coat were drenched in blood. Then another new tactic; he stumbled backward into the hill. They both hit the ground hard, and Vira scrambled out from under his shoulder. He shot an elbow into her rib cage and she limped away, out of his reach to regroup.

I clawed at the ground to get up.

Gravity declined to comply.

I was at one percent.

"Fuck this," Man-mountain said as he reached for his pistol and stood.

He swung the gun toward me and there was an explosion. A puff of crimson off his bicep spun Man-mountain sideways. He saw something he didn't like and raised the pistol, but there were three more explosions in rapid progression, and three more puffs of red in the center of his chest. Man-mountain dropped his pistol. He sunk to his knees, his features frozen in astonishment, perhaps coming to terms with his own demise.

"I got him, Wabs," Kippy said, walking into the clearing. "I got him."

She held the gun on Callum's driver until he dropped face-first into the dirt.

CHAPTER 51

Dispatcher: *Where is your emergency?*

Unidentified Male (breathing heavily): *There's been a shooting. Um, a bunch of screaming and then shots were fired.*

Dispatcher: *Where are you located?*

Unidentified Male: *I'm on the lake. Um, Rock Lake. Off old Route 9—um, the east road—but the shooting's not here, not at my cabin.*

Dispatcher: *Where's the shooting? Where's that address?*

Unidentified Male: *I don't know. I was on the dock and outta nowhere there were these thumping noises, like hitting a canoe paddle against a boat house or something and, um, dogs were barking up a storm, but they stopped and then came a scream—like, um, a guy, it was a male voice—screaming bloody murder.*

Dispatcher: *Where are you at now?*

Unidentified Male: *My wife and I, we've locked ourselves inside our cabin. There were more noises and then came the screaming again, but I think a different voice, um, maybe a different guy. And I ran inside for the landline when the shooting started.*

Dispatcher: *Could you tell where on Rock Lake the shots came from?*

Unidentified Male: *That's the problem—the sound carries around here, it carries and echoes and I couldn't see where it was* coming from. It could be the other side of the lake—um, the west side—or it could be ten cabins down. There's been dead silence since the gunshots and we don't know what happened to the screaming guys. Jesus Christ, I hope they're—um, Jesus Christ—the screams were . . . I hope they're still alive.

Dispatcher: *Okay, sir, I need you to calm down a second and tell me your exact location. Where are you at?*

Dispatcher (talking to someone else): *Reported gunshots and screams on Rock Lake. Repeat, gunshots on Rock Lake. I'll get you the caller's address off Route 9—the east side of Rock. Caller's not clear on where the shots were fired so sending all available units to circle the lake.*

CHAPTER 52

Okay, Mace is breathing . . . and he has a pulse . . . and he just moaned . . . thank you, God.

Kippy then looked from Maggie May—who lay whimpering against the side of the cabin, one paw twisted at an impossible angle—to Delta Dawn—who lay in the dirt, bleeding from her head, blinking drops of crimson from her eyes. It was all Kippy could do to keep from rolling Man-mountain over and emptying the rest of the Beretta's magazine into his face.

Instead, she darted inside Feist's cabin, tore through the undersized bedroom closet, grabbing at the towels she'd spotted earlier. She added a half dozen bottles of water on top of her pile and shot back outside, to Maggie, where she began wrapping a towel around the farm collie as though taking a newborn from a bath. She kept the towel-tucking away from Maggie's broken paw, and then dribbled water over Maggie's mouth, hoping little sips would help.

Tears tumbled onto the fur of Maggie's throat, and Kippy realized they were coming from her.

She moved Maggie as gently as possible near Mace—hoping that would provide her comfort and security, some kind of solace. Then she attended Delta—wrapping her in a towel, dribbling water onto her lips, using the rest of the bottle to rinse the blood away from Delta's face, away from her eyes—and also carried her near Mace.

Kippy then drenched the single washcloth she'd pilfered and wiped softly at the blood and dirt on Mace's face. His eyes fluttered, and then closed.

"Stay with them, Vira," she said, standing. "Stay with them."

Kippy cut into the woods, sprinting full bore, angling upward, heading toward the gravel road, toward where she'd abandoned the dog mobile. It was imperative she get Mace to whatever passed for a hospital or ER in Lake Mills as soon as possible. She'd feed whoever was on duty a line of shit— John Doe had been involved in a car accident or bad fall, a plane crash or whatever—and once the doctors began treating Mace, she'd make a speedy departure, find the nearest veterinary clinic and feed them a line of BS as well. She'd make sure the sister collies were in good hands, shake a finger at the dog mobile, and give them Paul Lewis's number.

Then she'd have to get serious about the flash drive—hit up the library again, see if they could rig her up with a PC that wasn't read only. Or . . . wait a minute . . . Callum's computer guy was locked in the Lincoln's trunk—didn't he have all sorts of gadgets she could utilize?

And speaking of Superintendent Callum, how the hell did his men find them so soon?

This was the second trap Kippy had walked them into in as many days. Wabs's death would be an open wound— something that'd never heal—but if Mace died or wound up with some kind of brain damage, or if Maggie or Delta were so critically injured they had to be put down, Kippy wasn't sure what she'd do.

She'd recently told Mace he had a screw loose, but Kippy hadn't meant it in a bad way and, as a cop, she'd witnessed an entire spectrum of loose screws. Sure, Mace was about as goofy as that new puppy of his, but he made her laugh—often out loud—and often when there really wasn't that much to laugh about. And the way he loved his dogs, his *kids* as he called them . . . Mace was a good guy.

And Mace had more courage in his little finger than the over-testosteroned lunkheads she'd been wasting her time with.

Kippy wished she could return to the moment Mace had kissed her in that over-scrubbed kitchen of his . . . she might have handled it differently.

And based upon the past couple of days, there were several things she'd handle differently.

Kippy swung open the dog mobile's door, hopped inside, twisted the key in the ignition, and headed back to get the gang.

CHAPTER 53

Evidently, I lost consciousness for several minutes.

Someone was licking at my hand, and then a soft nibbling began at the web between my thumb and forefinger. Vira gave a gentle bite, then a stronger one, trying to pull me back into the land of the living.

"I'm here, Vira," I said, opening my eyes and pulling my hand away. She'd left a couple of slight puncture marks and a tiny smear of blood. "Hey, that's not a very nice wake-up call."

I'd read once that casualty dogs in World War I could distinguish between the dead and unconscious. If a soldier was dead, the dog would move on; if the soldier was injured, the dog would return to friendly lines for help; however, if the soldier was dying, the dog would remain with him to offer comfort as he passed away—accompanying him—so he wouldn't feel left alone. There's something terribly bittersweet and wonderful in all that, but, as I stretched out my limbs, I hoped Vira wasn't operating in that mode.

I looked around. Man-mountain lay in the motionless heap where he'd collapsed. And my heart broke again when I saw that a bath towel Kippy must have pilfered from Feist's cabin had been wrapped around Delta Dawn. Her fur was awash in crimson, her head lolled from side to side as she tried to peek my way.

There was a low whimpering on my other side. Maggie May was loosely wrapped in another bath towel. Her right front leg hung at an unnatural angle.

"Oh, Maggie," I said, and put a palm on her back as gently as possible.

I sat upright. My face and neck were moist. Two empty water bottles lay near my feet, along with a damp washcloth that had likely been appropriated with Feist's old towels. Obviously Kippy's work, which begged the question—where the hell was Kippy? As if to answer my query, I heard the CACC truck before I spotted it backing down Feist's driveway.

Kippy stepped from the driver's seat. She looked ten exits past stressed out but tossed a crooked smile my way. "Nice of you to join us, Mace; you had me terrified," she said. "Time to get the hell out of here."

"I've got to get you to an ER."

I shook my head. "I need to get my girls to a pet hospital." I sat in the passenger seat, held Maggie in my lap, atop another of Feist's cabin pillows, with Delta, still bundled in Feist's beach towel, lying on my left side, and Vira in the back seat. I listened to Maggie yelp at every bump or pothole, but Delta's continued silence scared me even more. And to make matters worse, Maggie had started to pant. Like humans, dogs can sink into shock after an injury, which causes an insufficient flow of blood to the body's tissues, which can then cause significant damage to their organs . . . even death. I'd poured water in the cup of my hand, but Maggie had no interest. "That's my number one concern."

Kippy peeked my way. "You look like you fell off a cliff."

"Doesn't matter," I said. "Maggie and Delta are my number one concern."

Kippy provided a one-minute update on the way to Manmountain's car; she told me about Feist's flash drive, about

Cappelli Jr. being left cuffed to a tree, and how there was a computer guru or someone locked inside the Lincoln Continental's trunk.

Kippy had been a busy girl. Just like her to knock some pieces off the chessboard.

"Can you even drive?"

"I'll find a way," I said. "Your number one concern is to get those files to Agent Squires and get his ass out here before Callum sends more men."

Kippy backed the dog mobile into a driveway three or four doors down from Feist's cabin, past a Continental shrouded in the tree line, and halfway down the first bend where we could no longer be seen from the access road. Kippy clambered out with Vira and both jogged back up toward Man-mountain's sedan. I eased out of the passenger seat as softly as possible, lay Maggie and pillow back down, and buckled her in as best I could for our ride to town.

Then I stumbled to the front of the truck, bent over, stuck a finger down my throat, and threw up more green bile. I was anything but thirsty so I dumped the rest of the water bottle over my head. I inhaled gasp after gasp of country air and eavesdropped as I heard Kippy order someone to *shut the hell up.*

A minute later Kippy jogged back down the driveway, Vira at her heels. "I found some Advil and a .38 in the Lincoln's glove compartment."

She dumped four pills into my palm and handed me another bottle of water. I downed the pills with a sip of the water. Then she stared at me, eyes brimming with apprehension.

"What?"

"A squad car drove past," she said. "I heard the gravel and ducked behind a tire."

"Just one car?"

"I guess if they knew anything, they'd be out here in force."

"Some screaming," I said. "A few shots."

"Yeah. I assume someone called it in, but noise carries

around here and, hopefully, no one has any idea where the shots came from."

I took another mouthful of fresh air. "It's after school, so maybe kids are farting around with firecrackers or maybe some guy's sighting a rifle."

Kippy was a step ahead and said, "I'm going to jog over. If the squad car is at Feist's, Vira and I will come for you at the vet." She pointed up toward the Continental. "If we don't show up at the vet, that means we're still here."

I watched Kippy and my golden disappear into the woods from a side mirror as I turned the CACC truck left onto the access road. I called information when I hit the highway into Lake Mills and kept repeating the number they'd provided as I poked it into the burner phone.

"We're getting there," I said to a soundless Delta and poor little Maggie May, whose panting was now coming at a faster clip. "It's going to be okay, girls. I promise it's going to be okay."

The receptionist at the Lake Mills Pet Hospital answered and, after I informed her what was coming so she could prep the vets, I forced her to stay on the line so she could guide me in, providing directions like a human road map, right until I pulled up at their front entrance.

CHAPTER 54

Kippy cut through the wooded hill at nearly a full sprint, Vira by her side. Sixty yards out, she dropped to her knees. There was no squad car that she could spot from her vantage point, no startled officer radioing in news of his discovery. Kippy lifted the binoculars from the CACC truck up to her eyes and scanned about. There was no sign of activity, even if the squad car was blocked by Feist's cabin. There were no cops circling the structure with guns drawn, and no interest coming from the lakeside.

Police Superintendent Callum's driver still lay prone in the dirt.

Alone.

So Lake Mills PD gets a call, Kippy surmised, but the caller has no notion of where the screams and shots and hellishness came from, so a squad car or two or three are dispatched to circle the lake, to see if the officers hear any additional gunfire or if any cabin owner flags them down. Kippy had responded to similar calls herself—calls that ultimately led nowhere. It became clear she and Vira wouldn't be racing back, jumping in the Continental, and flooring it to the veterinarian clinic after all.

On the jog back, Kippy stopped by Cappelli Jr. "Your big friend is dead."

The news didn't seem to faze him one way or another.

Cappelli's concern had more to do with his own existential threat as Vira, snarling lightly, circled him twice . . . finally coming to a rest, her muzzle inches from his face.

"Don't let it hurt me," Cappelli Jr. lisped through swollen lips. "Please don't let it hurt me."

"Vira's a she, dumbass," Kippy said. "And members of her family got hurt in all this bullshit. If we get bad news from the vet, we'll be back for a final visit."

"I'm fucking bleeding here."

"You haven't lost more than half a cup of blood."

"Fucking bears'll smell it," Cappelli said. "They'll fucking smell it and come for me."

"Then you better hope they feed on your friend first."

The two left the sniveling Cappelli and returned to the back of the Lincoln Continental. Kippy rapped on the trunk.

"It's steamy in here," Callum's computer guy said from inside the luggage compartment.

"Your big friend is dead."

There was no response or acknowledgment.

"Your other friend is cuffed to a tree."

After a short moment, the voice from the trunk said, "Cappelli is not my friend."

"It's urgent I send files to Special Agent Len Squires, both his work and home email, maybe even text them to his smartphone," Kippy said, "but I don't have any addresses or phone numbers."

Another moment passed before the computer guy said, "I can help with that."

CHAPTER 55

"Maggie's here," I shouted to the room, carrying my wounded collie into Lake Mills Pet Hospital, striding past the reception desk where the girl I'd been on the phone with pointed at a woman in a white smock. The woman waved me toward a side room. "Delta's in the van," I continued shouting as a second lab-coated woman rushed for the door. "Head trauma. And watch her ribs."

Once inside the side room, I lay Maggie May as softly as possible onto the stainless-steel examination table, kissed her on the forehead, and got the hell out of the veterinarian's way. An assistant came in with a tray holding two hypodermic needles, which I assumed were for pain or antibiotics.

"Who did this to her?" the veterinarian asked, a hand on Maggie's neck and iron in her voice.

I could barely choke out the words. "A bad man."

"Has he been arrested?" she asked, a softer tone, perhaps realizing it'd not been me.

"He won't be doing this again."

"You don't look so good yourself, mister," the vet said, and went back to her examination as her assistant administered the shots.

"Do you have a restroom I can use?"

"Down the hall by where you came in."

I rushed back past the reception desk, past an elderly

woman holding a cat, past a magazine rack and coffee station, ducked into the restroom, shut the door, and dry-heaved into the toilet. My vomiting done, I hoped, I splashed water on my face and ran a hand through my hair. I glanced in the mirror. My head looked as though it'd be more natural at the end of a tether ball rope. The top of my T-shirt was red with blood and stained by some clammy green stuff I didn't want to think about.

I walked back into the lobby. The cat woman stared up at me. The receptionist was now facing the front windows, her back to me, whispering into her cell phone. The veterinarian and her assistant stood in the doorway of Maggie's examination room. The second veterinarian who'd gone for Delta stood outside another room.

They all stared my way.

And it sunk in that either the receptionist or cat-lady had recognized me.

I took a deep breath, pointed a finger toward the two veterinarians who'd begun treating my collies. "Take care of my girls."

And then I was out the door. I jumped behind the wheel of the CACC truck and as I sped out of the animal clinic's parking lot, I spotted the receptionist in the entryway, still talking on the phone, now with additional animation. If Paul Lewis had held tough in not reporting his missing dog mobile, it no longer mattered.

I sped down the street, but, once out of eyesight, I took the first left and another left at the next block, doubling back, stepping on the gas, and blowing through four-way stops. I heard sirens before I hit the highway leading back to Rock Lake; thank god they came from far off—behind me—a mile away. But how the hell big was the Lake Mills Police Department? I worried about any squad cars dispatched to the lake over reports of gunshots, prayed they'd found nothing and had already worked their way back to town empty-handed. It would not be amusing to pass one on the way back who'd just been clued in on the dog mobile. I pressed down on the accelerator—kicked the truck up to eighty—gunning to make the access road as soon as possible, hoping all squad cars were back in town, wasting valuable time threading the streets and avenues of Lake Mills in their initial search for little ol' me.

I slowed a little when I hit the gravel road, not much, and slammed the brakes before turning into the driveway with the Lincoln Continental hidden in the tree line. Kippy was talking on a cell phone and jumped backward onto the grass. Then she flagged me forward, told me to park the truck down by the cabin where it couldn't be seen from the road, before returning to her phone call. I almost hit the brakes a second time as I passed the Continental. A young male sat against a rear tire, sucking down a bottle of water. A laptop was off to the side, out of his reach. His legs had been duct-taped from his knees down to his ankles.

I parked the CACC dog mobile in a grove of pine next to a boat shed at the bottom of the hill where it wouldn't be seen from the lake or from the road above. We were lucky no one was home at this particular cabin—which, compared to Feist's shack—looked like the Courtyard Marriott. I could only imagine how screwed we'd have been if we'd attempted these antics over a weekend or during summer vacation.

"How are they?" Kippy asked, her and Vira coming to greet me as I headed up the driveway.

I shrugged and mumbled a hasty account of my recent ordeal.

Kippy held up what I took to be the computer guy's smartphone. "Special Agent Squires wants us to sit tight," Kippy said. "He says they'll be here in an hour."

Kippy jogged back up to bring the Continental and her computer-guy captive down by the cabin so no local cops could spot them in the tree line if they returned to the lake. A wave of light-headedness washed over me and I sat down on a patch of grass. I stared into the woods, in the direction of Feist's cabin. The sky had become overcast and the forest locked foreboding, like something Hansel and Gretel had once trekked through.

Vira was in my lap a second later, wiggling and licking at my face. Tears came to my eyes and I hugged my golden retriever for all I was worth.

CHAPTER 56

Unfuckingreal.

The last thirty-eight hours had been unfuckingreal.

Police Superintendent Gerald Callum knew something was wrong when Cordov Woods didn't check in at the established time. Uncharacteristic. The big man hadn't called in, nor had he returned Callum's call—not that Callum was dumb enough to call Woods from his own phone or leave a message, but Woods would have recognized the burner number and moved heaven and earth to get back in touch with him. And that could only mean one of two things, both of which sent Superintendent Callum's blood pressure skyrocketing— Cordov Woods had either been taken into custody . . . or Cordov Woods was dead.

There could be no third option.

Come eight o'clock that first night, Callum had called in a marker from a Wisconsin state trooper and had him cruise past Peter Feist's cabin on Rock Lake. The statie reported back an hour later.

"What the hell have you gotten me into, Callum?" the trooper said. "The place is crawling with feds. A bunch of the pricks were lining the road. Christ, one of them snapped a pic of my ID panel." A long second passed before the trooper continued. "Do not call me again. I don't know you. I've never met you." The Wisconsin trooper clicked off.

So Callum spent a sleepless night speculating . . . and plotting.

If Cordov Woods were in custody, Woods would keep his mouth shut—he wouldn't say jack shit. And if Cordov Woods were dead, well, then the man would have even less to say. And as far as Woods chauffeuring Callum about town now and again, hell, that was a staffing issue—it had nothing to do with him. Superintendent Callum could call upon a full rotation of drivers—each of whom he knew about as much as he knew the old guy who shined his shoes at Union Station.

Callum could survive Cordov Woods. Of that he was certain.

But the kid with the hacking skills worried him. Callum had never met Jethro in person, for obvious reasons, but the computer whiz would damn sure know chapter and verse about the data Superintendent Callum had him ferreting into—manipulating . . . revising . . . deleting. And the kid could sing a helluva siren song to Special Agent in Charge Len Squires, only it wouldn't be the Federal Bureau of Investigation the siren sent crashing into the rocks, it'd be Callum himself. But if the kid had no proof, he'd just be another punk trying to cut a deal.

Callum would deny everything and lawyer up.

Officer Gimm and the dog man were still considered fugitives. The latest news he'd caught on the television that morning had been the dog man's ex-wife pleading with him, evidently interrupting her latest honeymoon to stand before cameras and beg Mason Reid to turn himself in to the police before anyone else got hurt. It had been a faultless performance; Reid's ex couldn't have done better had Callum coached her himself. Sure, Rock Lake may be *crawling with feds,* but without solid evidence, Callum calculated, SAC Squires wouldn't be able to pry Gimm and the dog man out of the box Callum had placed them in.

Being in the dark—not having a clue what was going down outside his office walls—was definitely unfamiliar territory. It was madness and Superintendent Callum had spent the next day on pins and needles, holed up in his office, having canceled all appointments. But by evening, Callum had begun to feel more confident and in charge of the situation—more like himself—when the call he should have known was coming finally occurred.

"Where's my kid?" Frank Cappelli Sr. demanded without salutation.

"What?" Callum replied.

"Don't play dumb, Gerald," Cappelli Sr. said. "Your guy borrowed my kid to help fix the bullshit yesterday . . . and I've not heard from him since."

"I spoke with Cordov this morning," Callum said into the cell phone he used only when speaking with Frank Cappelli Sr. "He said everything went well and they got back late last night."

"The bullshit got resolved?"

"Like I said, everything went well," Callum replied. He knew Cappelli Sr. wasn't about to mention any names over the phone. *Bullshit* was just a generic bucket Cappelli used. It stood for Siskin and Feist and Gimm and Reid. "No more worries. It's done."

"Then where's my kid?"

Callum felt his brain freeze. "Cordov said he dropped your son off at a bar or someplace."

There was a long pause before Cappelli Sr. said, "I spoke with Skokie. No new guests have arrived."

"Cordov's bringing the guests today," Callum said, knowing full well the mob boss was referring to the crematorium. "Hell, he's probably there right now as we speak."

Another lengthy pause. "Today is my wife's birthday, Gerald," Cappelli Sr. said. "We're having a party. And my kid would never miss his mother's birthday party. Never."

Callum felt his heart thump in his chest. "I don't know what to say, Frank. Maybe he met a girl."

There'd been a long silence between the two men.

"So we're on for tomorrow?" Cappelli Sr. said.

"Tomorrow?" Callum asked.

"If my kid's not back, you and I are on for tomorrow," Cappelli Sr. confirmed and hung up the phone.

It was then that Police Superintendent Gerald Callum had begun to panic. Who wouldn't after a call like that? If the unthinkable occurred and Cordov Woods had managed to get Cappelli's son killed, Callum was a dead man. If Cappelli's son was in police custody, Callum was a dead man.

Callum had phoned home, told his wife he had to work late and not to wait up. Callum then sat at his desk all night, working the bottle of Baileys without coffee this time. He could make a run for it of course. Callum had some money tucked away, actually quite a bit of cash, but he wondered who'd find him first—whose knock it would be on the motel room door—the FBI or Cappelli Sr.'s people.

Then Callum's thoughts metastasized like cancer around dog man and that goddamned golden retriever of his. He'd worked so hard, for so many decades, only to have it come crashing down around his ears . . . and all because of some goddamned thing that belonged on a leash.

Unfuckingreal.

He wondered if he should alert Carter Weeks, because if the dog man or Officer Gimm or that computer whiz kid they called Jethro had any hard evidence, they would most certainly be spilling the beans to SAC Squires as to what truly went down at City Hall. But then Callum thought *fuck it*. If it was truly over, he might as well let Carter Weeks—the man he considered his nephew and protégé—enjoy his last day or two as the Honorable Mayor of the Great City of Chicago.

As Superintendent Callum finished off the last of the Baileys, he heard the sounds of a new day dawning, the sounds of his staff in the outer office arriving for work. One of Callum's cell phones pinged on his desktop, and he recognized the number from where the text message had been sent—his man in the Special Prosecutions Bureau . . . his man who'd kept tabs on Peter Feist.

FBI agents sweeping the building. I'm in a bathroom stall. What the fuck is going on?

Callum leaned back in his chair and tried to process that message through a haze of exhaustion.

And alcohol.

And fury.

That's when he heard the commotion in his outer office—lots of movement and muffled commands.

Police Superintendent Gerald Callum opened his right-side desk drawer and peered inside.

CHAPTER 57

THREE WEEKS LATER

Bill loafed under the picnic table while Vira, Delta, and Sue sat next to me on the backyard incline, and we all watched as Maggie May pranced about the lawn on her remaining three legs. Maggie was now a tripod dog. Her right front leg had been so badly mangled by the late Cordov Woods that it had to be amputated by the Lake Mills veterinarian.

Maggie May is now . . . adjusting.

My vet, the eternally competent Doc Rawson, reviewed Maggie's file and agreed that Lake Mills had made all the right moves. She also explained how front-leg amputees have more difficulty adjusting as front legs account for the majority of a dog's balance and strength. Doc Rawson gives Maggie glucosamine for her joints, and Kippy and me and Vira and Delta and Bill and even Sue give Maggie plenty of TLC—tender loving care.

Delta Dawn got off easy. Thank god dogs are hardheaded critters. My farm collie underwent the full neurological exam, got to enjoy intravenous fluids, a regimen of pain relievers, a handful of stitches, as well as medication to decrease any brain swelling. Hell, as far as I know, Delta and I probably share the same concussion meds.

It's good to finally be back home. Sure, a safe house can be fun at first, but it gets old quickly. I'd spent the first two nights at Northwestern Memorial Hospital being monitored for MTBI—mild traumatic brain injury—yup, a concussion. Other damages on the docket included deeply bruised ribs, likely from my repeated introductions to the back wall of Peter Feist's cabin; twelve stitches under my left eye where Cappelli Jr. had begun his carving; various other nicks and scratches; and a chin that still felt as though it'd been smacked with a meat mallet. I even got two stitches where Vira bit me back into consciousness.

But as I watched my farm collie hobble about the backyard, I realized just how lucky I had been.

I also got to dodge most of the paperwork. I scored an ambulance ride to Northwestern Memorial with paramedics flashing lights in my eyes while Kippy walked Special Agent in Charge Len Squires and his team of investigators through the crime scene and other events of a long and turbulent day. FBI agents did question me twice at Northwestern. I answered all of their queries as honestly as possible but left out any theories vis-à-vis Vira's *special* ability.

Quite frankly, I felt a little let down. I didn't get the impression the agents were really that interested in yours truly. Among other things, files off of Feist's flash drive included both an audio file and a typed transcript of David Siskin's deposition. These are what Kippy and Superintendent Callum's computer guy, Jesse Aarestad, sent to SAC Len Squires's iPhone in order to pique his interest.

And pique Squires's interest they certainly had.

But what focused SAC Squires's interest like a laser sight was the treasure trove of Police Superintendent Gerald Callum data Jesse Aarestad, the young computer whiz who insisted upon being addressed as *Jethro,* had backed up to the cloud for safekeeping. Aarestad was a tad peculiar, not unlike your basic tech-nerd cliché, but he was bright enough to realize that a day might come when he'd need some kind of leverage, so he'd backed up to his personally customized and encrypted cloud service every file he'd hacked, cracked, or deleted for Superintendent Callum's benefit. There's even a video from City Hall with me in a featured role as *Terrified Male Yanking Fire Alarm*.

Aarestad's concealed files also led SAC Squires to the leak inside Cook County State's Attorney's Office—Superintendent Callum's Judas on the Special Prosecutions Bureau—who turned out to be none other than Peter Feist's right-hand man and executive administrator: Marty Kolles—the same son of a bitch that got all choked up when giving a eulogy at Feist's funeral. Squires figured they had enough to put Kolles away for three twenty-year terms. Consecutive terms, of course.

Kippy figures that Jethro Aarestad will ultimately skate.

The others? Not so much.

One of the reasons I'm home instead of watching bad movies at my CPD safe house is due to what happened to Frank Cappelli Sr. several nights ago. Although Cappelli Jr. remains in custody, Cappelli Sr. was arrested in SAC Squires's initial sweep, but he posted bail within hours. Perhaps it would have been best for Cappelli Sr. and his wife of thirty years had he not. The maid discovered them both—still in bed—last Friday morning. The missus had taken one shot to the forehead; Frank Cappelli Sr. took three. SAC Squires believes a decision had been made by others in the Outfit—said decision being that Cappelli Sr. would not be taking them down with him in case he got the notion that the feebs might lighten his sentence—or the sentence of his psychotic son—were he to sing them some lullabies. Squires figured no assassin had snuck past Cappelli's security team as much as Cappelli's security team had been ordered to stand down by the new powers that be.

As for Frank Cappelli Jr., he'd been singing like a canary. Alas, it was all *low-hanging fruit* per Agent Squires or *candy ass shit* per Officer Kippy Gimm. Perhaps it would knock five minutes off his four consecutive life terms.

About the time I was signing out of Northwestern Memorial,

SAC Squires made his move. Police Superintendent Gerald Callum must have caught wind of it as he pulled his service revolver and held it against the side of his head—the crooked cop thought to take the coward's way out—but he hesitated long enough for one of Squires's men to zap him with a Taser. Callum dropped to the floor and squirmed about next to an empty bottle of Baileys.

I'm sure Stateville Correctional Center will welcome the former Chicago police superintendent with open arms.

On the second day of my safe house interment, Kippy kidnapped me on a surprise field trip to the offices of the Michael J. McCarron Investment Group . . . the place where it had all begun. Just like Man-mountain let slip behind Feist's cabin at Rock Lake, *Cappelli's pal*, Michael J. McCarron, was far from the frightened church mouse everyone—Siskin, Feist, Kippy, and myself—had believed him to be. In fact, based on Aarestad's systematic recordkeeping, the shingle that hung outside McCarron's door would have been more accurate had it read *Cappelli & McCarron Investment Group*. Michael J. had been in league with the devil for quite some time and ran to the mob boss when it became apparent that his Minneapolis partner, David Siskin, would neither be coerced nor intimidated, when it became obvious that Siskin wasn't going to play ball . . . and may well have already contacted the authorities.

Frank Cappelli Sr., in turn, had contacted his *partner* in law enforcement—Superintendent Gerald Callum—for remediation. Callum immediately checked in with his people on the inside—originally got nada—but then Marty Kolles called him back the next day to inform him David Siskin had showed up at the Special Prosecutions Bureau first thing that morning as an unscheduled walk-in, had sat patiently in the waiting area for nearly an hour, and was now in a closed-door meeting with Special Prosecutor Peter Feist.

And a situation such as that could not be ignored.

"What the hell is this all about?" McCarron demanded of Special Agent Squires as he was hauled out of his high-back

brown leather chair, and frog-marched from behind his mahogany desk, cuffed, and read his rights. And though Mc-
Carron protested his innocence as his executive secretary
cowered outside the door of his office, both hands over her
mouth—the quivering of his voice and look in his eyes told
a far different tale. McCarron must have spent the past two
days sweating bullets, hoping he'd somehow miraculously
slipped through the cracks, and praying that Cappelli Sr.
truly practiced that renowned code of silence his family
preached . . . Omertà.

Kippy and I thanked SAC Squires for allowing us to be
there as his team took out the final piece of trash—Michael J.
McCarron . . . the man who'd set everything in motion.

Mayor Carter Weeks was the only one to go gently into that
good night when the FBI came knocking. Last I heard from
Kippy, she mentioned Weeks would agree to plead guilty if the
charge of murder in the first degree was taken off the table
and replaced with a smorgasbord of corruption, conspiracy,
bribery, and racketeering charges, but, due to the severity of
the crimes—David Siskin, Peter Feist, Dave Wabiszewski—
that may be a plea bargain too far.

Ultimately, the mayor had been in Superintendent Callum's
back pocket—been his puppet—since the get-go, from back
when Weeks first began representing Ward 25 after his father's
death.

It was Chicago-style politics at its nastiest.

I'd attended a memorial service for Officer Wabiszewski.
The first hour was intended for family and close friends, but
the group was kind enough to let me slip in. I'd never been
prouder of Kippy as she spoke for fifteen minutes straight
about how much Wabs had meant to her, how much he'd
taught her, how a million years could pass and she'd never
forget him. I sat off to the side and worked my way through
a packet of Kleenex. Afterward, a procession of fellow officers
came by to express their condolences, to share a memory or
two, to mingle. Not being one of the boys in blue—and knowing

this was a first step in the healing process for Kippy—I quietly made my goodbyes and snuck off into the night.

I walked over and picked up the limping Maggie May and gave her a kiss on the forehead. Kippy is stopping by later. We're thinking of barbecuing chicken as the overcast weather is nothing a jean jacket can't handle. Hopefully, Bill will allow us to enjoy ourselves and not screw it by rolling in some skunked-up carcass thus forcing us to reopen the car wash. Paul and Sharla are also coming over with one of Sharla's homemade desserts. It'll be nice for them to meet Kippy under more *traditional* circumstances.

Whenever my thoughts turn to Kippy, I remember how she came to visit me on my second and final night at the hospital with Vira in tow.

"I brought Honey Bear to cheer you up," she'd told me that night, using her term of endearment for Vira.

"Her name is Vira," I replied.

"Well, we'll see about that," she said. "Anyway, I figured you could use a therapy dog."

"Vira's the perfect therapy dog."

"Hey, I've got some news for you."

"What?" I wondered if something further had broken in the case.

"I've been giving it a lot of thought lately," she said, taking my half-eaten plate of hospital corn, mashed potatoes, and meatloaf off the tray next to my bed and setting it on the floor for Vira to complete. "Remember when I told you I was off guys?"

"I have a murky recollection of that."

"I think I may be ready to get back on," she said.

"Back on guys?" I asked.

Kippy smiled and sat next to me on the bed. "You're turning red."

"It's the meds," I said. "Any guy in particular?"

"There is this one fellow," she replied, taking my hand in hers. "He's kind of cute, but I may have to buy him a comb."

"Does this fellow know how lucky he is?"

Kippy leaned in and kissed me on the lips. Then we stared at each other a long moment. It might have been the mild sedatives they'd been feeding me, but I swear I heard the shattering of our *just-friends* covenant.

"You're really turning red," Kippy said.

I glanced down at Vira for moral support. She peeked back up at me—as if to say *is there anything you can do on your own?*—and then went back to licking clean the hospital plate.

ACKNOWLEDGMENTS

First and foremost, I need to acknowledge the entire gang at St. Martin's Press—from senior editor Daniela Rapp to copyeditor Sarajane Herman to editorial assistant Cassidy Graham to marketing manager Sara Beth Haring to associate director of publicity Hector DeJean. You are all extremely talented and wonderful to work with. I can't thank you enough. I must also recognize my agent—the incredible and forever-upbeat Jill Marr at the Sandra Dijkstra Literary Agency. And, lest I forget—mega kudos to my photographer, beta reader extraordinaire, and wife, Cindy Archer-Burton, as well as my sounding board, editor, and father, Bruce W. Burton. A heartfelt thanks to each and every one of you.